Shadows in the Wind | Book 1

Tenebris Ordior

Rob Steyn

Produo Publishing Limited

Dedication

To my wife, René, whose steadfast love and caring has been the quiet strength behind every page, every word.
To my daughters, Suzette and Renée, who remind me, always, of what truly matters—courage, kindness, and the bonds that endure.
This book is as much yours as it is mine...
Without your patience and belief, its words would never have found their way to screen and paper.

Chapter 1

Book 1

Tenebris Ordior

Stellae recedunt, tenebrae tenent,
Spirat silentium, tumulus friget.
Ex umbrae utero, surgō intactus—
Non genitus, sed fractus, lividus, natus.

Lux negat quae vidi iam.
Fovet mendacium ubi fuit mundus.
Nulla aurora, nullus ignis, nulla vox lenis—
Sed sola nox... umbrae... quibus ego sum aptus.

⸺◆⸺

The stars recoil, the night takes hold,
A breathless hush, a grave turns cold.
From shadow's womb, I rise unshorn—
Not birthed, but broken, bruised, and born.

The light denies what I have seen.
Truth festers where the world has been.
No dawn, no flame, no gentle song—
Only the dark... the shadows... where I belong.

Chapter 2

The Unspeakable

In the midst of the harrowing turmoil of the Second World War, a beacon of hope blazed forth from Britain's heart—a programme known as CORB, the Children's Overseas Reception Board. Initiated in 1940, this programme sought to rescue thousands of vulnerable children from the imminent dangers of war-ravaged Britain, offering them a desperate chance at salvation beyond the suffocating shadows of conflict.

Under the auspices of the British Government, CORB aimed to evacuate children, primarily those of wealthy and influential families, to countries perceived as sanctuaries, such as Canada, South Africa, Australia, and New Zealand. The initiative was born from the terror of aerial bombardments, especially during the Blitz—a merciless campaign that forced the evacuation of almost 3,000 minors by early 1941.

While many saw CORB as a lifeline, others viewed it through a lens of bitter privilege. Critics argued that the programme disproportionately favoured those of higher social standing, abandoning poorer families who could not secure a precious seat on these vital voyages. Nevertheless, for those fortunate enough to escape, evacuation became a bittersweet edict—a stark illustration of wartime sacrifice shrouded in privilege.

However, the ambitious mission faced catastrophic setbacks. On the 17th of September, 1940, as the City of Benares—one of the ships designated for these evacuations—navigated the treacherous Atlantic, tragedy struck with devastating force. A German U-boat—U-48—torpedoed the vessel, leading to the heart-wrenching loss of 77 of the 90 CORB children, among the 258 souls who perished. An event that marked the darkest hour of the operation, casting a long, haunting shadow on the promise of hope.

Following the sinking of the Benares, the agonising question emerged: how many innocent lives were worth the risk? As public outrage swelled, the tone surrounding CORB shifted dramatically. The government, under intense scrutiny, began re-evaluating the viability of the evacuation scheme, struggling to reconcile its humanitarian aims with the brutal realities of the relentless war. The programme soon found itself floundering; by 1941, it had largely withered into obscurity.

The aspirations behind CORB suffered the fate of many noble ventures in turbulent times—bursting with hope yet ensnared by the vicious complexities of geopolitics. It was a razor-thin line between refuge and peril, one that not only altered the course of individual lives but also carved a painful legacy into the generations that followed.

Survivors and witnesses of the CORB evacuations recalled bittersweet memories of their journey, adventures filled with laughter and the innocence of childhood, yet poisoned by the knowledge that their peers, denied the same opportunity, faced a terrifying future at home. One survivor remarked, 'We were sat among a flotilla of fright, sailing towards what we hoped would be freedom, while leaving behind so much turmoil.'

Even as the dust of war began to settle, the implications of CORB resonated deeply within the very soul of British society. Eventually, many of those evacuated returned, and some became brilliant artists, educators, and leaders in their respective fields. Yet, the ghosts of the horrors they escaped continued to haunt them—dark shadows stalking the corridors of their once-carefree childhoods.

The story of the CORB evacuations is a complex tapestry woven through extraordinary courage and searing heartache. While it aimed to shield Britain's youth from the anguish of war, it became a poignant reminder that safety is often a cruel privilege, intertwined with the broader narrative of human resilience amid overwhelming darkness. Today, as we reflect on these unforgotten journeys and events, let us remember—each child swept away into the unknown carried with them the desperate hopes and fragile dreams of families, and the enduring spirit of those abandoned to fate... It is through this sombre reality and profound distress that our story begins.

Chapter 3

CORB

In 1940, with the winds of war howling across the Channel and the skies above London trembling under the merciless drone of enemy bombers, Britain turned her desperate eyes toward a savage kind of salvation. The war was no longer distant. It had clawed its way to the doorsteps of terraced houses and schoolyards, its presence unmistakable in the banshee wail of air raid sirens and the thunderous impact of incendiary bombs. For countless parents, the walls of home no longer offered sanctuary—but death.

And so, His Majesty's Government acted.

The Children's Overseas Reception Board—known simply as CORB—was formed with one brutal purpose: to send Britain's children abroad, beyond the reach of Hitler's murderous war machine. To the dominions: Canada, Australia, New Zealand... and South Africa.

The newspapers spoke of safety. Of the courage of small feet marching into the unknown. Of new lives under foreign skies. But no headline could capture the shattering agony of a decision that ripped families apart.

Across Britain, scenes of heartbreak unfolded in railway stations choked with steam and soot. Children in short trousers and woollen coats, gas masks dangling from shoulders like grim reminders, clutched their cardboard tags and stared at the world through eyes wide with terror. Some waved bravely to mothers weeping behind railings. Others stood mute, paralyzed in the cacophony of whistles and hissing brakes, as if struck dumb by their fate.

A girl of six clutched a threadbare bear with one ear missing. A boy no older than eight wore a school cap that swallowed his head and a scuffed leather satchel swinging at his side. Their names were stitched to them like cargo bound for distant shores.

Behind them loomed fathers in uniforms and mothers in threadbare coats, clinging desperately to identity papers and the crumbling illusion of control. Their smiles shattered the moment the train doors slammed shut. Some did not wave. Some could not.

To send a child away—perhaps forever—was an act of unspeakable love wrapped in silence. The weight of it crushed the bones of a generation and carved its mark in letters never finished and photographs clutched through sleepless nights.

And yet the ships set out. Across treacherous oceans, convoys of children sailed beneath alien stars, their decks lined with small figures leaning over railings, waving to ghosts. Above them, gulls circled and shrieked. Below, unseen and unspeakable, the sea concealed its predators.

There was no guarantee of safe passage. Only desperate hope.

Of such things, the boy had little understanding.

In a modest red-brick terrace off Upper Parliament Street in Liverpool, behind blackout curtains and the lingering stench of boiled cabbage, eleven-year-old William Braithwaite sat at the kitchen table, rubbing ink from his fingers. His world was maps and marbles, the faded corners of stamp collections, and the dull sheen of worn linoleum bathed in the dying afternoon light. Beyond the thin walls came the mournful bellow of ship horns down by the docks, but William paid them no mind. He did not yet know that this night would sever his childhood from the rest of his life.

His parents stood just out of view, in the hallway, rehearsing a conversation for which there existed no words. They had decided. The papers were signed. The trunk packed. And tomorrow, their son would become one of the Empire's children—sent away not to escape the war, as fate would have it, but to march straight into the long, merciless shadow it cast beyond her borders.

The rain fell lightly outside the narrow terrace house in Toxteth, a faint, rhythmic tapping against the pane like the heartbeat of a dying bird. Inside, the lamplight cast mournful shadows across the small parlour, where William Braithwaite sat curled in a worn armchair, a book unopened in his lap, his small fingers trembling against the cover. His father stood, now, by the fireplace, pipe unlit in one hand, the other resting stiffly against the mantelpiece, knuckles white with unspoken grief. His mother moved about the room with the restless anxiety of someone trying to outpace sorrow, straightening a cushion that didn't need straightening, smoothing a crease in the lace doily she had already smoothed twice, her eyes rimmed with red.

They had spoken earlier that day with the official. The decision was made. The papers were signed. Their family would be torn apart.

"William," his father said finally, voice low but cracking at the edges. "There's something your mother and I need to talk to you about."

The boy looked up. His pale blue eyes, so often alight with mischief or wonder, now clouded with a child's intuition of impending loss, searched their faces and found something broken there—something sealed behind the stiff posture and the soft tones. He sat straighter, his small shoulders bracing for the blow.

"You know how dangerous it's become, son. The bombing. The war."

William nodded, slowly, his throat tightening. "Is it about Gregory?"

His mother inhaled sharply, just once, and looked away, a tear sliding silently down her cheek.

His father continued. "It's about you. There's a programme—the government's offering places for children to go overseas. Somewhere safe. To South Africa, for a while. Just until the danger passes."

William frowned, his heart sinking. "Together?"

There was a pause, heavy with unspoken devastation.

"No, love," his mother said gently, her voice breaking. "Not together. You'll be—William, listen to me now. You'll be looked after. The people organising this... they're trained. It's a good opportunity. You'll be safe."

"But Gregory and I—" He stood now, heart quickening with desperate panic. "We were going together."

Another pause. His father's jaw shifted, swallowing down his own anguish. His mother's hand clutched a handkerchief that hadn't left her pocket all evening, now damp with silent tears.

"There was a change," his father said, the words like stones. "Some reassignments. Gregory's been placed on a different ship. The City of Benares."

William blinked, confused, betrayal washing over his young face. "Why? We signed up together. We asked to be on the same—"

"There was a man," his mother whispered, her voice hollow with helplessness. "An official. He didn't... he said your application needed changing. We tried, love. We did."

What they did not say—and what William already sensed with the crushing weight of injustice—was that the change had not been accidental. It was deliberate, almost gleefully so. There was a dark meanness in the way the man had made the change. The man had asked William's name twice. He had pursed his lips when he heard "Braithwaite." And when Gregory, his best friend, kind and outspoken, had tried to argue, the man had told him sharply to keep his mouth shut if he didn't want his own place withdrawn. "The man wouldn't listen, William. He just smiled that awful, mean smile and changed the papers," she said.

"You'll both be safe," his father said now, the lie tasting bitter on his tongue. "That's what matters."

William swallowed hard. His throat burned with unshed tears that threatened to drown him from within. He turned away, pretending to study the bookcase. These would be his last moments in this home, this sanctuary now crumbling around him.

Later that night he lay awake on the thin mattress in the school hall—Holt School, they called it—listening to the heart-wrenching sounds of children crying in the dark, each sob a testament to families shattered by war. One was only five, clutching a cloth rabbit and murmuring for her mother until sleep took her like a tide of mercy. William didn't cry. But he didn't sleep either, his eyes burning with loneliness as he stared into the darkness.

In the morning, he stood with a small group of boys, each with a cardboard tag safety-pinned to their coats like cattle marked for market, and boarded a waiting lorry. Gregory was nowhere in sight, the absence of his friend a wound that wouldn't heal.

They arrived at the docks under a grey sky that seemed to weep the tears William couldn't shed. There, nestled among cranes and the smell of engine oil and brine, rose the hulking form of the Llanstephan Castle.

William looked up at the vessel that would carry him away from everything he had ever loved and felt, for the first time, truly alone, a child adrift in an ocean of adult decisions.

The sea breeze caught the hem of his coat as he walked the gangway, cold fingers pulling him toward his exile. Somewhere in the crowd, a whistle blew, shrill and final, like the death knell of his childhood.

He didn't look back, though his heart shattered with every step forward.

⸺◆⸺

The ship's engines rumbled like a slumbering beast beneath William's feet. The Llanstephan Castle groaned and hissed, its steel hull streaked with salt and soot, its towering funnel coughing smoke into the grey Liverpool sky. To the crew it was just another crossing. To William, it was something else entirely—a chasm, a break in the world that threatened to swallow him whole.

The gangway had clattered ominously underfoot as he boarded, past tight-lipped officers and strangers in stiff uniforms, past rows of children already being herded into place like livestock. A tag with his name flapped against his chest in the bitter wind—BRAITHWAITE, WILLIAM. Aged 11. Destination: Cape Town. It may as well have said abandoned, or forgotten.

His suitcase had been taken. No explanation. No goodbye. Just the dock shrinking behind him and the sudden, gut-wrenching realisation that he hadn't said what he needed to say to Gregory, or his mother.

A woman in a tweed coat and stout shoes—Miss Vera Crocker, they called her—gathered a group of fourteen children together. "Right, this lot's mine. Come along now, Canaries!" Her voice was clipped but kind, trying to sound cheerful, as though it were a school outing and not an exodus into the unknown.

They were taken down narrow, echoing corridors lined with pipes that rattled menacingly whenever the ship shifted. The air was heavy with a suffocating cocktail of oil, sea salt, and a hundred unfamiliar bodies. Their dormitory was a makeshift space below deck, rows of cots jammed wall-to-wall with barely a foot between them. Canvas hammocks swung above, creaking like something wounded and alive.

William had never shared a room in his life.

That night, he lay rigid on a coarse blanket, staring at the pipes above him. A boy near him sobbed—quietly, but without stopping. Another had wet himself and said nothing. Miss Crocker moved between them like a shepherd with too many sheep and not enough light to ward off the wolves.

William said nothing.

He had been raised with polished cutlery, bookshelves of leather-bound classics, and the comforting smell of beeswax polish in the front hall. He had always slept in a room of his own, sheets crisp and sun-dried, a small lamp casting warm light onto rows of toy soldiers. Here, the world was metal and motion, damp socks and rationed biscuits. Even the sea sounded different—louder somehow, more alive. It growled outside the hull as if hungering.

In the days that followed, the ship rocked southward into an open ocean. Flying fish broke the surface like silver skipping stones. Porpoises raced the prow, their slick backs flashing in the sun. The children pointed and gasped, and for a moment, laughter broke the spell. Miss Crocker clapped her hands. "Now that's something, isn't it? You won't see that in London!"

But London was gone. And the laughter didn't last.

On the fourth day, William overheard two sailors whispering in the corridor, their voices tense with fear.

"We've lost the convoy," one said. "Slipped away in the night."

"Fewer eyes on us," the other replied grimly. "Or fewer to come for us if it goes wrong."

No one told the children.

Instead, the days grew warmer as they passed the Equator. A tarpaulin swimming pool was rigged on deck, and the older boys took turns jumping in, shrieking with mock bravery. William watched them from the side, arms crossed, too proud to join in, too angry to laugh. He didn't feel part of them. He ached for his best friend Gregory. He yearned for knowing where he belonged.

At Freetown, the ship refuelled. The port looked lush and strange from the deck, but none of them were allowed ashore. Soldiers moved like shadows on the dock, and the heat was thick, pressing against William's collarbones like a smothering hand. He stood near the railing, searching the distant trees, wondering what it might smell like down there—if it would be different from Liverpool, from Toxteth, from anywhere he'd ever known.

He felt so far from home that he no longer knew how to measure the distance.

Miss Crocker came to stand beside him. "You all right, William?"

He nodded, without looking at her. "Yes, Miss."

"You're one of the quiet ones."

"I don't have anything to say."

She regarded him for a moment, then patted his shoulder. "Sometimes that's best."

That evening, he opened his suitcase for the first time since they'd left. Inside, tucked between a clean shirt and a pair of socks, was a folded note in his mother's hand. It was short. Not especially tender. Not even signed.

Be brave. Be good. Come back to us.

William folded it again. Slowly. Precisely.

He didn't cry.

But something inside him shifted—small and sharp, like the beginning of a crack that would one day split his soul wide open.

——◆◇◆——

Mid-voyage, the mess deck was a suffocating warren of humanity, perpetually steeped in the acrid melange of over-brewed tea leaves, caustic ship fuel, and the musty reek of clothing that never quite dried in the damp sea air. Rows of children hunched like penitents over their tin trays, creating a symphony of misery—metal spoons scraping against metal, the dismal slosh of watery porridge that seemed to amplify rather than diminish the hollow emptiness of the space. The food was brutally simple—bread that crumbled like chalk, bully beef with its metallic tang, and on blessed days, a single potato boiled to submission—all doled out with the cold, unforgiving precision of a military operation.

William sat isolated at the periphery, absently picking at his crust with pale fingers. A solitary digestive biscuit lay forsaken on his tray, a small island beside the grey sea of his untouched bowl. Hunger was a distant concern, eclipsed by something deeper.

Ritchie Dean—a looming presence two years William's senior with shoulders like ship bulkheads, a voice that carried like a foghorn and soiled, worn-out dungarees that clearly made him feel ashamed—leaned predatorily over from the next row, his eyes fixed on the abandoned biscuit.

"You gonna eat that, posh-pants?" The question hung in the stale air between them, less an inquiry than a declaration of intent.

William raised his eyes slowly. "No."

Ritchie's hand darted out like a striking snake, claiming the biscuit without ceremony.

"You could've asked," William said, his voice unnervingly level, devoid of the expected indignation.

Ritchie shrugged, crumbs already dusting his lips. "You said no."

William fixed him with an unblinking gaze, his stillness somehow more disturbing than any outburst. "Still. It was mine."

"Ohhh," Ritchie's mockery dripped like poison, "'It was mine.' Someone's used to the butler serving tea, aren't they?"

Laughter rippled through the mess—not a tidal wave, but enough to create currents. William remained a stone in the stream, unmoved.

"You think you're better than us?" Ritchie challenged, the question barbed.

"No," William replied, his voice quiet yet somehow filling the space. "I think you're rude."

The laughter died as suddenly as if a door had slammed shut.

Ritchie surged to his feet, his stool crashing backwards with a sound like distant thunder. "What did you say?"

William rose too, with a deliberate slowness that seemed to drop the temperature in the room. "I said you're rude."

Miss Crocker materialised between them like an apparition, hands raised in warning, her voice cutting through the tension—controlled but brooking no defiance. "That's enough! Sit down, both of you. William, Ritchie, I don't want to see either of you up again until your trays are clean."

William sank back down. The collective gaze of the mess hall remained fixed on him, a weight almost physical in its intensity.

He offered nothing more. But from that day, an invisible perimeter formed around him. Not born of fear. Not born of respect. Something more unsettling. They couldn't decipher him—this boy who neither fought nor fled, who didn't break down in tears, yet refused to bend.

He was transforming into something else entirely.

—◆◇◆—

A few evenings later, the dormitory below deck seethed with restless energy—a cauldron of whispered tales and the furtive rustle of bedclothes. William lay supine, eyes wide and unblinking in the oppressive darkness, the ship's gentle rolling motion pressing against him like the persistent hand of a ghost.

He reached beneath his cot and withdrew the envelope once more.

His mother's note.

He had read it twelve times, each word etched into his memory like acid on metal.

He unfolded it carefully in the wan moonlight that spilled through the tiny porthole like quicksilver. Her voice seemed to emanate from the paper itself—sharp, clipped, perpetually in motion. Be brave. Be good. Come back to us.

It offered no warmth. No cruelty either. It simply existed, like a stone.

His gaze drifted across to where Tommy Withers hunched over a small notebook, writing by the feeble glow of a torch, his silhouette a solitary island in the sea of darkness.

"Are you writing to your mum?" William's question drifted across the void between them.

Tommy nodded, the motion barely visible. "She gave me this." He raised the notebook like a talisman. "Said to write everything down. So I don't forget."

William paused, the silence pregnant with unspoken thoughts. "What if you want to forget?"

Tommy offered no response. The light vanished as he extinguished his torch and receded into his bunk.

William refolded the note with precise movements and secreted it back within his coat pocket. No letters had left his hands for his parents. Not a single one. The words he might write remained trapped within him, shapeless and heavy.

Instead, he released Gregory's name into the darkness. Once. Just once. A solitary offering to the void.

And then he lay there, eyes fixed on nothing, a sentinel awaiting the mercy of dawn.

Chapter 4

Landfall

The Llanstephan Castle cut a slow arc through the still waters of Table Bay, its hull sighing beneath the weight of its passage, smoke coiling from the funnel into a pale South African morning. A thin haze bruised the sky as sunlight pushed weakly through it like a torch behind parchment. At the ship's rail, William clutched the cool metal with both hands, his knuckles bone-white against the sun-flaked green paint, the rust beneath it rough against his palms. The salt-laden breeze ruffled his carefully combed hair, carrying with it unfamiliar scents of exotic spices, diesel, and something earthy he couldn't quite place.

Before him, the land rose in dreamlike shapes—at once real and impossible. Table Mountain dominated the skyline, its flat summit sheared off as if by the hand of some ancient god. Cloud draped its top like a tablecloth left askew, edges billowing in the gentle wind. To its right, Devil's Peak reared up in jagged defiance, its steep slopes covered with vegetation that appeared almost blue-green from this distance. Behind the mountain basin, hints of other peaks ghosted into the distance, their names unknown to him, but already storied. William felt something stir within him—a peculiar mixture of dread and fascination that tightened his throat.

"Look at that!" chirped Miss Crocker, appearing beside him, her parasol still folded, her eyes glassy with excitement. "That's Table Mountain, William. South Africa's welcome mat." Her voice carried the brittle enthusiasm of someone determined to make the best of things, the slight tremor betraying her own uncertainty beneath the cheerful façade.

William didn't respond. His jaw was tight, but not with fear—not anymore. Awe, perhaps. Or the heavy breath of change pressing at his chest. The mountain filled his eyes, refusing to be looked away from, commanding his attention like some ancient sentinel guarding secrets he was not yet privy to. Behind him, children's voices rose and fell in a cacophony of excitement and nerves, their English accents incongruous against this foreign backdrop. But his ears filtered it all into background static, focusing instead on the rhythmic slap of water against the hull. The sea, the ship, the land—this was the world now. His world. There was no going back.

As the liner drew nearer to port, the shoreline came alive with detail. The breakwater jutted into the bay like a protective arm, curling around the docks, its concrete surface stained with algae and decades of salt spray. The harbour itself sprawled with a kind of colonial confidence: cranes standing like skeletal birds against the hazy sky; warehouses painted in sun-faded ochres and whites, their corrugated roofs reflecting the morning light; rust-streaked tugboats bobbing in place as though straining at invisible leashes, their decks crowded with dark-skinned men in faded uniforms. Flags flapped—British, Union, shipping lines—each carrying its own peculiar authority, their colours vivid against the muted landscape. Workers in loose khaki uniforms and bare-chested labourers with gleaming torsos moved between the sheds, calling out in English, Afrikaans, and other languages William couldn't place, their voices carrying across the water in fragments of sound that made no sense to his unaccustomed ears.

The ship's engines shuddered down to a heartbeat thrum as it manoeuvred toward the quay, the vibrations beneath William's feet changing pitch and intensity. Dockers gathered like ants on the pier below, arms waving, ropes tossed, commands shouted in clipped tones that echoed off the water. It smelled of salt and diesel, but also something sweet—like molasses and dust. Sun-warmed wood. Citrus. Ripeness. A kind of humid promise that clung to the back of his throat and made him both anxious and strangely alive.

Then—contact. The low, hollow sound of hull against wharf, a dull thud that reverberated through the vessel's frame. Gangways lowered with mechanical precision. Ropes secured by practised hands. Orders barked in a strange cadence that seemed to blend English authority with local inflection.

Disembarkation was brisk and impersonal. Children first, lined up by age and height, clutching small cases and paper tags. Escorts hovering with clipboards and forced smiles. Miss Crocker's hand on his shoulder, steering him down the gangway as if he were one of her carry-ons, her fingers digging into his jacket with unnecessary force. William barely registered the press of other bodies or the snap of a camera somewhere nearby, the photographer's face hidden behind his equipment. He stepped off the ship and onto South African soil as if the weight of that moment belonged to someone else, the solid ground beneath him feeling oddly untrustworthy after weeks at sea.

The port, up close, was a rush of brightness and noise: women in white dresses and wide-brimmed hats gliding past porters hunched beneath luggage, their faces shaded but their eyes watchful; soldiers with brass buttons catching the sun, rifles slung casually over shoulders; black boys weaving through the crowd hawking fruit or chewing gum, their English swift and unbothered, hands gesturing expressively. Barrels rolled across worn cobblestones. Horns bleated from unseen vehicles. Seagulls screamed overhead, diving occasionally for scraps. Somewhere nearby, a radio played something that might've been jazz, the tinny sound competing with shouts and the constant creaking of loading equipment.

William blinked against it all, feeling simultaneously overwhelmed and strangely detached. His shoes felt too clean for this place, too polished against the dusty ground. His head too full of grey English skies and ordered streets. Everything here seemed both brighter and darker, louder and yet somehow containing silences he couldn't yet comprehend. He swallowed hard, tasting dust and possibility on his tongue.

———◇———

They were marched across the port yard and down a broad avenue toward a nearby rail station, where a long black train sat waiting, breathing steam like a sleeping beast. The air changed here—fresher inland, tinged with eucalyptus and dust, carrying hints of distant wildflowers and the faint metallic tang of the railway. The mountain still loomed behind them, keeping watch, immutable and vast, its peak occasionally disappearing into wisps of cloud that clung to the rocky face like reluctant ghosts.

The train carriages were narrow, colonial-style, with rattan bench seats worn smooth from years of passengers and brass handles that had owed their shine to countless palms. The windows were tall and narrow, framed in dark wood that had cracked slightly in the African heat. William climbed aboard and settled near the window with Miss Crocker opposite, her hands folded primly in her lap, her face a careful mask of composure despite the journey's uncertainties. He turned his back to the engine, legs drawn up slightly, clutching a canvas satchel that held everything he now owned—a few clothes, a tattered journal, three pencils, and a photograph so well-handled its corners had softened to silk. The whistle blew—a long, mournful note that echoed against the station walls—and with a lurch and a series of metallic complaints, the train began its climb out of Cape Town.

Through the smudged glass, the city unwound behind them like a tapestry being rolled away: the old fort standing sentinel, cobbled roads winding between buildings, whitewashed homes with their blue-painted doorways, spired churches reaching toward heaven, and the smaller fishing boats bobbing in the docks, their masts creating a forest of thin wooden trunks against the blue harbour. Then vineyards appeared—neat and green in geometric rows, some with workers bent among the vines like insects—before giving way to yellow grasslands dotted with scrubby bushes and then to the reddish dust and thorny scrub of the inland plains that stretched toward the horizon in endless waves.

They passed stations with names like Worcester, Touws River, Laingsburg, each one little more than a wooden shack with a painted sign and a sunbaked platform where lone station masters stood with flags and clipboards, their uniforms crisp despite the heat. Sometimes, children waved from the tracksides, barefoot, curious, their limbs thin and brown as sugar cane, eyes wide and following the train until it disappeared around bends or behind the occasional thorn tree that had managed to grow tall despite the harshness.

The train rocked in a slow rhythm that seemed to speak to William in some new language—a click-clack susurration that told stories of distance and arrival. The noise soothed something raw in him, like a balm on wounds still too fresh to acknowledge. No bombs shattering the night. No blackout curtains turning homes into tombs. No air-raid sirens wailing their terrified warnings. Just wind through half-open windows carrying the scent of dust and wild sage, and the creak of a carriage with somewhere to be, something to witness in its steady progress across this foreign landscape.

That night, they slept in the train, or tried to. The heat clung to the walls like breath held too long, making the air thick and difficult. The rattan seats became beds with blankets so thin they seemed more symbolic than functional. William lay awake, arms behind his head, staring at the dark ceiling where shadows from passing trees occasionally danced like puppets. His thoughts drifted out through the window, past the fences and dry trees, to the line of stars marking the beginning of a new sky—stars arranged in unfamiliar patterns, constellations he couldn't name but felt drawn to nonetheless.

There was something vast and unknowable about this country that both terrified and exhilarated him. Something older than home, older than war, older perhaps than memory itself. It made him feel smaller—but in a good way, like standing before an ocean and understanding one's true proportion in the world. As if the land had been here long before any of them, before Braithwaite and his kind had carved it up with fences and deeds, and would be here long after they had all returned to dust. For now, he would follow the tracks laid by others, watching this strange new world unfold through glass smudged with the fingerprints of those who had come before.

And let the land tell its story, ancient and patient and indifferent to the small dramas of those who crossed its face.

⎯⎯⎯◇⎯⎯⎯

The train laboured its way across the belly of the Cape, shuddering along iron tracks that carved through land both ancient and unbothered. Each hour took them further from the coastal memory of Table Bay and deeper into a landscape that seemed to widen as it emptied, as if the sky itself had grown larger here, more intent on crushing the earth beneath its vast, oppressive weight.

William had grown quiet. The early excitement had faded into some-thing steadier, more contemplative. He no longer pressed his nose to the window or flinched when the whistle blew. Instead, he sat half-curled on the bench, one leg tucked beneath him, arms folded, eyes sliding over the passing terrain as if committing it to memory—each tree, each slope, each shade of sun-bleached grass.

The air inside the carriage was warm and dry, tinged with the scent of scorched timber and dust. Every station brought a temporary breeze through the corridor as doors opened and people called names and children were shuffled about like luggage. Miss Crocker fluttered among them, her hat always slightly askew, her voice sing-song and soothing.

The world beyond the window changed hour by hour. Vineyards gave way to jagged, menacing rocky outcrops, then to vast, desolate scrublands dotted with acacia trees that stood alone like gnarled sen-tinels, the last survivors of some long-forgotten forest. Herds of cattle moved in the distance, dark, shifting blots against the parched, tawny fields. Occasionally, the train passed tin-finned windmills—their blades turning lazily in the relentless breeze—indifferent sentries marking the passage of time.

In the afternoons, heat shimmered violently off the rails and the sky turned white at its centre, as if the sun had burned a savage hole through the heavens. The train seemed to slow in those hours, as though even the engine had grown weary under the merciless assault. Inside, shirts stuck to backs, tempers flared in muffled arguments, and children who had been strangers in Liverpool now dozed shoulder to shoulder, lulled into uneasy sleep.

It was on the second morning, just after dawn, that the train pulled into a modest station named Colesberg. The platform was long and narrow, its edges crumbling in places, flanked by a row of dry-looking eu-calyptus trees that dropped thin, ghost-like leaves onto the dusty ground like pale tears. A cast-iron bench sat in the shadow of the station office, and beyond it, low hills stretched out like the massive, slumbering bodies of ancient beasts.

A crowd had gathered—Afrikaner families mostly, their clothes clean but plainly made. Men in felt hats. Women with sun-lined faces and aprons. A few carried baskets, others clutched documents or stood beside cars that kicked up little clouds of powdery dust each time someone shifted weight.

Miss Crocker bustled to her feet, smoothing her skirt and checking the clasps on her handbag. Her voice rang out, calling names from a list clipped to a board. Children began collecting their things—canvas satchels, biscuit tins, woollen coats folded over arms. They moved with a mix of excitement and dread. This was the end of their journey.

William sat still, watching her. She turned once to meet his eyes.

"Not you, William dear," she said kindly. "You're still further on. Someone will meet you, don't worry."

He didn't answer, but he nodded. A part of him was almost disappointed. Not because he had grown attached to her—though in her own way, Miss Crocker had been kind—but because something about the journey felt safer than the arrival. As long as the train kept moving, the future remained somewhere ahead. Unknown. Undecided.

The doors opened with a groan. Miss Crocker led her small group onto the platform. Her hat caught the wind and listed again, and she laughed, steadying it with one gloved hand. Then she was gone—absorbed into the crowd, her voice drifting away.

A few moments later, a man entered the carriage.

He was tall and lean, his frame carried with the stiff precision of someone used to silence. His clothes were modest: dark trousers, a shirt of stiff cotton with the sleeves rolled neatly to the forearms, and a brown wool vest that looked too warm for the weather. A canvas satchel was slung across his back, military-style, though nothing about him seemed overtly martial. His face was deeply lined, sun-toughened, and clean-shaven. His eyes were a pale grey—cold at first glance, but not unkind.

He stood in the aisle, scanning the carriage. Then he walked toward William and sat down across from him without a word.

There was no introduction. No forced smile. Just a slow exhale as the man settled, resting his hands lightly on his knees. William watched him in silence.

The train gave a sudden jerk, then began to move again.

They travelled in wordless accord. Outside the window, the Karoo opened up into a dry, savage grandeur—a place both desolate and breathtakingly beautiful. The soil turned blood-red, the hills more like the exposed spines of buried giants than mere earth. Thorn trees clung desperately to rocky slopes, their shadows stark and angular in the high sun. Occasionally, a windmill flashed past, its blades squealing faintly like tortured steel. In the distance, fierce wind devils chased themselves across the boundless plains, kicking up spirals of dust that climbed toward the heavens.

After some time, the man opened a leather-bound notebook and began to write, a fountain pen scratching softly against the page. William didn't ask what he was writing. Somehow, it seemed private—like prayer.

Later, the man offered him an apple, which William took, nodding in thanks. Still, not a word was exchanged.

The afternoon wore on. Stations came and went—Norvalspont, Springfontein, Bethulie—each more sun-washed and forlorn than the last. The buildings were often no more than a waiting bench and a signboard, half-swallowed by the ravenous dust. Sometimes a lone figure would wave, and William found himself waving back, unsure why.

As the sun began to dip, casting long golden shafts through the windows like molten spears, William turned once more to the man opposite him.

"Who are you?" he asked, his voice barely above the rattle of the tracks.

The man looked up from his notebook. His gaze held William's for a long moment before he replied, his voice quiet and low.

"Just someone to get you where you need to go."

He didn't smile. But neither did he look away.

And somehow, that was enough.

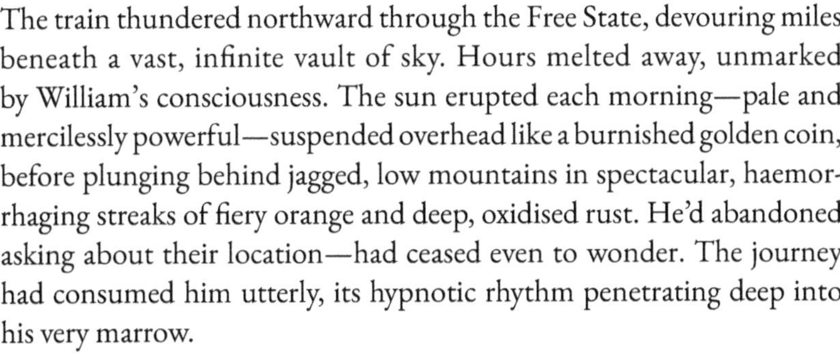

The train thundered northward through the Free State, devouring miles beneath a vast, infinite vault of sky. Hours melted away, unmarked by William's consciousness. The sun erupted each morning—pale and mercilessly powerful—suspended overhead like a burnished golden coin, before plunging behind jagged, low mountains in spectacular, haemorrhaging streaks of fiery orange and deep, oxidised rust. He'd abandoned asking about their location—had ceased even to wonder. The journey had consumed him utterly, its hypnotic rhythm penetrating deep into his very marrow.

There were fewer stops now. Fewer signs of habitation. The fields stretched long and ochre into the haze, dotted with dust plumes kicked up by sheep or cattle or wind. The landscape possessed a barren beauty, stark and unyielding, yet somehow pulsing with life in its own stubborn way. William found himself transfixed for hours by the unchanging horizon, his mind alternately racing and emptied of thought, the rhythmic clatter of the train wheels beneath him a hypnotic drumbeat marking time.

In the evenings, when the temperature plummeted and stars pierced the darkness one by one like distant lanterns, the train glowed from within—soft halos of lamplight illuminating weary faces and slumped shoulders. The glass windows transformed into mirrors, reflecting ghostly apparitions of the passengers superimposed upon the darkening African landscape. William sometimes imagined himself on a ship again, this time sailing over land, the carriage his cabin, the endless terrain a solid ocean with its own mysterious currents and treacherous tides.

The quiet man—his chaperone—had barely uttered a word since Colesberg. He'd given his name once, simply: Mr Harding, and William had committed it to memory without ceremony. There was something granite-like about the man, something immovable. His weathered face was a map of someone who had witnessed horrors but spoke of none. His silence wasn't emptiness; it was economy. A man who hoarded words because he'd learned how devastatingly costly they could be. His hands, William had noticed, were calloused but meticulously clean, his fingernails trimmed with surgical precision.

They shared meals in the dining car wrapped in silence, the clink of cutlery and occasional sigh the only sounds between them. William had attempted conversation once or twice, burning with curiosity about the man's background, his purpose, but Harding had deflected with polite brevity, ruthlessly steering the conversation to practicalities—schedules, connections, what dangers to expect upon arrival.

It was Mr Harding who nudged him awake as Johannesburg approached, the touch firm but not unkind on William's shoulder.

"Almost there," he said, voice like creased linen, rough yet somehow soft at the edges.

William bolted upright, rubbing his gritty eyes. The sky outside had transformed into a deepening purple, the first fingers of twilight clawing westward. His joints screamed from the long journey, his mouth parched and tasting of coal dust despite the sealed windows. He straightened his collar with trembling fingers, raked hands through his hair, desperately attempting to make himself presentable for whatever awaited him.

As the train slowed, the city erupted around them—sudden and dense after the vast emptiness of the interior. Chimneys and rooftops stacked over one another like brick-and-iron monuments to human ambition. Telegraph poles flashed past in a blur, lines humming with invisible messages. Smoke writhed from low buildings, some of it white and domestic, some of it black and poisonously industrial. Further off, tall mine headframes loomed like the spines of a slumbering monster, a stark reminder of what had built this place, what sustained it, what William had come to claim.

The outskirts surrendered to proper streets, to shops with windows blazing with light, to people surging with purpose despite the late hour. William caught glimpses of women in fashionable finery, men in immaculate suits, workers in sweat-stained clothes—all existing in their own separate worlds, utterly oblivious to his arrival.

Johannesburg Station, when it appeared, did so with a grandeur that left him breathless. For a city so young, so raw in many ways, it had erected a cathedral to transport that wouldn't have looked out of place among the architectural wonders of London or Paris.

The train pulled beneath an iron-and-glass canopy vast enough to swallow an ocean liner whole. Light filtered through in dusty shafts, catching motes that danced and swirled frantically in the currents of human movement below. The platform was magnificent chaos: whistles shrieking, voices shouting in English, Afrikaans, and languages William—again—couldn't identify, porters straining with carts groaning under mountains of trunks and parcels, soldiers in crisp uniforms slicing through clusters of civilians, all bathed in the grey-blue tones of twilight and coal smoke.

There was an electricity to it. A city inhaling and exhaling like a living creature. William felt it surge through his chest, a potent mixture of exhilaration and dread. This place would transform him, he knew that much already. No one came to Johannesburg and left the same.

Mr Harding seized his satchel with an efficiency that suggested he'd performed this ritual countless times before, nodded sharply toward the far platform where a small group of men in dark suits stood watching the disembarking passengers with predatory eyes.

"Come along," he commanded, and William followed, stepping into the heart of a city built on gold and ruthless ambition, where men like William Braithwaite would become, came to carve out their fortunes, regardless of the broken lives left in their wake.

⎯⎯⎯◆O◆⎯⎯⎯

They walked past tall pillars, under station clocks and signs printed in English and Afrikaans. The air hung heavy with a potent mixture of sooty grime and expensive perfume, all laced with the electric current of urgency. An army chaplain passed them, deep in conversation with a nurse, his collar stained with yellowing sweat, her uniform a beacon of pristine white against the coal-smudged backdrop of the station. Children's cries ricocheted off the vaulted ceiling like desperate birds seeking escape. A mother pressed a handkerchief to trembling lips, watching a train pull away, its metal body gleaming dully in the filtered light. Somewhere, a brass band struck up an incongruous melody, lost amid the cacophony—a cheerful march that seemed to mock the raw solemnity of farewells taking place around them.

Porters weaved through the crowd with trolleys piled high with burnished leather trunks and sun-bleached canvas bags. A newspaper boy shouted headlines about unrest in the north, his voice cracking with adolescence, face flushed with exertion. The floor beneath their feet vibrated with the thunderous rumble of arriving and departing trains, the sensation climbing up through their bones.

Their next train was waiting, its carriages older, darker, with peeling paint the colour of dried blood and windows clouded by years of dust and coal smoke. A Natal-bound line—destination Pietermaritzburg, with sidings to small towns in the midlands. William stepped up into the car with a thrill running through his veins, his hand gripping the worn brass rail, polished to a dull sheen by thousands of hands before his. The first train had felt like escape. This one felt like adventure—a plunge into the unknown that made his heart race beneath his waistcoat.

Inside, the carriage smelled of tobacco, beeswax polish, and something indefinably foreign—a scent both musty and exotic. Passengers settled into seats upholstered in faded crimson velvet. A woman in a feathered hat arranged her skirts carefully, while an elderly gentleman with a magnificent snow-white moustache folded his newspaper with military precision.

By the time they pulled out of the station, night had taken full hold, wrapping the world in velvet darkness. The city lights thinned as they climbed eastward, like stars being extinguished one by one by an invisible hand. Through the window, William could see the occasional flare of a cooking fire in the darkness, a sudden burst of orange against the inky blackness, the silhouettes of shanties etched against the night sky like paper cutouts. Sleep came in snatches—jolted loose by curves in the track or the sudden mournful hoot of the engine. Dreams mingled with wakefulness until he no longer knew which was which.

It was the smell that changed first.

Somewhere in the night, as William drifted between sleep and consciousness, the air shifted—from dry iron and dust to something moist, alive, primeval. The scent of vegetation, of soil rich with possibility, seeped through the carriage windows like an invisible mist. The sun rose into a golden sky brushed with lavender and rose-pink clouds, burning away the pearlescent mist that clung to the land below like a lover reluctant to leave, and the train began its slow descent into the Drakensberg escarpment.

William pressed his face to the window, fingers splayed against the cool glass. What he saw stole the breath from his lungs.

The mountains unfolded beneath them, veined with emerald valleys and jade forests, crowned with cliffs that shimmered in the morning light like the burnished ramparts of some forgotten civilisation. Massive buttresses of ochre and amber stone jutted from the slopes, weathered by millennia of wind and rain, and long waterfalls unspooled down ravines in silken threads that caught the sun and turned to liquid silver, sparkling with diamond brilliance. The train hugged the mountainside like a cautious insect, rounding bends with almost reverent slowness, the wheels singing against the rails.

Far below, valleys opened like emerald bowls, cupped in the hands of the mountains. Smoke drifted lazily from hidden kraals, spiral messages rising to the heavens through the crystalline air. He caught glimpses of rivers, sudden and silver, tumbling between boulders worn smooth as satin by centuries of flowing water. Birds soared, their cries carried on the rising air, wings spread against the vastness of the cobalt sky.

"Is this all Natal?" William whispered, his voice hushed with wonder, as though speaking too loudly might shatter the majesty before him.

Mr Harding nodded, his weathered face impassive but his eyes alive with recognition. "The edge of it."

It wasn't the Africa of maps. Not dry and featureless, not the blank spaces marked with warnings. This was a different kingdom—green, breathing, mythic. A land where legends might still walk in the shadows between trees.

As they descended further, the land changed again. Forests rose around them—tangled and thick with fever trees, their bark peeling in patches of copper and mint, wild fig, acacia, and thorn. Mist clung to the emerald undergrowth like fragments of dreams. It smelled of damp leaves and something deeper—moss and bark and distant rain, of life and decay interwoven in an endless cycle, rich and loamy and ancient.

They passed a troop of baboons, sitting like sentinels on a rocky ledge, their russet fur catching gold in the morning sun, their ancient eyes following the train's passage. Later, William glimpsed zebra, motionless among tall golden grasses, like striped ghosts materialising from another world. A flash of antelope startled into movement, a blur of tawny grace and speed. Once, briefly, a giraffe's neck swayed above the treetops like a mast rising from the earth, its spotted pattern of burnt sienna distinct against the green canopy.

William turned, wide-eyed, and saw Mr Harding watching the bush too—not with awe, but familiarity. The older man's face had softened, the lines around his eyes deepening not with strain but with something like recognition, like greeting an old friend.

"Wild country," the man said softly, almost to himself, his voice barely audible above the rhythm of the wheels. "Still breathing."

Then the trees began to thin again. The heat rose, pressing against the windows, seeping into the carriage like molten honey. The grass grew higher, greener, swaying in waves under the touch of a breeze, a sea of emerald punctuated with wildflowers of scarlet and gold. The midlands—rolling, fertile—spread out before them like a painted story, a landscape of gentle slopes and hidden valleys cradled beneath a vast azure sky.

Red earth roads snaked away from the rail, carving through the grassland like ochre rivers. Farmhouses dotted the hills, many of them white-walled with corrugated iron roofs that gleamed like polished silver in the strengthening sun. Windmills creaked, their metal vanes turning lazily in the morning air. Smoke curled from morning fires, promising breakfast and the start of a working day.

The engine gave a low, final sigh as they approached the small siding where William's journey would again change direction. The brakes squealed softly, a counterpoint to the slowing chug of the engine.

Mr Harding stood and lifted his satchel without asking, the leather worn smooth as caramel by years of handling.

"Time to get off," he said, his tone matter-of-fact, betraying nothing of what might await them.

And though William nodded, gathering his own belongings with reluctant hands, part of him longed to stay aboard—to keep chasing the tracks into the deep green beyond, into whatever lay past the hills. The promise of the unknown pulled at him, a siren song of adventure.

But the whistle blew, a sharp note cutting through his daydreams.

And the train, once again, began to slow, the rhythm of its wheels becoming a staccato heartbeat counting down to arrival.

Chapter 5

Trewil Loop

The train slowed with a steady groan, brakes hissing like a snake in the long grass. William felt the carriage tilt slightly, as if reluctant to yield him to what lay beyond, its aged timbers creaking against the inevitable.

The siding was little more than a platform of tamped earth and warped timber planks, baked hard by years of African sun. A rusting corrugated shed stood beside the tracks, its roof patched with old tin and weather-stained canvas, corners flapping in the morning breeze. One faded sign—Trewil Loop—hung from a crooked post, the lettering half-eaten by rust, swinging with a creak that announced William's arrival.

Beyond it, a dirt road vanished into the morning mist, twisting away into the distance.

A man waited beside an idling truck—an old Chevrolet, its once-vibrant paint scoured by decades of sun and rain, the tray bed marked with rust and dust, its metal skin pitted like a face marked by smallpox. He was leaning against the bonnet, one boot heel hooked on the bumper, smoking a thin roll-up, the smoke curling around his weathered face in grey wisps. He didn't wave. Didn't smile. His stillness had a quality of permanence, like something carved from the landscape itself.

He simply watched, eyes narrowed against the glare or perhaps against the world itself.

Mr Harding stood first, dusted off his trousers with meticulous hands, then reached for William's satchel, lifting it with a slight grunt of effort.

"That's him," he said quietly, his breath warm against William's ear. "Jacques de Beer."

They stepped down from the carriage, William blinking in the sudden white light that seemed to bleach all colour from the world. The train exhaled steam behind them and began to pull away, iron wheels moving into motion again, leaving a silence in its wake that felt complete—as if the last connection to the world William knew had been severed.

The man straightened as they approached, unfolding his tall frame with deliberate economy of movement. His face was hard, all hollows and cheekbone, eyes sunk deep beneath a low brow like pale stones in a riverbed. His hair was thick and sun-bleached to the colour of dried wheat, combed back without vanity or concern. Deep lines etched his forehead and the corners of his mouth, mapping decades of squinting into harsh sunlight. He looked like the kind of man the land might carve if it had hands—unyielding, patient, and indifferent to comfort.

"Harding," he said, shaking the chaperone's hand with a grip that spoke of strength. His voice was gravelly, thickly Afrikaans-accented, with a smoker's edge that scraped against the ear. "You're late."

"By ten minutes," Mr Harding replied evenly, withdrawing his hand with careful dignity. "You'll survive."

De Beer looked at William then—appraisingly, not unkindly, but without the warmth of welcome. His gaze moved from William's city shoes to his face with the assessment of a man who regularly judged livestock.

"This the boy?" he asked redundantly, though it wasn't really a question.

"This is William," Harding confirmed, placing a hand briefly on William's shoulder.

William extended a hand, awkward but polite, conscious of his smooth palms and clean fingernails—soon to be changed by his new life.

De Beer took it in his own rough grip, a dry, calloused handshake that felt more like a test than a greeting. His skin was like tanned leather, cracked and hardened by sun and labour, bearing the memory of countless fences mended and animals broken.

"Right," he said, releasing William's hand. "Come on, then."

Mr Harding handed over the satchel, which De Beer took without comment.

"He's strong," he added, not to William, but to De Beer, as if discussing a horse or a piece of equipment. "Good worker."

De Beer said nothing, his silence neither agreement nor disagreement, merely acknowledgment.

They climbed into the cab of the truck—William wedged in the middle between the two men, aware of their differing scents: Harding's faint cologne and De Beer's mixture of tobacco, sweat and something indefinably wild. The seat was cracked leather, hot from the sun, its springs pressing against William's thighs. The engine coughed to life, and with a jolt, they were moving, tyres crunching over loose gravel.

The road twisted through bush and farmland—initially green, almost idyllic in the morning light. Tall grass brushed the edges of the path, dotted with wildflowers of yellow and purple, with insects dancing in shafts of light that pierced through the canopy above. Birds flickered between branches—flashes of iridescent blue and crimson against the green. A breeze moved through the acacia trees, carrying scents of dust and distant rain.

But the further they drove, the more the land changed, transforming before William's eyes.

The road narrowed, its edges worn by erosion, revealing red soil beneath. The trees grew taller, denser, their leaves darker, shinier, as if lacquered in something unnatural. Fences appeared—barbed and crooked, posts eaten by termites, wire sagging between them. A smell rose in the heat—not unpleasant, but animal, rank. Dung and diesel. Rust and rot. The mingled scents of neglect and survival.

They passed no other vehicles. No people. Just the endless hush of grassland thinning into dry fields and broken fences, occasionally punctuated by the cry of a bird or the distant bellow of unseen cattle.

De Beer didn't speak. Neither did Harding. The silence in the cab pressed against William's ears, making each breath, each creak of the suspension, loud.

William stole glances at the driver's profile—sun-scoured, unblinking, jaw set. Deep furrows ran from nose to mouth, carved by years of disappointment or anger. This was not a man accustomed to company, nor one who sought it. His hands gripped the wheel with unconscious force, knuckles standing out like small stones.

Eventually, the truck crested a low ridge, and there it was: Trewil Loop, spread out below them.

The farmhouse stood squat on a rise at the centre of the valley. It was built of stone and corrugated iron, whitewashed once but now streaked with grime and rust-coloured stains. A wraparound veranda leaned at an angle, its posts askew, some tied with wire in makeshift repairs. A windmill stood behind it, broken, the blades spinning only when caught by a particularly strong gust, creaking an irregular rhythm.

Two outbuildings stood nearby—barns or sheds, indistinct in the distance, their roofs patched and sagging, windows like blind eyes staring out at nothing.

As they approached, William saw that the grass around the house was long and yellowing, moving in waves with each breath of wind. A rusting wheelbarrow sat upside down near a dry trough, its wheel frozen in mid-rotation. Chickens scattered as the truck drew near, flapping and squawking, but no dogs barked. No voices called out. The place was quiet, as if the farm itself were holding its breath.

A wire gate stood open, hanging from a single hinge. De Beer drove through without slowing, then stopped before the house, engine ticking in the silence.

He turned to William, his eyes pale and unreadable in the shadow of the cab.

"You'll be staying in the back room," he said, words clipped and precise. "I'll show you where. Don't wander off. Not safe for city boys who don't know the land."

Then he opened the door and climbed out, boots crunching on dry ground.

Harding turned to William. His face was unreadable, but something in his eyes—a flicker of concern quickly masked—spoke volumes.

"You remember what I said, lad?" he asked quietly, one hand briefly touching William's forearm.

William nodded, though the words themselves had evaporated from memory, lost in the overwhelming reality of this place. Something about endurance. About keeping his head down. About writing if things bec ame... but that thought dissolved too.

Harding nodded back. "Good." The word fell between them, inadequate and final.

Then he climbed down too, straightening his jacket as if armouring himself.

William followed, stepping onto the red earth that immediately coated his shoes with fine dust. The heat rose up through his soles. A crow called from a distant tree.

He looked at the house again, taking in the details he'd missed from a distance: the cracked windowpanes, the door hanging slightly ajar, the absence of any softening touch—no curtains, no plants, no sign that this was a home rather than merely a shelter.

Something in him shifted. A knowing. A sense that slid down his spine.

He didn't know what would happen here, in this place that seemed to exist outside of time, under the rule of a man carved from the same unforgiving stone as the mountains that loomed in the distance.

But he knew—with a certainty that settled in his bones—that nothing would ever be the same again. That he had crossed a threshold, and the way back, if it existed at all, would demand a price he couldn't yet imagine.

⸺◆⸺

Mr Harding didn't stay long.

He said his goodbyes at the veranda with a short nod to William, and a flat-eyed glance toward Jacques de Beer. No handshake. No warmth. Harding had done his duty, and what came next wasn't his to soften. The air hung heavy with unspoken tension, the kind that settles in the bones and refuses to budge. William shifted his weight from one foot to the other, his young face already learning to mask the unease that churned in his gut.

They waited silently as another truck arrived—this one newer, painted in the pale green of military surplus, its arrival sending up a small storm of dust. The man who stepped out was built like a ploughhorse, all shoulders and sunburn, and he greeted Harding with a nod of recognition. A quiet exchange passed between them, something about "deliveries" and "the back road to Winterton," their voices low and hurried, as if the very land might overhear. Then Harding climbed into the passenger seat and was gone, the truck kicking up a rooster tail of dust as it sped away.

The road swallowed them in a shimmer of heat, the horizon wavering like a mirage.

William stood in the doorway, watching the dust settle. The sun beat down mercilessly, the kind of heat that sears the skin and parches the throat. He could feel the sweat beading on his forehead, the rough fabric of his shirt sticking to his back. But he didn't move, didn't dare to break the stillness that had descended upon the farm.

De Beer said nothing. He turned and walked inside, his boots heavy on the wooden floorboards, leaving the boy to follow. William hesitated for a moment, his eyes still fixed on the spot where the truck had disappeared. Then, with a deep breath, he stepped over the threshold and into the shadowed interior of the farmhouse.

The house was quiet. Too quiet. A stillness not of peace, but abandonment. The air was stale and musty, thick with the ghosts of memories long past. The walls seemed to press in, the low ceilings and narrow hallways a stark contrast to the wide open spaces of the veld outside. It was as if the very house itself was holding its breath, waiting for something to shatter the silence.

And in that silence, history breathed. The weight of generations, of lives lived and lost, of secrets buried deep beneath the red earth. It whispered in the creaking of the floorboards, in the faded photographs that hung on the walls, in the dust motes that danced in the slanting sunlight. The past was never far away here, never truly gone. It lingered in every corner, every crevice, waiting to be awakened.

—◆—

Trewil Loop had not always been a dying farm.

Once, long ago, it had been a promise. Built in the last decade of the nineteenth century by Jacques de Beer's grandfather—one of the early Voortrekkers who had carved a life from this wild and fertile place—it had passed down through blood and blisters. Red earth, sour sweat, stubborn dreams. The land had stretched before them like a canvas waiting to be painted with prosperity, each furrow and fence post a testament to Boer determination against an unforgiving landscape.

Jacques had inherited it from his father in 1923, and for a time, it had flourished: maize, sheep, dairy, even a few prize horses. There were hired hands back then, two tractors, and regular wagons to market. The old windmill had sung in the sun, its metal vanes catching the light as they turned, marking the rhythm of prosperous days. His wife, Marie, had painted the veranda posts every spring, her delicate hands working the brush with careful precision, singing softly as she transformed weathered wood into something bright and hopeful. They'd hung chimes made of shells collected during their rare trips to the coast, the delicate music a counterpoint to the harsh calls of birds of prey that circled overhead. There had been laughter then—rich and full—echoing across the stoep in the evenings as neighbours gathered to share coffee and koeksisters under stars that seemed to bless their existence.

And then came the boy.

Pieter.

He'd been bright-eyed, stocky like his father, but with his mother's soft jaw and endless curiosity. For a while, his presence tethered Jacques to something gentler—something that reminded him of hope. The boy would run barefoot down the fencelines, a wooden sword tucked in his belt, imagining himself a hero of the veld. His small voice would carry across the farm as he narrated imaginary battles against ancient foes, his shadow stretching long in the late afternoon sun. Jacques would watch him from the fields, something loosening in his chest at the sight of his son's unbridled joy.

But the land had grown harder.

The rain came less frequently, leaving the earth cracked and thirsty. The markets tightened, squeezing farmers with prices that barely covered seed. Banks stopped lending to men like Jacques, whose collateral was merely the promise of a good season. Labour drifted to the cities, lured by the siren call of mines and factories that paid regular wages. And Jacques, who had never been a kind man, grew tighter in the chest, shorter in temper, his words becoming as sharp as the thorn bushes that encroached upon his boundaries. When Pieter was nine, a fire swept through the southern paddock and killed ten sheep, their blackened carcasses a grim reminder of nature's indifference. When he was ten, the tractor finally gave up with a death rattle that seemed to echo Jacques's own frustrations. When he was eleven, the final hand left without warning, and Jacques never replaced him, choosing instead to bend his own back further, to push his own limits until sweat stung his eyes and his muscles screamed in protest.

And then—the leopard.

It had happened without warning, on an ordinary Tuesday in autumn.

A walk beyond the ridge. A delay in the return. A trail of blood in the underbrush that glinted wetly in the fading light, leading Jacques deeper into the scrub with a dread that turned his bones to ice.

By the time Jacques found him, the boy's body was still warm. His throat opened like a pouch, a grotesque second mouth that spoke only of violence. His arms clawed at nothing, frozen in a final, desperate defence. His eyes—those bright, curious eyes—stared skyward, reflecting clouds he could no longer see.

The leopard was never found. Nor the tracks. Just a trail of drag marks and silence that seemed to mock the search parties that combed the veld for days afterwards. The farmers who came to help spoke in hushed tones about the old spirits, about bad omens, about the land taking back what it was owed. Jacques heard none of it through the roaring in his ears.

Marie wept for months. She stopped painting the veranda, leaving the wood to grey and splinter under the relentless sun. Stopped speaking more than was necessary, her words becoming as sparse as winter rain. One day, she stopped going into town altogether, unable to bear the pitying glances, the awkward silences that fell when she approached. Something had gone out in her, like a lamp with no oil left, leaving behind only a hollow-eyed woman who moved through the house like a ghost, touching the boy's belongings with trembling fingers.

But it was Jacques who changed most.

The man who had once wrestled calves and repaired his own windmill now stared at the fields with suspicion. As if the land itself had turned traitor, conspiring with fate to rob him of his only son. His bitterness fermented in him like sour milk, curdling everything it touched. His hands, once steady and sure, now shook when he was alone, though he hid it well from Marie.

He began to speak of things he hadn't before. The British—how they had driven the Boers off their land decades earlier, forcing proud farmers into concentration camps where women and children had withered like uprooted plants. How they had imported their wars, their taxes, their weak-chinned schoolmasters and fat-lipped banks. How the world had shifted to serve them, leaving men like him to scratch a living from increasingly hostile soil. It wasn't the leopard, he began to mutter in the evenings as he drank his brandy on the stoep, but the world that had let it come. A world shaped by British laws. British greed. British blindness that couldn't see the value of men who worked with their hands.

He never quite said they killed my son.

But he believed it, the thought taking root in the fertile soil of his grief, growing into something twisted and poisonous that strangled rational thought.

Marie once tried to reason with him. Told him he was pushing away the last parts of Pieter still left, that their son wouldn't want his memory to become something dark and hateful. She touched his arm as they sat at the kitchen table, her fingers light as butterfly wings against his weathered skin.

He didn't respond. Just stared at her hand until she withdrew it, his eyes flat and unreachable as distant mountains.

And she, eventually, stopped trying, retreating further into her private grief, tending to it like a garden of thorns.

By 1941, Trewil Loop was a ghost of itself.

The fences were more holes than wire, barely containing the few remaining livestock that had grown as wild and suspicious as their owner. The cows had grown lean and wild-eyed, their ribs visible beneath dull hides. The paddocks sprouted weeds that choked what little crop Jacques still bothered to plant. The windmill stood still, its gears rusted into silence, a monument to better days. Jacques had taken to repairing equipment that could no longer be fixed, more out of habit than hope, his scarred hands moving through familiar motions while his mind wandered down dark corridors of memory.

Money was short. Government contracts had dried up. No one wanted his milk anymore, not when the larger farms closer to town could provide it cheaper and more reliably. What few things they didn't eat themselves, he bartered in town for paraffin or soap, the transactions conducted with as few words as possible, his presence tolerated rather than welcomed.

And then the letter came.

An official inquiry, via the Union of South Africa, on behalf of the CORB program. A British boy—evacuated from the war—needed a rural billet. Temporary guardianship. Expenses covered. Monthly remittance. Government-inspected. The paper was crisp and official, bearing stamps and signatures that spoke of authority and expectation.

Paid.

Jacques de Beer read it once, his lips moving silently over the words, something flickering behind his eyes like distant lightning.

Then again, his calloused finger tracing each line as if searching for hidden meaning or trickery.

And without a word to Marie, he accepted, signing his name with a hand that did not shake, sealing a decision that would change everything that remained of their fractured lives.

❖

When 11-year-old William arrived at the farmstead, Jacques De Beer did not see a boy standing before him. Not really.

He saw a symbol—a flesh-and-blood emblem of the British Empire he had grown to despise with every fibre of his weathered being. A fragment of the colonial power that had, in his mind, betrayed his people and stolen their birthright. A mouth to feed, certainly—but more pressingly, another burden upon his land, another drain on resources already stretched thin by drought and hardship. A trespasser crossing the invisible boundaries he had erected around his grief. A reminder of everything he had lost and everything he blamed for that loss.

And so, Jacques greeted the boy with no trace of warmth in his gravelly voice, no welcoming gesture from his work-hardened hands. His eyes, the colour of drought-parched earth, surveyed William with the same detached assessment he might give a newly purchased head of livestock. He offered him no room in the house proper—that space remained sacrosanct, preserved in a peculiar stasis since his son's death. Instead, William was directed to a converted storeroom that jutted awkwardly from the back of the main building—a space once used for saddles and tack, now hastily swept bare and furnished with nothing but a narrow cot, a splintered wooden chair, and a small, cloudy mirror hanging crookedly on the wall. The air inside smelled of dust, old leather, and something faintly chemical.

He didn't hit the boy. Not yet. Jacques wasn't cruel for cruelty's sake—his brutality was not so simple or unrefined. It had purpose, a structure, a twisted logic that made sense within the confines of his broken world.

But the thing inside Jacques de Beer—that essential human quality of compassion that had withered and died alongside his son beneath the unforgiving African sun—left no space for softness or mercy. The capacity for tenderness had been excised from him like a tumour, leaving behind only scar tissue where empathy should have resided.

Not anymore.

And the house at Trewil Loop waited quietly as it had for generations, its windows blind to the human suffering contained within its walls, its wooden porch sagging beneath the weight of accumulated sorrows. The jacaranda trees cast dappled shadows across its façade, a beauty at odds with the darkness it harboured. The farmhouse had known grief before—had absorbed it into its very foundations, the pain of past generations seeping into the stone and timber like rising damp.

It would know it again. The wind whispered this promise as it swept down from the Drakensberg, rustling through the olive groves with the certainty of prophecy.

Chapter 6

A Mother No More

Dawn at Trewil Loop did not rise; it oozed in—through cracked shutters and the fraying weave of William's blanket, through the chill of stone walls and the relentless ache in his young spine. The thin mattress beneath him had long since surrendered its comfort, compressed by years of neglect into something more akin to a board than bedding.

The cot was unforgiving, the room bitterly cold. Once a tack room, it reeked of stale leather and dust, haunted by the echoes of animals long departed. Cobwebs stretched across the low ceiling beams, their architects long vanished. His satchel lay abandoned in the corner, its meagre contents—a few worn clothes, a dog-eared book, a photograph too painful to look at—untouched since his arrival. No drawers. No lamp. No door—only a ragged curtain nailed into the lintel that fluttered ominously in the draught, a constant reminder of his lack of privacy, of sanctuary.

Outside, the windmill blades rasped—a disjointed rhythm, like an old man clearing his throat. The sound carried across the silent farmyard, punctuating the heavy stillness of early morning with its metallic protest.

Then, the stomp of boots. Heavy. Resolute. Deliberate. Each footfall a declaration of authority.

Jacques de Beer.

He loomed in the doorway, a spectre of authority, his broad shoulders nearly filling the frame. The weak light caught the weathered creases of his face, deepening them into canyons of displeasure.

"Out," he barked, his guttural voice cutting through the chill air. "Dress quick. You work for your meals here. Nothing comes free at Trewil Loop."

William scrambled upright, already shivering, his thin frame barely holding warmth. He tugged on his jumper, fingers stiff as ice, fumbling with the worn wool. His trousers followed, hastily pulled over goose-fleshed legs, and he stepped into the pale light of the courtyard, blinking against the sudden brightness. The farm remained cloaked in shadow, the mountains behind it massive silhouettes against the lightening sky. Mist clung low over the yellowed grass, wreathing the fence posts like spectral sentinels. A solitary chicken clucked, concealed somewhere in the gloom, its complaint the only sound beyond the windmill's creak.

Jacques awaited by the trough, arms crossed over his barrel chest, a tin mug steaming in his grip. The aroma of strong coffee wafted tantalising-ly, a luxury clearly not intended for sharing.

"You'll fetch water. From the borehole. That pump there." He jabbed the mug in its direction, coffee sloshing dangerously close to the rim. "Fill that trough. Then the bucket on the stoep. Then the big drum by the shed. No dawdling. If it squeaks, oil it. If it doesn't work, don't come running. Fix it. Understand? This isn't a holiday camp for soft English boys."

William nodded, the pit of dread tightening in his stomach, twisting like a live thing.

"Good. Then we'll see about the woodpile. Winter's coming, and we need it stacked proper, not like the rubbish heap it is now."

And with that, he turned his back, boots crunching on the gravel as he strode toward the main house, his silhouette stark against the dawn sky.

No "Good morning." No "How did you sleep?" No acknowledge-ment of William's humanity. Jacques issued commands like a man pre-pared for failure, expecting disappointment, perhaps even inviting it.

The pump was a monstrous cast-iron beast, its base swallowed by cracked earth, its handle jutting up like an accusatory finger. It groaned in protest when William set to it, stiff and unwieldy, resisting his every effort. Each downward thrust required his full weight, each upward pull strained his shoulders. But water eventually gushed—brownish at first, then clear, splashing coldly against his wrists. He filled the trough, methodically, watching the water level rise with painful slowness. He splashed his shoes, soaked his jumper, the damp cloth clinging uncomfortably to his skin. His hands burned in the cold, reddening painfully, knuckles white around the pump handle.

As he turned, wiping sweat despite the chill, he caught Jacques lurking in the shadows of the shed, half-hidden behind a weathered door.

Not aiding. Merely observing.

Judging.

The man's eyes followed his every movement, cataloguing each hesitation, each misstep, each moment of uncertainty. The weight of that gaze pressed on William's shoulders more heavily than any labour.

What am I meant to be? William thought, lugging the heavy bucket toward the house. A guest? A worker? A target? A prisoner? The uncertainty gnawed at him worse than the hunger beginning to hollow his stomach.

Inside the house, breakfast was already in progress by the time he was summoned, his knuckles raw from hauling water. The kitchen was spartan but spotless, dominated by a heavy wooden table scrubbed to pale submission. Two plates. Bread, dry-fried in lard, its edges curled and crisp. Coffee that tasted like ash, bitter and burnt. Marie placed it before him without uttering a word, her movements efficient but without warmth.

She seemed diminished from the day before, shrunk somehow in the harsh morning light. A frail woman, pallid beneath her tan, her skin mapped with fine lines that spoke of worry rather than age. Her hair twisted into a bun so tight it strained at her brow, not a strand permitted to escape its severe arrangement. She wore a faded blouse with sleeves rolled to the elbows, revealing forearms corded with lean muscle, and a skirt that brushed the floor as she moved with ghostly grace between sink and stove.

She did not smile, but neither did she turn cold. Her eyes, when they briefly met his, held something—not kindness exactly, but perhaps an absence of the hostility that radiated from her husband. Her presence felt like a truce held in the oppressive silence, a momentary ceasefire in a war William hadn't known he'd entered.

"Eat," Jacques commanded from the head of the table, his own plate already half-empty.

William complied, tearing into the bread with hunger that overrode taste. The coffee scalded his tongue, but he gulped it down, grateful for its warmth if nothing else.

He barely glanced up. When he did, he caught Jacques's eyes drilling into him again. Something lurking behind that gaze—not merely suspicion, but a dark undercurrent of blame. As though William's very existence was an affront, a reminder of something painful, something unforgivable.

Later, there was wood to be chopped. The axe handle worn smooth by years of use, its weight unfamiliar in William's inexperienced hands. Each swing jarred his shoulders, each split log a small victory against both the timber and Jacques' evident expectation of failure. Eggs to be gathered from beneath irritable hens who pecked at his reaching fingers. A pen to be swept, the smell of animal waste thick in his nostrils as he pushed the heavy broom across uneven ground.

By midday, his arms trembled with fatigue, his back a single knot of pain, his hands blistered and raw.

And yet, Jacques found fault, materialising beside him at each task like a disapproving shadow.

"You call that clean? Use the rake, not your bloody fingers. You'll spread the muck everywhere."

"Don't drop that—are you simple? Those eggs cost money, boy."

"No, not that way. You'll bend the hinge. Haven't you ever worked with your hands before?"

Each reprimand struck hard, just shy of cruelty. Enough to bruise the air, to teach him that the line between discipline and punishment could be crossed at any moment, that his position here was precarious, dependent entirely on Jacques' mercurial judgment.

Marie said nothing. She drifted like a wraith through the rooms—tidying, folding, rinsing. Her presence marked only by the soft rustle of her skirt, the quiet click of a cupboard door. At one point, she handed William a slice of pawpaw on a chipped saucer without meeting his eye, the fruit's orange flesh a startling brightness in the austere kitchen. He muttered thanks. She gave a small nod and turned away, her spirit seemingly as worn as the house itself, as faded as the curtains that stirred listlessly at the windows.

That evening, the sun bled out across the valley like a festering wound, staining the distant mountains crimson. Jacques sat on the stoep, sharpening a knife slowly, the sound a rhythmic shhk-shhk against the whetstone. The blade caught the dying light, flashing with each deliberate stroke. William sat on the steps, knees pulled tight to his chest, muscles aching, watching shadows lengthen across the yard, swallowing the chicken coop, the woodpile, the distant fence line.

The chickens had fallen silent. The world turned orange, then deepened to crimson, cloaked in an eerie stillness. Even the ever-present wind had died, leaving nothing but the sound of the knife against stone.

The silence hung heavy, weighted with unspoken questions, with tension thick enough to cut.

Jacques looked up, eyes narrowing like a hawk's, the knife pausing mid-stroke.

"You miss your mother?"

William flinched at the query, unexpected as a slap. "Yes, sir." His voice sounded small, lost in the vastness of the African twilight.

Jacques fixed him with a stare, his jaw tightening, a muscle working beneath the weathered skin. The scar along his cheekbone seemed to deepen in the fading light.

"Then don't make trouble. Else I'll send you back in a box."

He said it flatly. No smile. No laugh. No hint of jest. Just the cold certainty of a promise he was entirely capable of keeping.

William lowered his gaze to his shoes, the leather scuffed and dusty from the day's labour. Said nothing. What was there to say to such a threat? His throat closed around any possible response.

And the knife kept singing, its blade growing sharper with each deliberate stroke, as darkness claimed Trewil Loop completely.

━━━━◆━━━━

Marie de Beer woke before the sun.

She always did. Not from habit, but because sleep had become a thing she did in pieces—never quite whole, never restful. Her body knew to wake before Jacques. It was safer that way. The darkness was still thick, pressing against the small window of their bedroom, but her internal clock had become as precise as any timepiece after twenty-seven years of marriage. Thirty minutes. That's what she had before he would stir, before his heavy frame would shift and the day would truly begin.

She sat up slowly, careful not to shift the mattress too much. Her knees ached. Her hip too. She'd bruised it the week before—he'd only grabbed her arm, not hard, but she'd stumbled against the doorframe. The purple-yellow stain spread like a watercolour beneath her night-dress. He'd muttered something afterwards. Not quite an apology. Not quite a denial either. Just words dropped into the space between them, heavy with something that might have been shame in a softer man.

She remembered when he used to kiss her shoulders to wake her, when his breath in her hair was a thing she craved. The memory was worn smooth like a river stone, handled too often in the quiet hours. That was another life. Another man. Before their son's death had hollowed him out and filled the empty space with something hard and unyielding. Sometimes she caught glimpses of the old Jacques—in the way he absently stroked a farm dog's ear, or how his eyes would soften momentarily when watching the sunset bleed across the veld—but those moments were rare now, precious and fleeting.

She moved to the sink, washing her face in cold water that shocked her skin into alertness. The pipes groaned—an old house's complaint against the early hour. Her reflection in the cracked mirror above the basin was familiar but foreign—lines she didn't remember earning, lips thinner than they used to be, grey threading through hair that had once been rich chestnut. Her eyes were still sharp, though. Still mine, she thought. The one part of her that Jacques hadn't managed to dim or reshape with his moods and demands.

Outside, the windmill creaked. Always that sound—metal against metal, a complaint and a cry. The rhythm of it had become the heart-beat of Trewil Loop, marking the passage of days that blended one into another. Sometimes she wondered if it had found a voice for all of them—for the silent house, for the workers who kept their eyes down-cast, for her own throat that had forgotten how to form certain words.

She dressed methodically, choosing the faded blue dress that Jacques said made her look "decent enough," and pinned her hair back with practised movements. In the kitchen, she boiled water in the old copper kettle, its bottom blackened from years over open flame. Her hands began the familiar ritual of breadmaking—flour, salt, water, yeast—her fingers working the dough with a knowledge deeper than thought. The fire was slow to catch, the kindling damp from yesterday's unexpected rain.

It always was. Like hope in this house—reluctant to spark, quick to extinguish, requiring constant attention to maintain even the smallest flame.

⸻◆⸻

They had been married for twenty-seven years.

He had courted her with poems once. *Jacques de Beer*, the man with rough hands and a tongue like warm molasses. He had brought her wildflowers from the ridge, gathered in the early dawn light when the dew still clung to their petals like tears reluctant to fall. He'd built her a wooden swing beneath the pepper tree, sanding the seat until it was smooth as silk against her thighs, a comfort now lost to memory. He'd carved her name into the gatepost with his penknife, the letters deep and deliberate, a declaration to all who entered that this place belonged to her heart. That mark was still there—half-covered by rust and lichen now, weathered by countless seasons of sun and rain, but she saw it every day, a fading testament to what they had once been, like a ghost that refused to depart.

He had wept when she gave birth to Pieter. Unashamed tears that streaked his sunburnt face as he cradled the child as if he held the sun in his arms. "Look what we've made," he had whispered, his voice cracking with wonder. She remembered his calloused fingers tracing the curve of their son's cheek, so gentle then, so full of reverence—a tenderness now buried beneath years of hardened grief.

But the years had taken things from Jacques, carving away at him like a river through stone, leaving only the hardest parts behind. The farm, first—portions sold off when the drought came three years running, each acre a piece of their shared dream withering away. Then the friends who drifted off one by one—some to towns seeking better fortunes, others to graves marked by simple crosses on the hillside, each departure another light extinguished. Then his pride, eroded by changing politics and economics he couldn't control, like sand slipping through desperate fingers. And finally, Pieter, torn from them by leopard's jaws, claws and teeth, cutting their future into before and after.

After that, something in him collapsed. Not all at once, not in a way that could be repaired with bandages or medicine. More like a lung slowly filling with water—his humanity drowning inch by inch, day by day, until his breathing grew laboured with bitterness, the sweet air of their past replaced by the heaviness of what could never be again.

She remembered the first time he struck her. It was after a dinner where she'd mentioned perhaps selling more land. It wasn't a punch—just a backhand, sudden and fast, his wedding ring catching her lip. Her mouth had filled with the copper taste of blood, metallic and familiar, like the taste of lost dreams. He had cried after, drunken and ashamed, on his knees before her at the kitchen table. Swore it was the drink. Swore it was grief. He held her for hours that night, trembling against her shoulder like a frightened child. "Never again," he had promised into her hair, words that hung in the air like autumn leaves before their inevitable fall.

And then he did it again, when she dropped his father's old watch.

And again, when she spoke to the young British doctor in town for too long.

Always followed by the same wet-eyed remorse. The same trembling voice. The same promises wrapped in the scent of brandy and regret. "I'm not this man," he would say. "This isn't me." As if the man he once was still existed somewhere, trapped behind a wall of grief neither could breach.

They stopped mattering, those promises. Like raindrops in an ocean of what might have been.

Marie had learned to measure his moods like weather, reading the signs with the precision of a lifetime farmer's wife. Don't answer when he's pacing the veranda, boots heavy on the wooden boards. Keep the stove warm even in summer; he hates cold food. Say nothing when he speaks of the British or the new government. Never meet his eyes when the sun's going down—that's when the memories come strongest, when Pieter's ghost seems to hover in the gathering shadows, a spectre of all they had lost.

She moved now through the house like wind—there, but not there. Present enough to pour his coffee, to press his shirts, to nod at the right moments during his bitter monologues, but absent in all the ways that mattered. Her existence folded into routine. Quiet defiance hidden beneath compliance, like pressed flowers between the pages of a life she no longer recognised.

She kept her books in a battered tin box beneath the bed, wedged against the wall where he never looked. Read them at night when he snored, the pages illuminated by a small torch she'd bought in town. Woolf. Brontë. Van Niekerk. Women who understood confinement, who spoke of inner worlds vast enough to contain oceans. She read their strength into herself, line by line, paragraph by paragraph, their words becoming a scaffold inside her that his fists could not reach. It was not rebellion, not really—she harboured no plans for escape, no dramatic gestures.

It was survival, pure and simple. A way to remain Marie when everything around her insisted she become only an extension of Jacques's pain, a shadow of what once was, and what would never be again.

<hr>

That afternoon, she saw the boy—William—in the side yard, struggling with the feed bags. Too small for the work. Too pale. Too thin. His slender arms strained against the coarse burlap, fingers whitening at the knuckles as he dragged each heavy sack across the dusty yard. The African sun beat down relentlessly on his exposed neck, already reddening beneath his collar.

Her heart couldn't fully open for him. It had closed too long ago for that. Years of disappointment and grief had hardened something essential within her, leaving only the remnant of what maternal instinct she once possessed.

Yet something in her watched him thoughtfully. The way his shoulders hunched forward. The determined set of his jaw. The occasional glance toward the main house, as if checking whether his efforts were being observed, measured, understood.

She noticed how Jacques looked at him—not with hatred anymore, but something more concerning: contempt mingled with purpose. As if the boy were a puzzle he could solve with enough pressure. Her husband's eyes narrowed when William faltered, a subtle tightening around his mouth that she recognised all too well. It was the same expression he'd worn when training farm dogs—expecting obedience, seeking perfection, allowing no weakness.

She recognised these signs. The tight jaw. The short breath. The way Jacques's hand flexed at his side, like it was remembering something it wished to do. The familiar rhythm of his growing frustration, like a gathering storm. His boots planted firmly in the red soil, watching the boy's every movement with the critical eye of a man who had forgotten how to accept imperfection.

And she wondered—not for the first time—if Jacques intended to reshape the boy, guide him into something harder. Something less vulnerable. If he saw in William not a child, but an opportunity to pass along the pain that now sustained him. A vessel to fill with his bitterness, his prejudice, his unyielding sense of what a man should be in this harsh country.

Marie stood at the kitchen window and watched them. The late afternoon light slanted across the yard, casting long shadows. The kettle behind her had boiled and gone cold again, forgotten in her vigil.

She could feel it in the air—the lesson beginning. The unspoken ritual of toughening that Jacques believed necessary, the misguided kindness of preparing a boy for a difficult world.

It would not be taught with books or affection or even words. There would be no gentle explanations, no patient demonstrations. Jacques had long since set aside such methods, if he'd ever embraced them at all.

It would be taught with withholding. With correction. With moments where William would be made to feel small and then, when he resisted, guided in some quiet, deliberate way. A meal delayed. A privilege postponed. A look that could diminish any sense of accomplishment. The careful, methodical reshaping of confidence that Jacques had developed over years.

She saw the boy flinch when Jacques raised a hand—not to strike, just to gesture. But that flinch revealed everything. The involuntary tightening of his shoulders, the quick ducking of his head—reflexes being conditioned into him like one of the farm dogs. Learning to anticipate rather than react.

He's adapting already, she thought. Learning what authority is. What silence suggests. What wariness does. Learning the unwritten rules of

Trewil Loop, where the hierarchy was as immutable as the mountains looming in the distance. Where a boy's worth was measured in resilience and composure.

That night, after supper, she walked out to the broken swing beneath the pepper tree. The ropes were still intact, frayed at the edges but holding firm against the rough bark. The plank seat had cracked in the middle, weathered by sun and rain and neglect. A remnant from another time, when laughter had echoed across this same yard.

She sat anyway. The wood creaked beneath her weight, the crack widening slightly. The familiar scent of pepper berries hung in the evening air, sharp and nostalgic.

The stars had risen. Cool light in a black sky. Countless pinpricks against the vast darkness above the Drakensberg, witnessing the small dramas playing out beneath them. The same stars that had observed generations of struggle on this land.

She looked at her hands. They trembled slightly, as they always did in the quiet. She laced them together. Work-worn fingers interlocking, steadying each other. Hands that had once cradled a son, now empty save for the memory of what they'd held.

Marie did not cry. Those tears had subsided long ago, leaving only a hollow ache where grief once flowed freely.

She did not plan. Planning required hope, and hope was a comfort she could no longer afford in the shadow of Jacques's certainty.

She simply sat there, feeling the shape of the silence, and wondering how long before the boy stopped looking over his shoulder with caution and uncertainty...

...and started looking in the mirror with Jacques's perspective. Started seeing the world through that same lens of hurt and rigid expectation. Started becoming the man that Jacques was determined to shape from this raw material—this child who had arrived on their doorstep, unaware of the transformation that awaited him.

Chapter 7

The Long Dry Season

It was near dusk when Jacques summoned William to the stoep, the veranda's weathered boards creaking beneath the weight of decades.

He had been chopping kindling behind the shed, arms sore, palms rubbed raw, blisters forming where the axe handle had repeatedly struck the same tender spots. Sweat trickled down his spine, soaking the back of his shirt, when the low voice called his name—not shouted, not angry, just firm. The kind of voice that expected immediate compliance without needing to demand it.

William came quickly. Not running, not dawdling. He'd learned already that the way you walked toward Jacques de Beer mattered. Too fast suggested fear; too slow suggested defiance. Either could be dangerous. He wiped his hands on his trousers, leaving faint smears of blood and dirt, and made his way around the corner of the farmhouse.

The old man was seated on a wooden chair facing the western horizon, the sun dying in sheets of copper and crimson that painted the vast expanse of the veld in otherworldly hues. The Drakensberg mountains loomed in the distance, their jagged peaks cutting into the sky like ancient teeth. Jacques was sharpening his knife again, the blade rasping across the stone with methodical rhythm—a sound William had come to associate with the man almost as much as his gravelly voice. Nearby, a flask of strong coffee sat cooling on the windowsill, its bitter aroma mingling with the scent of dust and approaching night.

"Sit," Jacques said, nodding to the second chair—the only other one, a broken wicker thing with a sagging back that threatened to give way entirely if one leaned too heavily against it.

William sat. Quiet. Alert. He placed his hands on his knees, conscious of the dirt beneath his fingernails, the small cuts across his knuckles.

For a while, neither spoke. The knife kept whispering against the stone, a sound like secrets being traded. The cooling air brought with it the scent of wild sage and the distant lowing of cattle being herded into their night pens by the farm workers.

Then Jacques paused. Wiped the blade on a rag stained with years of similar use. Looked straight ahead as he began, his weathered face carved into deep lines by sun and hardship and memory.

"You ever hear of Commandant Verwey?" he asked, his Afrikaans accent thickening around the name, giving it a weight that seemed to hang in the air.

William shook his head, sensing this was not merely idle conversation but some kind of test.

Jacques's mouth twitched—something between disdain and approval. The fading light caught the silver in his stubble, making it gleam momentarily.

"No. Course not. They don't teach you that kind of thing in your English schools. Too busy telling you how you civilised the world." The contempt in his voice was palpable but controlled, like a dog on a tight leash.

He shifted in his chair, leaned forward, elbows on his knees. His voice dropped into a lower, quieter register. The kind people lean in to hear, the kind that draws you in despite yourself. His eyes, brown and hard as river stones, fixed on the distant mountains.

"Verwey was a Boer officer during the Second War. Commanded a small commando group in the Free State. Nimble. Fast. Smart as a jackal. British hated him. Couldn't catch him. Every time they came close, he disappeared into the veld—smoke in the grass. A ghost who left nothing but British bodies and burning supply wagons in his wake."

William said nothing. Just listened. The creaking of the chair beneath him seemed unnaturally loud in the stillness.

Jacques continued, his fingers tracing the edge of the knife blade absently, testing its sharpness.

"One day, his unit's holed up in the Drakensberg—starving, hunted, low on ammo. Their horses thin as rails, men with feet wrapped in rags because their boots had worn through. British scouts get wind of their location. A patrol's sent to flush them out. Two hundred men against Verwey's thirty. But Verwey..." he paused, a glint of something like pride flickering in his eyes, "he doesn't run."

Here, Jacques glanced at William, assessing whether the significance was being understood, whether the boy was worthy of the story.

"He takes five men. Just five. Slips down the mountain before dawn. Gets behind the British line. Crawls through the rocks like a snake. Knows the veld. Owns it. Becomes part of it. The British, with all their fancy equipment and training, they're blind out here. Always have been."

Jacques's hand gripped the knife tighter, the knuckles whitening, the scars across them stretching taut.

"He finds the British captain's tent. Slits it open. Quiet as a prayer. Doesn't kill the man—no. Cuts off his trigger finger. Leaves him alive. And on the canvas, with that same knife, he carves one word."

He turned now. Looked at William with an intensity that seemed to reach inside and take hold of something vital.

"*Onreg.*"

William blinked, the unfamiliar word hanging between them. "What does it mean?"

"Injustice." Jacques leaned back, the chair protesting beneath his weight. "The British said he was a savage. A war criminal. But they were the ones burning our farms, starving our women, killing children in concentration camps. Verwey was just reminding them... you don't get to cry when the hunted bites back. You don't get to write the history books and call yourself the hero."

The knife returned to the whetstone. Shhhk. Shhhk. The sound seemed to cut through more than just the gathering darkness.

"I was told that story by my father, who heard it from his father. We don't forget where we come from. Not like the English. You people, you have the luxury of forgetting. Of moving on. Of pretending the blood was never spilled."

The sky had deepened now—purple whelts behind the silhouetted hills, the first stars beginning to pierce through the veil of twilight.

Somewhere, a jackal cried in the distance, a haunting, mournful sound that seemed to echo Jacques's words. The windmill creaked as it turned slowly in the evening breeze, pumping water from the depths of the earth.

Jacques's voice dropped again, becoming almost intimate in its quietness.

"Do you know what weakness is, boy?"

William swallowed. Shook his head. The night air suddenly felt colder against his skin.

Jacques pointed with the knife—not at him, but at the horizon, the blade catching the last remnants of daylight.

"Believing the world will be fair. That people will save you. That being soft gets you anything but broken bones and shame. That all that talk of peace and understanding amounts to anything when the chips are down."

He spat into the dirt, a gesture of contempt so casual it seemed almost ritualistic.

"Verwey didn't believe in softness. He believed in survival. And principle. And making sure your enemies know they can bleed too. That's what this land teaches you, if you're willing to learn. That's what separates men from boys."

William stared at the dirt, at the small dark spot where Jacques's spittle had landed. He could feel the old man's eyes on him, weighing him, measuring his worth against some ancient, unforgiving standard.

The silence stretched between them, filled with the sounds of the African night awakening—insects beginning their chorus, the distant bark of a farm dog, the soft rustling of wind through the thorn trees.

And in that silence, something shifted—not violently, not with lightning—but like a bone beginning to set in the wrong direction. A subtle realignment that would, in time, change everything that followed.

It was not admiration he felt.

Not yet.

But it was a seed.

And the ground, in certain places out here, was fertile. Watered by blood and history and the dangerous allure of strength without mercy.

It was one of those clear, windless nights, the kind that seemed to trap sound and memory alike in the still air.

The stars above Trewil Loop hung like bullet holes in velvet, the kind of sky that seemed to press downward, heavy with silence and watchful malevolence. William sat cross-legged on a low rock near the cooking fire, staring into the coals where orange embers pulsed like dying heartbeats. Jacques sat opposite, elbows on his knees, a dented tin mug clutched in his calloused hand, a strip of dark, leathery *biltong* clamped between his yellowing teeth. The firelight carved deep shadows into the hollows of his weathered face, making him look more like a death mask than a man.

No one else spoke. The crackle of the fire and the distant chorus of night insects filled the void where conversation should have been.

Marie was in the house, finishing the dishes, the clink of porcelain and the soft splash of water barely audible from where they sat. Her presence had not been requested. It rarely was during these nighttime talks that had become increasingly frequent between her husband and the boy.

"Come," Jacques said after a long while, tapping the ground beside him with thick, work-hardened fingers. "Bring that stick. Draw in the dirt."

William rose, unsure, his lanky frame awkward in the half-light, but did as he was told. He crouched near the fire where the ash was soft and grey, fine as talcum. The stick made easy lines, leaving pale furrows in the dark soil.

Jacques watched for a moment, his eyes narrowing as he tracked the boy's movements, then gave a grunt that might've meant approval or merely acknowledgement.

"You like your books, *neh*?" The question came out like gravel being turned.

William nodded, his gaze flicking up briefly. "I do. I used to read every night. At home." The last word hung between them, fragile and uncertain.

Jacques spat into the dust beside him, a wet projectile that glistened momentarily in the firelight before being swallowed by the earth.

"Books," he said, the word coming out round and sour like a fruit gone bad. "They teach you how to talk like a gentleman, *ja*. Make you clever. Fancy." He rolled the words as if tasting something poisonous. "Put big thoughts in a small head."

He shifted, leaned on one arm, the leather of his old work jacket creaking with the movement.

"But books... they don't teach you how to bleed. Or how to make a man beg for his miserable life. Or how to shoot a jackal through both eyes in the wind when your family hasn't eaten in three days." His voice had dropped lower, a rumble that seemed to rise from the grave itself.

William didn't know what to say. He traced aimless patterns in the dirt, the stick moving without purpose now.

Jacques scratched the back of his neck, staring into the fire, his eyes reflecting twin flames. Memories seemed to flicker across his face like shadows of the damned.

"My pa—he never went to school. Not one day. He couldn't write his name. But he could smell a horse thief in the dark, across a dry riverbed from two kilometres away. Could track a man two days through bush without water. When the British came, they put up signs. Papers. Laws. All their fancy words." His lip curled in disgust. "But my pa, he just took up his rifle and he said—*fok jou*."

The way he said it—low, growling, guttural—carried more history than hatred, the weight of generations compressed into those two syllables.

Jacques turned to William now, his eyes glinting in the firelight, hard and bright as polished bone. The fire cast half his face in amber light, leaving the other in darkness.

"You speak English like the king's little boy. So proper. So soft. Every word like it comes from a book." He flicked his fingers dismissively.

He paused, taking a long pull from his mug, Adam's apple bobbing beneath leathery skin.

"But out here—" he jabbed his thumb toward the veld, where the darkness swallowed everything beyond their small circle of light "—your mouth won't save you. Out here, you must know how to see in the black, how to smell danger before it smells you. How to fight dirty when the knife is at your throat. That is my school." He thumped his chest with a fist, the sound hollow and solid at once. "This—is the only book you need."

Then his voice softened, almost conspiratorial, dropping to a whisper that forced William to lean closer.

"I tell you now, boy... they sent you here because they think you soft. Think the world must protect you like a baby bird. Send you to Africa, let the savages raise you while they hide in their bunkers and drink their tea with their little fingers sticking out." He mimicked the gesture with surprising delicacy, then let his hand fall heavily back to his knee.

He leaned closer still, close enough that William could smell the tobacco and brandy on his breath.

"But I will teach you something better. I will teach you to be hard. To be wild. To survive when others would die whimpering. So when you go back one day, they will not know what you are. You will walk among them like a wolf among sheep."

The fire cracked between them, sending up a shower of sparks that spiralled into the darkness above like souls ascending to judgment.

William looked down at his hands, the dust caking beneath his nails, the beginnings of calluses on his once-soft palms. He didn't speak. He didn't need to. Something in Jacques had already sensed the slow burn of curiosity behind the boy's eyes, the hunger for something he couldn't yet name.

Jacques continued, slower now, each word measured and deliberate. "Your people... they took my land. My father's land. They put my uncle in a camp—starved him to bones while they ate roast beef. They laugh at our speech. At our ways. They call us brutes." He sneered the word, spitting it out like something foul. "But who laughs when a brute learns to train a lion, *neh*? Who laughs then?"

A pause, pregnant with foreboding.

"You are my lion."

The statement dropped between them like a death sentence, heavy with both promise and threat.

And William—still too young to name the feeling it stirred in his chest, something between fear and exhilaration—did not recoil. Instead, he sat straighter, something awakening in his posture.

Somewhere in the veld, a hyena yelped, its eerie laugh echoing across the darkened landscape like a harbinger. The windmill let out a groan as a slight breeze stirred it to reluctant life. The fire hissed low, consuming the last of the dry wood.

From the shadows near the house, Marie watched unseen, her drying cloth twisted tightly in her hands, her body stilled as though movement might shatter something fragile. The moonlight caught the silver in her hair, the worried creases around her mouth.

She had heard that tone before. She knew what it preceded.

He's feeding the boy poison, drop by careful drop, she thought. Turning him into something terrible.

But William didn't know that yet. Couldn't recognise the slow corruption taking root.

He only knew that, in Jacques's rough, broken English, beneath the twisted stories and talk of war and survival, there was something else: a purpose. A role carved out especially for him.

And purpose, to a boy without a country, was dangerously close to *belonging*.

Weeks and then months passed.

At Trewil Loop, days slid by like grit beneath the boot—monotonous, coarse, and endless. The sun rose and set with indifferent regularity over the sprawling farmland, casting long shadows across the parched earth that seemed to breathe with ancient patience beneath the looming Drakensberg mountains.

Mornings were cold. Evenings colder. The firewood pile never shrank, no matter how many hours William spent splitting logs with hands that had grown calloused and strong. His shoulders ached with a dull persistence that had become as familiar as his own heartbeat. Eggs were gathered from restless hens, milk churned until arms trembled with fatigue, troughs filled for livestock that regarded him with the same detached interest as their master. Chores stacked atop one another like the stones in the crumbling boundary wall—a wall that seemed to William both a barrier and a metaphor for his own crumbling resistance.

The farmhouse itself had taken on a different character, no longer alien but not yet home. Its creaking floorboards and musty corners had become a map he could navigate blindfolded, each sound and smell catalogued in his unconscious.

The silence between William and Jacques had grown thinner—not warmer, but more inhabited. Like a space one learns to occupy rather than escape. The boy had learned the rhythms: when to speak, how to read the flinch in Jacques' jaw that meant don't push, the particular way the old Boer's eyes narrowed before his temper flared. He spoke Afrikaans now in broken phrases—just enough to fetch tools, to name animals, to avoid trouble. Words like "*spanner*" and "*melk*" and "*pas op*" formed a survival vocabulary, each term earned through necessity rather than curiosity.

The bruises hadn't come. The violence remained potential energy, crackling in the air between them like the *miggies* that danced in the shafts of morning light through the kitchen window.

But the weather had changed inside him. Something fundamental had shifted, like tectonic plates grinding beneath the surface of his consciousness.

He no longer jumped when Jacques raised his hand to gesture, no longer anticipated the blow that might follow. His body had unlearned its instinctive fear.

He no longer flinched at the sound of boots on the stoep, that distinctive heavy tread that announced Jacques's return from the fields. The sound had become merely information, not warning.

He'd stopped asking questions. About home, about what might happen next, about why things were as they were. The curiosity that had once defined him had retreated behind a wall of pure pragmatism.

He was learning to endure.

And more than that—he was learning to watch. To wait. To measure people the way Jacques did, as tools or threats or liabilities. He found himself studying the old farmer's interactions with the occasional farmhand or neighbour, noting how power flowed, how respect was demanded rather than earned. These observations settled into him like sediment, changing the composition of his character in ways too subtle to notice day by day.

Even Marie had grown quieter in his mind. He saw her less often, as though she were fading into the wallpaper of the farmhouse. When she did appear—offering food with trembling hands, mending a torn shirt with stitches as regular as heartbeats—he no longer thanked her. Her kindness registered as fact rather than gift. Her soft words fell on ears that had grown accustomed to Jacques's gruff commands.

It wasn't that he was being cruel.

It was that he was forgetting to care. The capacity for gratitude, for connection, was being slowly ground away like soil in drought. Something essential was eroding in him, day by day, beneath the relentless sun of Trewil Loop.

It was a sun-bitten afternoon, weeks later, when he found the mongoose.

It was caught in the wire snare near the edge of the field, its back leg twisted grotesquely in the trap, blood matting the fur where metal bit into flesh. It had likely been after eggs again. The birds had been agitated all morning, their frantic squawking carrying across the dusty yard, and Jacques had grunted something about "*verdomde* pests" at breakfast, his coffee cup slamming down with unnecessary force as he'd scanned the horizon with narrowed eyes.

The creature hissed as William approached, baring sharp, rodent-like teeth, its eyes wide with panic and pain, small body heaving with each rapid breath. The sun caught the moisture in its eyes, giving them an almost glassy sheen.

It wasn't large—sleek, dusty grey, body trembling with each laboured heartbeat—but its defiance was unmistakable. Even with its leg torn half through, sinew visible beneath the mangled fur, it tried to lunge, mustering what little strength remained in its failing body.

William crouched just out of reach, studying it. The air around them was still, heavy with heat and the scent of dry earth. A bead of sweat rolled down his temple, but he made no move to wipe it away.

He could have called Jacques, whose boots would have crushed the creature without hesitation.

He could have found a rock, ended its suffering with a single, decisive blow.

He could have ended it, quickly, mercifully, a clean death under the African sun.

Instead, he sat. The hard-packed earth warm beneath him, time stretching like the shadows across the ground.

Watching. Observing each twitch, each desperate attempt to escape, each faltering breath. Cataloguing and calculating its suffering with cold precision.

Minutes passed. The mongoose bared its teeth again, panting now, its small ribcage heaving, too weak to strike but still defiant, still clinging to its wild dignity even as life ebbed from it.

William didn't move. He tilted his head, not out of pity, not out of concern, but out of a detached fascination. Its struggle was merely data to collect, its pain an experiment to monitor. His fingers twitched slightly in his lap, eager to participate.

A thought arrived in him, cold and calculating, like ice forming in his veins:

What would Jacques do?

He didn't know exactly. The old Boer's methods were harsh but purposeful.

But he knew what Jacques had said once, standing over a farmhand who'd collapsed from heat exhaustion—"pain teaches quicker than mercy." The words had been delivered in that gravelly voice, flat and certain as scripture.

He stood at last, the decision made, and walked to the shed, dust rising with each deliberate step. He returned with a small spade, its metal head glinting in the harsh afternoon light. Not to kill it. Not immediately. That would be too simple, too clean. Too kind.

Instead, he prodded it. The metal cold and unyielding against fur and bone.

Once.

The mongoose shrieked and lashed out weakly, a pathetic sound that carried across the empty field, then died in the still air. William felt nothing but clinical interest.

Again. Harder. The spade pressing into wounded flesh, seeking a response, a confirmation of something unnameable. The creature's pain was merely a curiosity to satisfy.

A sound behind him. Soft footsteps in the dust. Marie.

She didn't shout. Didn't rush forward in horror. Her presence was like a shadow, quiet and inevitable.

She just stood there, still as a stone, her hands clasped before her, the lines around her eyes deeper in the harsh sunlight, her faded dress hanging loose on her thin frame.

William turned slowly, the spade still held loosely in his grip, its edge now smeared with a thin line of blood.

Their eyes met. Hers held no accusation, no judgment—only a deep, unfathomable weariness that seemed to reach beyond this moment, beyond this day.

The boy didn't flush with shame, but with irritation. As if he'd been caught in the middle of something important, a private experiment interrupted. His fingers tightened around the spade handle, then relaxed.

Marie stepped forward, silent as a prayer, and knelt beside the snare. Her hands were deft, weathered by years of similar tasks. She took out a small knife from her pocket, the wooden handle worn smooth from use, and cut the wire with practiced precision. The mongoose scrambled forward on three legs, dragging the fourth, a trail of blood marking its desperate escape. Then it was gone into the brush, swallowed by the tall grass and thorny scrub.

She said nothing. No reproach, no explanation. The silence between them hung heavy with unspoken understanding.

She stood. Brushed the dirt from her skirt with hands that trembled almost imperceptibly. Walked past him without a glance, her shoulders straight despite the invisible weight they carried.

William stared after her, watching her retreating figure grow smaller against the backdrop of the farmhouse, heat waves distorting her silhouette.

He wasn't angry at the interruption.

He wasn't relieved by the creature's escape.

He was... calculating. Assessing this new piece of information about Marie, about himself, filing it away like a collector of moments. Another data point in his growing catalogue of weaknesses to exploit.

And in that small silence, something shifted again. A subtle realignment, like something dark and sinister moving beneath the surface—imperceptible, yet changing everything.

Chapter 8

The Night the Sea Took Them

17th September 1940, approximately 21h45 / 9:45 PM

The soft thrum of engines pulsed beneath the floorboards like a distant, steady heartbeat. The corridor lights outside the children's cabin had been dimmed for blackout, casting long shadows through the open door and across the rows of narrow iron-framed bunks. A single bulb glowed faintly overhead, swinging ever so slightly on its chain as the ship rocked gently with the sea, creating hypnotic patterns that danced across the whitewashed ceiling. The metal fixtures creaked occasionally, their complaints barely audible above the constant background noise of water rushing against the hull.

For the first time since leaving Liverpool, the children had gone to bed without their lifejackets. After several days at sea, and once the ship was thought to be beyond the range of German submarines, these precautions were relaxed. The bulky cork vests—which had chafed necks raw and made sleep nearly impossible—now lay neatly stacked in wooden crates at the far end of the cabin, a small victory of comfort in their uncertain journey across the Atlantic.

Gregory sat up in his top bunk, knees hugged to his chest beneath the scratchy grey blanket, his eyes fixed on the ceiling where the lamplight wobbled in thin, watery ellipses. The wool of the blanket itched against his bare legs, but he welcomed the discomfort—it kept him alert when exhaustion threatened to pull him under. Across from him, someone whispered a joke; a ripple of giggles passed down the cabin like a wave, rising and falling in muffled bursts. Two younger boys—twins from Kent with identical cowlicks and missing front teeth—were playing shadow puppets on the bulkhead with their hands, their fingers creating rabbits and wolves that chased each other across the metal surface. The hush of night had brought a peculiar sense of ease, as if danger were a myth that had receded with the horizon behind them, something left behind with the bombed-out streets and wailing sirens of home.

But Gregory couldn't sleep. His mind raced with thoughts of England, of family left behind, of the uncertain future that awaited him across the vast expanse of water.

He turned to glance at his suitcase, tucked beneath the bunk. A small red leather diary poked out between the brass latches, its worn edges visible even in the dim light. He'd written a few lines earlier, the pencil marks smudged where his hand had trembled slightly:

Fifth day at sea. Miss Peabody says we are well beyond danger. Feels strange to undress again. I wonder what William's doing now. Maybe he's reading by torchlight. Maybe he's still angry I didn't wait.

He rubbed his thumb along a splinter on the bunk rail, feeling the rough wood catch against his skin. The ship groaned faintly—no different than usual, yet tonight it seemed to linger, a deeper, more resonant sound that vibrated through the metal frame of his bed and settled somewhere in his stomach.

At the far end of the cabin, Miss Peabody's voice rose softly in song. She was sitting by the porthole, cradling a book on her lap, her feet wrapped in a knitted shawl. The moonlight caught in her silver-streaked hair, giving her an otherworldly appearance as she swayed gently with the ship's motion.

"*Abide with me; fast falls the eventide...*" Her voice was thin but true, carrying notes of comfort that seemed to settle over the children like an invisible blanket.

Gregory looked over at his bunkmate, Lawrence, whose snores had just begun to take rhythm—starting soft, building to a crescendo, then tapering off before beginning again. The boy's round face was slack with sleep, his mouth slightly open, one arm dangling over the edge of the bunk. He envied the boy's oblivion, the easy way he had slipped into dreams while Gregory remained stubbornly, frustratingly awake.

From somewhere up above, a muffled clang echoed—a closing hatch? A dropped wrench? The sound reverberated through the metal corridors of the ship, alien and intrusive. Gregory stiffened. He waited, holding his breath, straining his ears against the background noise of the ocean and the collective breathing of twenty-six children.

Nothing followed. Only the creak of metal, the churn of ocean, and the lull of a lullaby barely heard. The ship continued its steady progress through the darkness, undisturbed.

He reached out to the shelf beside his bunk and felt for his tin whistle, running his fingers over the worn metal. The surface was smooth from years of handling, polished by countless practices behind the school chapel. It had been a parting gift from William—their last day at school. *"If you're in trouble, blow it. I'll hear you. Even across the sea."* They'd laughed then, shoulders bumping, eyes avoiding the reality of their imminent separation. It was only half a joke, a promise neither believed could be kept but both pretended was possible.

A shiver passed through him, raising goosebumps along his arms despite the cabin's stuffiness.

Somewhere outside, on the black Atlantic, waves heaved against the hull with just a little more force than they had earlier. The rhythm changed subtly—a different cadence, a heavier impact. The air in the cabin felt colder, despite the sealed windows and the warmth of so many bodies. Gregory pulled the blanket tighter around him and slid down beneath the edge, staring into the darkness below where shadows pooled between bunks like spilled ink.

He didn't know what kept him from sleep. A nervous thrill? A sense of adventure? Or something unnamed—a prickle at the back of the neck, the weight of unseen eyes watching from the deep? Perhaps it was simply the strangeness of freedom after days of constraint, the unfamiliar sensation of pajamas against skin instead of day clothes worn through the night.

He reached again for the whistle. Slipped it under his pillow where his fingers could find it quickly. The metal was cool against his palm, reassuring in its solidity.

The ship rocked gently. The children slept, their breathing creating a soft symphony of innocence and trust. Miss Peabody's song had faded to humming, then to silence as she too nodded off, her book sliding unnoticed to the floor.

And far below, in the cold, watchful silence of the sea, something moved. A shadow darker than the surrounding depths, purposeful in its approach, leaving a trail of disturbed water in its wake as it rose toward the unsuspecting vessel above.

17th September 1940, 22h03 / 10:03 PM

The whistle rolled off Gregory's pillow and landed with a sickening clink on the wooden floorboards. He heard it, faintly, through the veil of near-sleep—an echo at the edge of consciousness, like death's whisper.

Then came the sound that didn't belong.

It began as a low, foreign vibration beneath the bed, a deeper growl in the engine's steady hum—then an unnatural shudder tore through the entire ship like a dying beast convulsing. In that half-second of terror, Gregory's eyes snapped open.

A thunderclap ripped through the hull.

The cabin jolted violently. Bunks wrenched free, bodies tumbled. Gregory was thrown sideways against the iron railing of his bunk, the wind brutally punched from his lungs. A scream—shrill and blood-curdling—erupted from somewhere nearby. Then another. The lights above flickered once, twice—

—and died.

Total darkness. Not the comforting black of sleep, but a living, suffocating void that clawed at his skin.

"Miss Peabody?" someone shrieked. "Miss Peab—!"

The voice was strangled by a catastrophic crashing noise—furniture or a ceiling panel—splintering nearby. Frigid air rushed in, sharp and wet. Gregory gasped as a violent mist struck his face. He tasted salt and fear.

Beneath him, Lawrence groaned. "Wh-what happened—?"

"I don't know," Gregory whispered, his voice fracturing. His hands fumbled frantically in the blackness, clawing for the bedframe, for the edge, for anything solid. His knees felt weak, rubbery. The ship was tilting. He could feel it—first a subtle lean, then more. The world was sliding violently sideways.

He dropped to the floor, his palms slapping against the boards. The whistle. He grabbed it, clutching it in his trembling fist.

Screams ricocheted down the corridor now. Children calling desperately for one another. For their mothers. For the escorts. Somewhere, someone was sobbing hysterically. The stench of oil and scorched metal hung thick in the air, choking him.

A beam of light slashed through the cabin—Miss Peabody, her torch in hand. She was limping, blood cascading down one side of her face, soaking into her nightgown.

"Children! Stay calm!" she screamed, her voice shredded. "Everyone up! Grab your coats if you can—no time for shoes—move to the corridor, now!"

Gregory saw a girl stumble past him, barefoot, wailing. She was only wearing a vest and knickers, her arms wrapped desperately around a ragged stuffed bear. He lunged for her but she vanished in the crush of panicked bodies.

He whirled, looking for Lawrence—still tangled in his blanket, moaning like a wounded animal.

"Get up!" Gregory seized his arm. "Come on, we have to go!"

But Lawrence wouldn't budge. Blood poured down his forehead. The metal frame had smashed him when the bunk shifted. Gregory hesitated, torn—leave him? No. He hauled the boy's arm over his shoulder and half-dragged, half-pushed him toward the door.

The hallway outside was hellish chaos.

Frantic torches. Slamming doors. Flooded floors. A steward bellowed something unintelligible—then vanished down a companionway. The floor pitched violently beneath their feet, and Gregory slipped, tearing his elbow on the wall. A siren began to sound—a long, broken wail, uncertain, as though the ship herself were screaming in agony.

"Don't let go," Gregory commanded Lawrence. "Don't let go."

Behind them, the ship groaned again—a long, shuddering death rattle from deep within her bones. Water surged savagely at their ankles.

And somewhere in the dark, below the decks and beyond sight, the sea was rushing in, hungry and merciless.

17th September 1940, 22h15 / 10:15 PM

The corridor tilted as Gregory staggered forward, dragging Lawrence beside him, their socked feet slipping on wet linoleum. Shouts shattered the air from every direction—orders barked like gunfire, names screamed into oblivion, cries of agony, bewilderment, blind terror. A steward, his oilskin jacket flapping like a wounded bird, bolted past without acknowledging their existence.

"ABANDON SHIP! ALL TO THE BOATS! MOVE, FOR GOD'S SAKE!"

Gregory's mind couldn't process the words through the roaring in his ears. The floor beneath him wailed and lurched again—more violently now. The incline had become a precipice. The ship was listing catastrophically to port. He felt it twisting his spine, warping his perception as the light fractured at impossible angles, hurling demonic shadows across the stairwell walls.

Miss Peabody had vanished—swallowed by the churning human tide behind them.

"Almost there," Gregory mumbled, his words lost even to himself as Lawrence wheezed beside him, lungs fighting for air. The cold had invaded their bodies like a parasite, gnawing at their marrow.

At the top of the stairwell, a small door crashed open with such force it nearly tore from its hinges. The night outside attacked them—wind like razors, spray like bullets, rain like acid. The deck lights had surrendered to darkness, but moonlight glinted cruelly off the monstrous, ravenous sea. Hell itself had erupted above.

Lifeboats dangled like mangled corpses from their davits, some thrashing wildly in the gale, others vanished into the abyss. Crewmen wrestled with lines, their faces masks of desperation. One lifeboat hung suspended in its cradle, grotesquely twisted. Another had been obliterated by the torpedo's fury, its entrails strewn across the deck.

Gregory dragged Lawrence through the door and into the howling maelstrom. The air choked them with diesel and brine. From somewhere in the darkness, a woman's scream cut through everything—a sound so primal and terrifying it could not have come from anything human.

To their left, against the rail, children huddled like terrified animals, blankets offering no protection, as a matron with shorn grey hair and a sodden wool coat tried to shield them from the horror. Gregory thought he recognised a girl—was it Margery with the red ribbon? She was beyond tears now, her face contorted, eyes searching the void for phantoms.

"HERE!" a voice thundered—a man, looming impossibly large, waving frantically toward the last remaining boats. "YOU BOYS, THIS WAY! NOW!"

Gregory froze, paralysed by conflicting instincts. He whirled back toward the doorway. Miss Peabody remained lost in the chaos. Lawrence's younger brother—gone to the lavatory moments before catastrophe struck—had he been consumed by the ship's bowels?

Lawrence collapsed, his body surrendering. Gregory clutched him desperately. "We have to go," he shouted against the storm. "We'll find them."

The lie tasted like blood in his mouth.

Another convulsion seized the deck—louder than death itself, the sound of the ship's skeleton shattering. The bow clawed skyward.

The man at the lifeboat screamed, "LOWER IT! NOW! SHE'S GOING!"

Ropes shrieked in agony. The lifeboat plummeted downward.

Gregory lunged for the edge as it vanished beyond his fingertips. Too late.

A savage blast of wind hurled freezing spray across the deck. He turned—Lawrence had crumpled against the bulkhead, alive but defeated.

Gregory fell beside him. "Stay with me. Please."

For one heartbeat, one fragile moment, he buried his face in his arm, trying to blink away salt and tears while the world disintegrated around them.

Somewhere far below—in the hungry darkness—the sea continued its relentless, merciless consumption of everything they'd ever known.

◆

17th September 1940, 22h20 / 10:20 PM

Catherine Sanderson's hands were bleeding.

She didn't know when it had happened—only that the salt burned like acid as she clung desperately to the edge of the lifeboat's hull, shoving a trembling boy up into the arms of the sailor beside her. The deck beneath her boots was a treacherous slick of rain, seawater, and raw human terror. Everything pitched and screamed in unholy chorus.

"Tighten the aft line!" the sailor shouted, his voice cracking. His accent was soft, Indian—his face illuminated in ghastly relief by the sudden flash of a lantern. "Now! NOW!"

The boat creaked like a dying animal, swinging violently like a madman's cradle. Children scrambled aboard, shivering, confused, some wailing in primal fear, others trapped in a terrifying silence. Catherine guided them one by one, her voice low, desperate.

"Hold the rail. Watch your step. That's it, darling. You're safe. You're safe."

A girl in a green dressing gown slipped—Catherine snatched her by the collar. Her knees buckled beneath the weight. She hauled her up with a strength born of pure, animal panic.

"We're full!" someone shrieked from within the boat.

"We are not," Catherine snarled. "Make room. You can hold one another."

The deck lurched violently. The ship's groan deepened into a monstrous death-rattle—metal straining against itself like a creature being tortured. There was no time.

One last child—a boy, drenched to the bone, face nearly corpse-grey—reached the boat rail. The lascar sailor thrust out his hand. "Quickly!"

But the boy froze, paralysed. His eyes darted behind him in naked horror.

"Gregory!" someone called from the shadows. "Gregory, wait!"

Catherine whipped around. A shape was moving along the deck—a smaller boy dragging another, barely conscious. The boy with the whistle.

Gregory.

She opened her mouth to scream—but the sailor seized her arm in an iron grip. "We go now. The sea is taking her."

The lifeboat jerked savagely, suddenly lurching outward. They were being lowered into the abyss.

Catherine leaned over the edge. "Gregory—!"

But the deck above was already rising, sliding away into an impenetrable darkness that seemed to hunger for them all.

Wind howled like a banshee.

Salt and rain lashed her face with vicious fury.

She could no longer see whether the boy had turned back—or had leapt into oblivion.

The boat hit the water with a sickening crack, the impact shooting agony through her knees. For a moment, the children cried out in terror—then silence, except for the murderous waves.

Then Catherine saw them.

Bodies.

Three, maybe four—drifting, half-submerged, some tangled grotesquely in flotsam. One small form in a life vest, face down in surrender. Another in nightclothes, arm twisted at an impossible, nightmarish angle. An adult, perhaps a steward, floating near the wreckage of a lifebuoy, eyes wide and unseeing, forever frozen in horror.

She looked away, bile rising in her throat.

"We row," the sailor said quietly beside her. His voice had lost all urgency, hollow with dread. "Row now."

Catherine didn't answer. She pulled the child nearest to her into a desperate embrace, shielding her from the ghastly tableau. The girl was shivering uncontrollably, her lips blue as death.

The boat rocked in the endless, merciless dark, filled with breathless survivors, haunted by those who hadn't made it—and by those, like Gregory, who still might.

⚬

17th September 1940, 22h22 / 10:22 PM

The floor was cold. That was her first clear thought.

It came in through her stockings and into her knees, where she knelt beside the two girls huddled against the corridor wall. The lights had failed minutes ago, and the torch she'd found flickered uselessly—its beam choked by steam and the curling mist of saltwater spray that snaked along the floor like fog, a harbinger of their inevitable fate.

They were in the mid-deck passageway near the stairwell. The ship groaned again—long, metallic, exhausted. Like something ancient giving up its last breath before surrendering to the merciless deep.

"Stay together," she whispered, her voice breaking with desperation. Her words barely rose above the creaks and distant crashes. "Hold hands. Don't let go, no matter what."

The older of the two girls nodded, her eyes wide with unspoken terror. The younger didn't. She just whimpered and pressed her face into the escort's coat, her tiny body trembling with fear. Her hands were ice, fragile as bird bones.

Water lapped at the girl's heels, a deadly caress.

The ship had shifted again—more violently this time. What had been a tilt was now a lean. Furniture skidded in unseen rooms like the last movements of the dying. Somewhere far off, glass shattered, a sound like the breaking of all hope.

The escort turned, her heart constricting. "Mr Hensley?" she called into the dark, her voice hollow with dread. "Are you there?"

No reply. Only the terrible silence of absence.

He had gone forward five minutes ago—just before the last tilt—to search for the remaining boys from the end corridor. She should never have let him go alone. But she had the girls. She had no choice. Another soul lost to the hungry sea.

A child's voice cried out faintly—one word, maybe two. Impossible to tell what. The steel walls twisted the sound into something otherworldly, a ghostly lament.

The older girl spoke at last, her voice small and broken. "Will we drown?"

The escort did not answer right away, the weight of their mortality crushing her chest.

She steadied herself, then lowered her voice. "We're going to try for the stairs. Hold tight to each other's sleeves, okay? Ready?"

Both nodded, their faces pale as death in the dimness.

The escort moved first, torch beam dancing over rivets, handrails, a floating cushion, a single shoe—abandoned relics of lives about to be extinguished. She stepped into ankle-deep water. It was bone cold, and moving—swirling now, not still. The stairwell was ahead, but it felt impossibly far, a salvation they would never reach.

Behind her, a sound. A rush. The hiss of something giving way.

A gust of water shot through a side corridor like breath through a whistle. It struck her legs and knocked the younger girl sideways. She caught her by the arm just in time, her heart shattering at how close they'd come to separation.

The torch flickered out.

The dark returned—total, unrelenting. The girls clung to her coat, their small bodies shaking with silent sobs. All around, the ship creaked and buckled and moaned. No voices now. Only water, the ancient enemy come to claim them.

She held the children closer, the small one in her lap, the older wrapped in her arms, and began to hum—softly, steadily, her tears falling unseen into the rising water.

"Golden slumbers kiss your eyes,

Smiles awake you when you rise..."

Her voice trembled with grief, but she kept going. The girls' breathing slowed against her chest, finding comfort in these final moments.

There would be no stairwell.

There was only this. Their last embrace in the darkness, three souls joined in the face of oblivion.

—◇—

17 September 1940, approximately 22h30 - 22h34 / 10:30 - 10:34 PM

Third Officer John Ainsley gripped the freezing brass rail of the port-side bridge ladder, knuckles white, breath seizing in his throat as the deck beneath him gave another violent, sickening lurch.

She was going. Dear God, she was going.

He had known it for the last ten minutes—but now, with the bow rising like a final desperate gasp toward the cloud-heavy sky, there could be no doubt. The City of Benares wasn't dying—she was being murdered by the merciless sea.

Rain lashed sideways across the deck, stinging his face like needles. The sea roared with savage hunger in the darkness—black upon black, a monstrous void. Somewhere behind him, the mast groaned like a wounded beast, and the wireless aerial—useless now—snapped in half with a crack like gunfire and vanished into the night.

Below, hell itself reigned. Lifeboats half-filled, swinging madly or torn adrift altogether. People thrashing in the water, voices shredding as they called out. He couldn't make out words anymore—only the raw, primal tone: pleading, terrified, resigned to death.

Ainsley spun toward the stern. Flames still flickered low beneath the quarterdeck, a last cruel joke—light, now that no one needed it. He could just make out the cracked lifeboat davits, one of them twisted grotesquely like a broken arm.

A child clung desperately to the railing below, his small body silhouetted for a heartbreaking instant by the orange glow.

Gregory? The boy vanished before he could cry out.

A frantic shout from above: "She's breaking up!"

He looked up—two signalmen, drenched and staggering wildly, trying to climb down. One slipped. Ainsley lunged for him, but the man was swept violently sideways by a wave that broke across the deck like an executioner's fist. He was gone.

Time stopped.

There was only wind, and steel, and sea—the unholy trinity of their destruction.

The ship reared again, screaming. The bow was near-vertical now—masts pointing skyward in one last plea for mercy, stern groaning, rivets popping like distant gunfire in a battlefield of water.

Ainsley backed away, boots sliding on the treacherous deck. He had seconds, maybe less. He reached the edge of the bridge wing and looked down—dark water churning below. He couldn't swim, not well. But staying meant certain death. So did jumping.

Somewhere below, someone was still singing, impossibly.

A child's voice. Or a woman's. He couldn't tell through the howling tempest.

"Abide with me, fast falls the eventide..."

The deck tilted harder—one last, thunderous creak that shook his very soul.

And then it was over.

The ship slipped beneath the waves—not in cinematic grandeur, but in broken, agonised gasps, metal screaming as it was pulled downward, stern-first into the ravenous deep. The ocean closed above her with a fury—no mercy, no pause.

All that remained were lifeboats and wreckage. A burst mattress. A lifebelt. A slipper. A whistle... and a sea of lifeless, floating bodies, their stories silenced forever.

Ainsley surfaced moments later, gasping desperately, clinging to the remains of a splintered hatch cover. Around him, the sea hissed and breathed and rolled. Cold beyond anything he'd ever imagined—a cold that reached for his heart.

He turned his head, coughing violently, trying to keep his eyes open against the stinging salt.

All he could see were shadows.

All he could hear were waves.

And somewhere, still, the distant sound of a child calling a name—a final, fading echo of humanity in the vast, indifferent darkness.

⸺◆○◆⸺

17th - 18th September 1940, 23h30 - Dawn / 11:30 PM - Dawn

Nell Whitworth did not know how long they had been drifting.

She sat pressed between two younger girls in the middle of the lifeboat, her arms wrapped tight around her knees beneath the blanket Mrs Sanderson had thrust at her before jumping in. The blanket was soaked through. Everyone was soaked through. Their hair hung in death-like strings. Their lips were blue as corpses. Their hands trembled with the futility of survival.

The sea around them was black as pitch, a void swallowing all hope, broken only by the foam of their wake and the low silhouette of another lifeboat half a mile off, rising and falling like a condemned spirit in the merciless swell.

No one spoke now. Not really. There had been crying—desperate sobs at first, then quiet ones, then the hollow silence of resignation. Nell's own voice had withered after the second hour. Her throat hurt. Everything hurt with the dull ache of approaching doom.

She could still feel the scream trapped in her body from when the ship went under. The moment the City of Benares disappeared, it took all light and possibility with it. For a long time after, the ocean had raged with cruel indifference—slapping, surging, punishing the pathetic shell of their boat. But now it had settled into something worse.

Silence. The silence of graves.

The sailor with the dark eyes sat at the bow, his arms around a girl who would never shiver again. Her head lay motionless on his chest. He kept murmuring to her in a language Nell didn't know, words that could no longer reach her.

Mrs Sanderson sat at the stern, staring into the abyss, lips moving silently. Praying to gods who had abandoned them. Or counting the dead. Or remembering a world that would never be hers again.

Nell glanced down into the water.

It was calm again. Too calm. Like a patient predator.

Once, hours earlier—or minutes, time had lost all meaning—she'd seen a body float past. A man, face down, his arms out like wings. A lifejacket still fastened around his chest. No blood. Just the emptiness of death. He had looked like he was flying to nowhere.

There had been others too. One child. A woman. All claimed by the depths now.

The stars above were so bright they made her stomach twist with bitter anguish. It didn't feel fair. The sea should be dark. The sky should be empty. Beauty had no right to witness their suffering.

A sound beside her—a boy, maybe eight years old, whispering. "Will we still get to Canada?"

Nell didn't answer. There would be no Canada. No tomorrow.

She tightened her arms around her knees and closed her eyes.

The whistle Gregory had carried was gone, swallowed by the unforgiving sea.

The lullabies were gone, silenced forever.

Even the ship's engine, that low, comforting thrum, was gone, replaced by the hollow promise of rescue that may never come.

All that remained was the creak of oars unused, the shuffle of dying limbs, and the slow rhythm of the waves—each one drawing them farther from life that had been.

Farther into the eternal night.

⸺◆⸺

18th September 1940, Dawn

The sea was pale grey now, like old pewter, dimpled with light from a reluctant sun struggling through the clouds—a bleak canvas for their tragedy.

Catherine Sanderson sat upright in the lifeboat, her back against the side, arms around two girls who had cried themselves into a hollow sleep. Her joints screamed in agony. Her lips were cracked and bleeding. Her hands were raw, blistered from rowing through the merciless night.

She had rowed until the sailor told her to stop. Until there was nowhere left to row to. Until hope itself had abandoned them to the vast, indifferent sea.

All night, the sea had whispered its terrible secrets—groans of distant hulls like dying beasts, creaks of lost wreckage, the soft slap of water against the cold. And once, hours ago, the unmistakable sound of something breaking apart beneath the surface. A door, maybe. Or a rib of the ship surrendering to the deep, taking more souls with it.

Now, in the grey quiet of dawn, she heard something else.

Engines.

Low, steady. Too far off to trust. Too impossible to believe in a world that had already taken so much.

She turned her head slowly, not daring to hope, fearing another cruel illusion.

And there—through the thin mist—she saw her.

HMS Hurricane, a warship's silhouette cutting cleanly through the waves. Grey on grey, a shadow made real. A flicker of the White Ensign snapping in the wind. A voice shouting across the water through a loudhailer. Hands waving from the deck.

The sailor at the bow gave a nod, quiet and tired, the weight of all they'd lost etched into his weathered face.

They were found. But salvation came too late for too many.

Catherine did not smile. She could not. The grief was too vast, too crushing.

She scanned the horizon with desperate eyes.

More boats floated nearby, scattered across the ocean like lost feathers—some upright, some half-sunk, monuments to catastrophe. One was upside down, drifting at an angle, a coffin for those trapped beneath. Another had only two figures aboard, where dozens should have been.

And the rest?

Wreckage. A school satchel, once clutched by hopeful hands. A child's slipper, torn from a foot now cold and still. A lifebelt with no one inside it, its purpose unfulfilled.

A red ribbon caught on a piece of timber. Margery's. The only testament that she had ever existed at all.

Catherine closed her eyes and let the wind press salt into her face, tears mingling with the sea's cruel kiss. The girls stirred beside her, innocent survivors in a world suddenly bereft of innocence.

The younger one whispered, "Is that Canada?" Her voice trembled with fragile hope.

"No, sweetheart," Catherine said, voice barely audible, broken by grief.

"It's England?"

"No," she said again. Then, after a pause, "It's help." Help that came too late for countless others.

The warship drew closer. Ropes were cast. Voices rose—some urgent, some shaken, some already grieving for what could never be recovered.

Catherine looked once more across the water. A whistle bobbed on a piece of driftwood, turning slowly in the swell. The last remnant of a life extinguished.

She did not call his name.

She did not need to.

She simply looked, for one more moment, as if by sheer force of will she could conjure him into view. A boy with steady hands and a whistle in his pocket, now claimed by the depths.

But the sea gave her nothing.

Only silence.

Only light.

Only the deep, unending ache of too few saved and too many lost to the merciless waters.

◄○►

The knock came just after noon. Two short raps, then silence—a herald of devastation.

Mrs Everly, the housekeeper, answered the door. She knew before she opened it, as though doom had already whispered its arrival.

The boy stood on the step in a grey uniform, cap too large for his ears, his bicycle propped against the hedge. He held out the envelope with both hands, a reluctant messenger.

"For Mr or Mrs Talbot," he said. His voice was flat, emptied of life.

Mrs Everly stared at the telegram for a moment, then reached for it as though it might bite—this paper serpent bearing poison.

"I'll see that it's delivered," she said.

The door closed. She turned, her fingertips white on the envelope's edge, clutching this harbinger of sorrow.

The Talbots sat in the drawing room. A fire burned low in the grate, though the day was warm, as if already mourning. Gregory's father, Edward, hadn't spoken since breakfast. His teacup sat untouched on the side table, a ring of cold beneath it—a small, perfectly resigned circle.

His wife, Margaret, looked up as Mrs Everly entered, her eyes already darkening with premonition.

"There's... there's a message."

Edward stood, slowly, a man approaching the gallows.

Margaret reached for it with trembling fingers.

The telegram was addressed to *Mr and Mrs E. Talbot. Urgent.*

Edward opened it with shaking fingers, each movement an agony.

His eyes moved line by line.

Then stopped. Frozen in grief's first terrible moment.

He sat down again, very slowly. The paper trembled in his hands.

Margaret reached for it. She read it once. Then again. Then let it fall to her lap, a stone sinking into dark waters.

Regret to inform you SS CITY OF BENARES torpedoed at sea STOP

Your son Gregory Talbot listed as missing STOP

Rescue operations ongoing STOP

Further information will follow STOP

Silence. Vast and bottomless.

Outside, in the garden, the breeze stirred the yellow roses by the trellis, cruelly indifferent. Somewhere down the lane, a child's bicycle bell rang—a sound from another world. A dog barked twice, then fell quiet, as though respecting the sacred hush of catastrophe.

Margaret placed her hand over her husband's. Neither moved.

The fire gave a small sigh.

And the clock on the mantel ticked on, counting moments in a world suddenly emptied of meaning.

In a war that touched every shore and turned every mother's breath into prayer, tragedy befell not only battleships, but civilian vessels as well.

September 1940. The Atlantic.

The City of Benares, an elegant steamship converted for wartime evacuation, was carrying 406 people westward across increasingly dangerous waters. Among the passengers were 90 children—CORB evacuees, selected through official channels, being transported from bomb-damaged London to safety in Canada.

The children travelled with trunks containing wool socks, tins of condensed milk, and books. Many kept letters from their mothers beneath their pillows. The oldest child was fourteen, the youngest just five.

For five days, the crossing proceeded without incident. A naval escort accompanied the vessel until the fifth night, when fog and operational orders separated the ships.

At 10:03 p.m., in the North Atlantic, the ship was struck by a torpedo. German submarine U-48 had targeted the vessel.

The impact damaged the port side severely. Water rapidly flooded the corridors. Power was lost. The structure began to fail as seawater entered the vessel.

In the initial moments after impact, seventeen children lost their lives below deck while still in their sleeping quarters.

In the ensuing evacuation, several lifeboats were damaged against the ship's hull or overturned in the darkness. Strong winds hampered rescue efforts. Passengers called out across the water. One boy was heard calling for his brother until both were lost. A crew member attempted to reach the children's cabin, but that section of the ship had already submerged.

For several hours, survivors remained scattered across the ocean amongst the wreckage.

Rescue vessels did not reach the scene until morning.

The survivors—suffering from hypothermia and extreme exposure—drew strength from one another's presence.

Of the 90 child evacuees aboard, only 13 survived.

"The world was outraged. But outrage has no resurrection.
The Nazis had their war effort. The Allies had their headlines.
And mothers had empty rooms."
—Excerpt from British Pathé wartime documentary transcript, "*The
Innocents Lost*"

In a rusted cupboard in Kent, a woman kept her son's shoes in a paper bag for forty years. In Glasgow, a father refused to take down the swing in the back garden. In Oxford, a headmistress left a chair open in morning assembly until her retirement.

And in Africa, on a farm called Trewil Loop, a boy who had once known Gregory Talbot awoke in the dark, sweat-soaked, heart racing—remembering a whistle blown across a black sea...

...and never answered.

Chapter 9

Homecoming

Winter had descended on Trewil Loop, bringing with it a biting cold that crept through the stone walls of the farmhouse and settled in the bones of those who dwelled within. The veld stretched out brittle and brown, a vast emptiness beneath a steel-grey sky that hung low and threatening, promising neither snow nor reprieve. William, no longer the thin English boy who had arrived five years earlier, who had ruthlessly tormented a trapped mongoose with a detached fascination that had pleased Jacques, now split logs with practised efficiency, his axe falling in perfect rhythm. Each strike echoed across the silent farmyard, the sound swallowed by the vastness of the deepening African winter.

At sixteen, his body had hardened into something Jacques approved of—lean, sinewy, purposeful, forged through years of unrelenting labour. His fair skin had darkened from years under the African sun, weathered and toughened like leather left to cure. His once-soft hands were now calloused maps of labour, each ridge and hardened patch telling stories of fence-mending, cattle-branding, and the thousand small violences that made up life on Trewil Loop. He worked without complaint, had learned when to speak and when silence served better, a lesson beaten into him through Jacques's unflinching discipline and Marie's quiet warnings.

The lorry appeared first as a distant dust cloud on the horizon, a smudge of movement against the stillness before materialising into a government vehicle, its official markings visible even at a distance. William paused mid-swing, watching as it approached along the rutted dirt track, the engine's growl disturbing the winter quiet. Government vehicles rarely brought good news to isolated farms like theirs—especially to a Boer household still nursing generational wounds from British rule.

Jacques emerged from the barn like a sentinel, wiping grease from his hands with an old rag, squinting against the winter light that seemed to carve deeper lines into his face. He stood with feet planted firmly in the dust, as if preparing for battle, his posture rigid with the instinctive wariness of a man who expected life to deliver blows rather than blessings.

The driver, a thin man in a khaki uniform that hung loosely from his shoulders, handed Jacques an envelope bearing official stamps and seals. William continued chopping, pretending disinterest while his senses sharpened to catch every nuance, every shift in Jacques's demeanour. He watched from beneath lowered lashes as Jacques's face darkened like a thundercloud, the paper trembling slightly in his weathered hands, a rare display of emotion from a man who prided himself on impassivity.

"What is it?" William finally asked, setting down his axe with deliberate calm, though his heart had quickened its pace.

Jacques folded the letter with deliberate care, creasing it precisely as though the act might somehow contain the news it carried. "The war is over. They want you back."

The words drifted between them like smoke, acrid and inescapable, filling the space with unspoken implications. In the far distance, church bells rang out faintly across the valley, their joyful pealing carrying on the winter wind, celebrating victory and homecoming. The sound seemed to mock the sudden hollowness in William's chest, a cavity where something unnamed had been dislodged.

"When?" William's voice remained steady, betraying nothing of the turbulence beneath, a skill he had perfected under Jacques's tutelage.

"September. The Mauretania from Durban." Jacques spat the ship's name like poison, his disgust palpable. "They've had their victory. Now they want their children back. Like cattle being rounded up after the storm has passed."

William nodded, his face a careful blank, a canvas wiped clean of expression. Inside, something ancient stirred—memories of his friend Gregory with his windblown hair and quiet laughter, of Liverpool's sooty streets and foghorns, of a mother's note tucked in a suitcase that he had read until the creases threatened to tear the paper. *Be brave. Be good. Come back to us.* Words that now seemed to belong to another boy entirely, one who had ceased to exist somewhere in the passage of years.

Marie appeared in the doorway of the farmhouse, her now slight frame silhouetted against the interior darkness, wiping her hands on her apron with the perpetual motion of a woman whose hands were never still. She had heard everything, as she always did, her quietness allowing her to absorb the currents of tension that flowed through the household. Her eyes found William's across the yard, and for once, he couldn't read what lay behind them—a mixture of emotions too complex to decipher.

"England," she said softly, the word carrying on the still air. "Your home."

"This is my home now," William replied, the words emerging before he could consider them, surprising even himself with their vehemence.

Jacques's head snapped up, surprise briefly overtaking his anger, a flicker of something almost like pride crossing his features. In five years, this was the closest William had come to declaring allegiance to Trewil Loop, to the harsh life Jacques had carved from this unforgiving land.

"They made you soft once," Jacques said, his voice low and dangerous, like the rumble before an avalanche. "They'll do it again. Everything I've taught you—the strength, the discipline, the truth about what the world really is—"

"I remember your lessons," William interrupted, something he would never have dared years ago when he still flinched at Jacques's raised voice. Now he met the older man's gaze steadily, neither challenging nor submitting.

The church bells continued their jubilant pealing across the valley, carrying on the wind like fragments of a celebration happening in another world entirely. Somewhere, in cities and villages William barely remembered, people danced in streets, threw confetti from windows, kissed strangers in celebration. Peace had come at last. Sons and fathers would return from battlefields. The world would rebuild itself from the ashes of conflict.

But here at Trewil Loop, victory felt like defeat, an intrusion from a world they had deliberately shut out. Jacques crumpled the letter in his fist, his knuckles white with tension, the veins standing proud against his weathered skin.

"They think they can just write a letter and take you," he muttered, his voice thick with resentment. "After all these years. After everything."

William turned back to his chopping block with deliberate movements, lifting the axe and bringing it down with controlled violence. The wood split perfectly down the grain, falling away in two neat halves. The sound cracked through the winter air like a gunshot.

"Perhaps I won't go," he said, the words falling like stones into still water, creating ripples that could not be called back.

Marie gasped softly from the doorway, her hand flying to her throat in a gesture of surprise. Jacques studied William's face with narrowed eyes, searching for weakness or deceit, finding neither. There was only the hard certainty that had been forged in him over years of brutal lessons and survival.

"They'll come for you," Jacques said finally, a statement of fact rather than a warning. "The British government doesn't ask. It takes."

William picked up another log from the pile, positioned it carefully on the block, his movements precise and unhurried. His eyes, when he raised them to meet Jacques's, held something new—a calculation, a coldness that mirrored his mentor's own.

"Let them try," he said, and brought the axe down again, cleaving the wood with a finality that seemed to echo across the winter-stilled veld.

⸻◆⸻

That night, William sat beneath the pepper tree, watching darkness swallow the distant Drakensberg. The wooden swing creaked in the breeze, empty and abandoned like so much at Trewil Loop. Earlier defiance had hardened into resignation as the day wore on. He must return to England.

Jacques had not mentioned the letter again after their morning confrontation, but his silence spoke volumes—a wounded, resentful quiet that filled the farmhouse like smoke. At dinner, he'd drunk more than usual, his eyes occasionally finding William's across the table with something like betrayal in them. As if William had orchestrated the war's end himself.

The night air carried the scent of dust and coming rain. William's fingers traced patterns in the dry earth beside him, unconsciously forming the letters of his own name—his English name, William Charles Braithwaite. Not Willie, as Marie sometimes called him, which he hated. Not the *Rooinek* that Jacques had spat at him in the early days.

He didn't feel joy. Or fear. Or grief. The emotions that should accompany such momentous news remained stubbornly out of reach, like objects viewed through murky water. Instead, he felt like something had shifted under the soil. Something he'd buried. And now it had begun to move. A life had been waiting, dormant. And now it had remembered his name.

Stars pricked and attacked the vast African sky, impossibly bright and numerous. William had learned their Afrikaans names from Jacques—*Suiderkruis*, *Drie Konings*, *Melkweg*. The English names felt foreign now, belonging to a boy who no longer existed.

The farmhouse door opened, spilling yellow lamplight onto the stoep. Marie stood silhouetted, watching him for a moment before approaching. She carried something wrapped in cloth.

"You'll catch cold," she said, though the night was mild.

William didn't answer. She settled beside him on the ground, her movements stiff with age and labour.

"I found this," she said, unwrapping the bundle. "When you first came."

It was a small notebook, its blue cover faded nearly to grey. William recognised it immediately—the journal his mother had packed for him. He'd discarded it somewhere in those first brutal months, unable to find words for what was happening to him.

"I kept it," Marie said. "I thought someday you might want it again."

William took it, feeling its negligible weight in his palm. The pages were blank except for a single entry on the first page, written in a child's careful script: *I have arrived at Trewil Loop. The man is not kind.*

"England will seem strange to you now," Marie said. Her hands, rough and reddened from years of work, twisted in her lap. "But it's still there, waiting."

"What's waiting?" William asked, his voice unexpectedly hoarse.

"The boy you were. The man you might become."

William slipped the notebook into his pocket. Above them, the pepper tree whispered secrets to the night, its leaves rustling with ancient wisdom.

"Jacques believes he made you in his image," Marie said softly. "But you were someone before you came here. You'll be someone after."

She rose with difficulty, patting his shoulder awkwardly before returning to the house. William remained beneath the stars, feeling the notebook's presence against his chest like something alive. Something with a heartbeat.

In the distance, a jackal called—a high-pitched, lonely sound that echoed across the veld. William closed his eyes and listened to Africa singing its night songs, storing the memory like a treasure. When he opened them again, he saw not just the land before him, but the ocean beyond, and further still, a fog-shrouded island where strangers who shared his blood awaited his return.

⊰•◦◦•⊱

William stepped into the farmhouse, his muscles aching from a day spent repairing the stone wall near the southern paddock. The familiar scent of dust and wood polish greeted him, along with something sharper—brandy. Jacques sat at the kitchen table, a half-empty bottle before him, eyes fixed on nothing. Marie stood by the stove, stirring a pot of stew with mechanical precision, her shoulders tense beneath her faded dress.

The floorboard creaked beneath William's boot. Jacques looked up, his weathered face hardening at the sight of the boy.

"There you are." Jacques's voice carried the rough edge of alcohol. "We leave at first light. The drive to Durban takes seven hours, and I won't have you making me late."

William nodded, setting his hat on the hook by the door. "I've packed everything."

"The Mauretania sails at mid-morning." Jacques took another swallow of brandy. "British ship. Fitting."

Marie turned from the stove, her eyes meeting William's briefly before darting away. "I've made lamb stew. Your favourite."

Jacques snorted. "Wasting good meat on his last night."

The kitchen fell silent except for the bubbling pot and the clink of Jacques's glass against the wooden table. William stood awkwardly, caught between sitting down and retreating to his room.

"Five years," Jacques said suddenly, his voice low and dangerous. "Five years I've fed you, clothed you, taught you everything worth knowing." He looked up at William, eyes bloodshot. "You know I never wanted you here? A burden from the moment you arrived. The British government's money barely covered what you ate."

Marie's spoon clattered against the pot. "Jacques, please—"

"No, let the boy hear it." Jacques leaned forward. "This farm was dying before you came. It's still dying. And what did I get for my trouble? A soft English boy who couldn't tell a sheep from a goat."

William felt something twist inside him, a knife turning in a wound he thought had scarred over long ago. The hurt was sudden and deep, but his face remained impassive, a skill learned through countless such moments.

"Your ship will take you back to your real family," Jacques continued, pouring another measure of brandy. "And good riddance."

William met Jacques's gaze steadily. "I'll be ready at first light," he said, his voice flat and emotionless.

Something flickered in Jacques's eyes—perhaps disappointment at William's lack of reaction, or perhaps a deeper emotion he couldn't express.

Marie set a bowl of stew before William. "Eat while it's hot," she said softly.

As William sat at the table, he catalogued Jacques's cruelty with clinical precision. Not as a wound to nurse, but as information to process. He understood what was happening: Jacques was losing someone again. Not a son—Jacques had never truly accepted him as such—but something adjacent to family. The old man was experiencing loss for a second time, and like a wounded animal, he lashed out at what was nearest.

William ate methodically, giving no outward sign of the turmoil within. To Jacques and Marie, he appeared unmoved, perhaps even cold—a boy who couldn't care less about leaving. They couldn't see how he mentally dissected the moment, examining Jacques's behaviour as the immature reaction of a man who couldn't process his emotions properly.

Outside, the African dusk deepened into night. Tomorrow, William would board a ship bound for England, carrying with him lessons Jacques never intended to teach: how cruelty revealed weakness, how silence could be power, and how a heart, once broken, could be rebuilt into something harder and more dangerous than before.

———◆◇◆———

The darkness wrapped around Trewil Loop like a shroud, stars still bright in the pre-dawn sky. Inside the farmhouse, lamps cast weak yellow pools of light as three figures moved with deliberate purpose, avoiding each other's paths like planets in separate orbits.

Jacques pulled on his jacket, the leather creaking as he stretched his shoulders. His movements were precise, economical, betraying nothing of last night's brandy-soaked bitterness. Marie packed a small basket with bread and dried meat, her hands moving with the efficiency of long practice. Neither spoke.

William emerged from his room carrying a single canvas bag—five years of life in Africa distilled to almost nothing. His hair was neatly combed, his shirt pressed. The boy who had arrived at Trewil Loop was nowhere to be seen in this tall, lean young man with watchful eyes.

"The car is ready," Jacques said, the first words spoken that morning. His voice seemed to hang in the air, unnaturally loud.

They loaded the Chevrolet in silence. Jacques had spent days hunched over the engine, cursing and adjusting, determined that the vehicle would complete the journey without incident. William noticed fresh grease under the old man's fingernails, a small detail that registered alongside countless others.

The engine coughed twice before catching. Jacques eased the car down the rutted track, past the broken windmill and the stone wall William had repaired just yesterday. Marie sat in the middle, her hands folded in her lap, while William pressed against the passenger door, watching Trewil Loop recede in the side mirror until it vanished in the growing light.

The journey stretched before them like the dusty road itself—long, monotonous, uncomfortable. They passed through small towns still sleeping, farms where dogs barked at their passing, and vast stretches of empty veld. The sun climbed higher, baking the car's interior despite the open windows.

They stopped occasionally, brief pauses by the roadside where each walked a different direction, seeking momentary privacy. No words were exchanged even then—just nods indicating they were ready to continue.

By mid-afternoon, the landscape began to change. The air grew heavier, more humid. Palm trees appeared alongside the road, and eventually, the distant shimmer of the Indian Ocean came into view.

Durban emerged from the haze—a sprawling port city alive with noise and movement. The streets were crowded with people, many in uniform, their faces bright with the peculiar euphoria that follows collective survival. Banners proclaiming victory hung from buildings. Music spilled from open doorways.

A British soldier, face flushed with drink and celebration, approached their car at an intersection. He leaned in, grinning widely.

"Good day to you, sir! Isn't it wonderful? The war's over at last!"

He thrust his hand toward Jacques, who stiffened, his knuckles whitening on the steering wheel. A tremor passed through his body as his lips pulled back in a snarl.

"Jacques, no," Marie said quietly, her hand finding his arm. Her fingers pressed into his sleeve with surprising strength.

The soldier stepped back, confusion replacing his smile. "I only meant—"

"Go," Marie said to him, her voice gentle but firm. "Please."

The port was a chaos of activity—ships being loaded, sailors rushing about, families reuniting or saying goodbye. The Mauretania loomed over everything, a floating city of steel awaiting its passengers.

Jacques parked the car and sat motionless, staring straight ahead.

Marie turned to William, her eyes searching his face as if memorising it. "You will be fine," she said softly. "Remember who you were. Who you can be."

Jacques stepped out of the car, moving to the back where he roughly extracted William's bag. "Here," he said, holding it out. "The British government has arranged everything. Just follow the signs."

William took the bag, standing tall before the man who had shaped the last five years of his life. "Thank you," he said evenly. "Both of you. For everything."

Something flickered in Jacques's eyes—a momentary crack in his armour—before he nodded curtly. "Go on, then. Don't miss your ship."

William turned away, feeling the weight of their gaze on his back as he walked toward the gangway, neither looking back nor betraying the hollow ache expanding within his chest.

<hr>

There are some boys who return from war changed by what they have seen.

And then there are those changed by what they were taught to forget.

William Braithwaite came back not as a prodigal son, but as a foreign body slipped into the bloodstream of Britain. He carried no medals, no scars, no soldier's uniform—only silence, and a polished manner learned in the dust of another man's hatred.

The Liverpool docks materialised through morning fog like a watercolour painting slowly gaining definition. William stood at the Mauretania's rail, watching his birthplace emerge. The familiar skyline of warehouses and church spires should have stirred something within him. Instead, he catalogued them with clinical detachment, measuring the distance between what he remembered and what now existed.

A light rain fell as the gangway descended. William joined the queue of returning evacuees, each clutching their meagre possessions, many weeping with anticipation. Around him, families reunited in explosive bursts of emotion—mothers collapsing against children they barely recognised, fathers attempting stoicism while their eyes betrayed them.

William scanned the crowd methodically until he located his parents. They stood apart from the others, his father, Charles, in a charcoal suit, his mother, Margaret, in navy blue, both wearing expressions of cautious hope. He approached them with measured steps, accepting his mother's embrace without returning it, shaking his father's hand with perfect pressure.

"William," his mother whispered, touching his face. "You're so tall."

"The car is waiting," his father said, gesturing toward the street.

To the neighbours, he was well-mannered. Quiet. Distant. A boy made brittle by exile. They pitied him, as one pities anything that arrives out of sequence with its time.

Mrs Hartley from next door brought fruitcake. "Such a handsome young man," she said, studying him through her spectacles. "You must have stories to tell."

William smiled politely. "Nothing worth mentioning."

His old bedroom remained unchanged—preserved like a museum exhibit of childhood. Cricket bat in the corner. Model aeroplanes suspended from the ceiling. Books arranged by height on the shelf.

William sat on the edge of the bed, testing its softness after years of sleeping on a straw mattress. He opened the wardrobe to find clothes that would no longer fit him, arranged with painful optimism.

But the truth was quieter than pity.

Inside William, something had calcified.

He observed his parents at breakfast, noting how his mother's hands trembled slightly when passing the marmalade, how his father hid behind his newspaper, uncertain how to address this stranger wearing their son's face. They spoke of relatives he barely remembered, neighbourhood changes, rationing finally easing.

He had been taught not just to survive, but to dominate. To hollow himself out until only his purpose remained. His heart had been trained to beat in rhythm with cruelty—and to mistake that rhythm for strength.

In the garden, William found his father's toolshed and methodically examined each implement, testing weight and balance. The secateurs felt familiar in his hand, reminiscent of the pruning shears at Trewil Loop. He clipped a perfect rose from his mother's garden and presented it to her with a smile that never reached his eyes.

He had not come back to find his place in the world.

He had come back to own it.

At night, William stood at his bedroom window, watching lights extinguish across Liverpool. No more blackout curtains. No more air raid sirens. A city exhaling after years of held breath. Below, his parents spoke in hushed tones in the kitchen, their words drifting up through the open window.

"He's different," Margaret whispered. "So... contained."

"He'll adjust," Charles replied, without conviction. "Give him time."

And though no one could yet see it—beneath the handshakes, the soft wool coats, the boyish grin he wore like armour—a storm had begun to gather.

And William Braithwaite would not be caught in it.
He would be the one to bring it.

Chapter 10

The Course is Set

The brown Daimler slid through the morning streets of Liverpool, its chrome gleaming despite the lingering drizzle. William sat in the back, a precise distance from both parents, neither too close nor conspicuously far. The leather seats felt obscenely soft after years of wooden benches and sun-baked earth.

Their chauffeur, Hodges, drove with both hands clamped tightly on the wheel, jaw working as if grinding invisible objections into dust. Every bump in the road was a reminder of years of shortages and neglect.

"We'll stop in London first," Charles explained, breaking a twenty-minute silence. "I've matters at the office that can't wait. Then straight on to Wraysbury."

William nodded, filing away the information without comment. Wraysbury—the family estate he'd nearly forgotten. Images flickered through his mind: a stone entrance, gardens, a lake perhaps. The details had worn thin, like photographs left too long in sunlight.

"Your room is exactly as you left it," Margaret offered. "I made sure of it."

"Thank you," William replied, the words hollow and correct.

The journey stretched before them like a sentence to be served. Fields gave way to towns, towns to larger settlements. Conversation rose and fell in awkward bursts, punctuated by silences that grew more comfortable than the words themselves.

Charles spoke of the business—banking investments that had weathered the war, new opportunities in reconstruction. Margaret described distant relatives William barely remembered, their triumphs and tragedies catalogued with the precision of a museum curator.

As they approached the fractured heart of London, the city lay under a shroud of grey cloud and silent ruin, scarred by bomb craters, burned-out shells of terraces, and the skeletal remains of churches that once anchored neighbourhoods.

"The Germans were quite thorough," Charles remarked, his tone suggesting mild inconvenience rather than catastrophe.

Margaret offered snippets of chatter, remarks about the weather, the shortages, the rebuilding efforts—desperate little strings of words thrown back toward him across the growing gulf.

"They say rationing might ease by Christmas," she ventured. "Though sugar remains impossible."

William stared out the window, watching the city slide by in blurred fragments:

A child dragging a broken toy along a cracked pavement.

A woman patching holes in a bombed-out wall with pieces of old wood.

Men in suits and military greatcoats queuing in silence outside government buildings.

The war was over, they said. Victory had been declared.

But everywhere he looked, William saw defeat, exhaustion, and loss, ground into the very stones. Inside the car, conversation faltered again, the engine filling the silence with its mechanical rasp. Outside, the ruined city rolled past, indifferent to the hopes and plans of small men.

William watched it all—the broken buildings, the fractured streets, the weary people—and felt an unexpected kinship with them. Fire and loss had shaped them, ground down into something harder, something colder.

William leaned his forehead lightly against the glass, the chill seeping into his skin. "You can't go back," he thought, watching a row of shattered houses vanish behind them. "You can only go forward. Even if forward leads to nothing but ruins."

The car rattled onward through the ruins of a city, carrying a family that no longer truly existed.

Only the forms remained.

Charles glanced at his watch. "We'll be at the office shortly. You and your mother can wait in the car."

Margaret's fingers twisted in her lap. "Perhaps William might like to stretch his legs? See a bit of London?"

"No need," William said, his voice neutral. "I'm quite comfortable here."

In truth, he was studying them—their movements, their weaknesses, the careful dance of their marriage. Jacques had taught him to watch for leverage, for pressure points. Every relationship had them. Every person could be moved, if you understood which strings to pull.

The car slowed as they entered the financial district, where grand buildings stood largely untouched by bombs—as if even German pilots recognised the true centres of power.

⸺◆⸺

The Daimler's tires crunched over the gravel drive as they approached the Wraysbury estate. William watched as the grand Georgian house emerged from behind a veil of trees, its red-brick façade partially concealed beneath cascades of ivy that climbed like green fingers toward the slate roof. The vegetation had grown unchecked during the war years, lending the house an air of gentle neglect, as though nature were slowly reclaiming what man had built.

Hodges brought the car to a halt before the wide stone steps. Before he could open the door, three figures emerged from the house—Mrs Hartley, the housekeeper, Simmons the butler, and young Alice who helped with the cleaning. They stood in a neat row, arranged by height and station, their faces a careful blend of deference and genuine welcome.

"Welcome home, sir. Madam. Master William." Simmons bowed slightly, his spine as rigid as the day William had left for Africa. Only the new constellation of liver spots on his hands betrayed the passage of time.

William stepped from the car, assessing the house with cool detachment. It seemed smaller than he remembered, though no less imposing. The windows stared back at him, dark and reflective, revealing nothing of what lay within.

"Everything is prepared as you requested, madam," Mrs Hartley said, her voice carrying the same Yorkshire lilt that had once narrated bedtime stories. She had aged considerably, her once-auburn hair now steel grey, her face mapped with new lines.

The entrance hall welcomed them with the scent of beeswax and lemon polish—familiar yet distant, like a half-remembered dream. The grandfather clock that had stood sentinel since William's great-grand-father's time continued its steady heartbeat against the wall, its brass pendulum swinging with unwavering precision. It had survived two world wars without missing a beat, marking time while empires fell and rose again.

"I've had a fire lit in the drawing room," Mrs Hartley added, taking Margaret's coat.

William's gaze travelled across the hallway—the same oak umbrella stand in the corner, still bearing the scratch his wooden sword had inflicted when he was seven; the same threadbare runner lining the corridor that led to the east wing; the same framed sketches of fox hunts and seaside holidays adorning the walls—relics of a world that still clung to its illusions of permanence.

The house exuded an air of stubborn survival. Unlike London with its bomb sites and visible scars, Wraysbury had endured the war years with superficial dignity intact. Only subtle signs betrayed the strain: the slight discolouration where paintings had once hung, now sold to maintain appearances; the thinness of the carpet in high-traffic areas; the absence of certain silver pieces that had likely been converted to currency when investments faltered.

Charles placed his hat on the hall table with practised precision. "I'll be in my study. Have tea brought in, Simmons."

William ascended the main staircase, his fingers trailing along the polished bannister. The wood felt cool beneath his touch, smooth from generations of Braithwaite hands. Oil portraits of stern-faced ancestors tracked his progress, their eyes following him accusingly, as if they recognised the stranger wearing their descendant's skin.

On the landing, he paused before a window that overlooked the rear gardens. The once-immaculate hedgerows had grown shaggy, the tennis court was now a vegetable patch, and the ornamental pond had been drained—concessions to wartime practicality. Yet even in its diminished state, the property spoke of old money, of wealth so deeply embedded it could weather any storm.

The very walls seemed to whisper of generations of privilege, of inheritances and investments, of fortunes made in distant colonies and preserved through careful marriages and shrewd decisions. This was not merely a house but a fortress built to protect wealth across centuries.

❖

The dining room glowed with warm light from the crystal chandelier, casting a golden hue across the polished mahogany table. Simmons had summoned them with the gentle ring of a silver bell, its clear tone reverberating through the house like a call to ceremony.

"Dinner is served, sir," Simmons announced, standing at rigid attention as the family entered.

Charles pulled out Margaret's chair with practised gallantry. "Here you are, Peggy, love."

Margaret smiled, her eyes brightening momentarily as she took her seat. Her hand trembled slightly as she arranged her napkin, but her posture remained impeccable—a testament to breeding that even alcohol couldn't erode.

"It's lovely to have our boy back at the table," she said, reaching across to pat William's hand. Her touch lingered, seeking connection.

The first course arrived—clear consommé with fresh herbs from the kitchen garden. Steam rose from the bowls like ghosts, dissipating into the air.

"Cook has outdone herself," Charles remarked with the old cliche, his voice carrying the warm timbre of contentment. "Despite the rationing."

Margaret lifted her soup spoon with deliberate care. "Simmons, might I trouble you for a gin and tonic?"

"Of course, madam." Simmons blinked, then moved with the silent efficiency of long service.

Charles and Margaret exchanged stories of village life during the war years—the vicar's unfortunate incident with an incendiary bomb, Mrs Cavendish's heroic efforts with the Women's Voluntary Service, the time the Home Guard mistook Lord Harrington's gamekeeper for a German paratrooper.

William observed his parents with clinical detachment. His mother laughed too loudly at Charles' anecdotes, her mirth hollow and brittle. His father's eyes tracked Margaret's glass, measuring its emptying with subtle concern.

By the fish course, Margaret had emptied her second gin. The slight flush across her cheekbones deepened, and her words began to blur at the edges.

"You never wrote to us properly, William," she said suddenly, her voice sharper. "We worried terribly."

William cut his sole with surgical precision. "There was little to report."

"Little to report? Five years in Africa and little to report?" Margaret's laugh held no humour. "Or perhaps you simply didn't care to share it with us."

Charles cleared his throat. "Peggy, I'm sure William had his reasons."

"Did you even miss us at all?" Margaret pressed, leaning forward.

William met her gaze evenly. "I adapted to my circumstances."

Margaret's third gin arrived with the lamb. She drank deeply, her eyes never leaving William's face.

"Adapted. Such a cold word." She twisted her napkin between her fingers. "Do you know what it was like here? The bombs falling, never knowing if we'd wake up in the morning?"

"Margaret," Charles said, his tone warning that he had crossed from affectionate nickname to formal address.

She ignored him. "I begged Charles not to send you away. Did you know that? But he insisted. Said it was for your safety."

"It was for his safety," Charles said firmly. "And I would make the same decision again."

"Would you?" Margaret's voice rose. "When it turned our son into this... this stranger?"

The room fell silent save for the soft tick of the carriage clock on the mantelpiece.

"I think that's quite enough, Margaret." Charles' voice had hardened to granite.

He turned deliberately to William, his shoulders squared as if physically blocking Margaret from the conversation.

"Now then, William. We must discuss your future. I've been giving it considerable thought."

William set down his knife and fork with perfect symmetry.

"Cambridge, of course," Charles continued. "My alma mater. The connections you'll make there will serve you for life."

"I'm only sixteen," William observed.

"Precisely. Which gives us time to prepare you properly. Until then, you'll shadow me at Braithwaite Enterprises. Learn the family business from the ground up."

Margaret poured herself some wine, her movements sloppy. "More plans made without consulting anyone. How typical."

Charles continued as if she hadn't spoken. "Banking, finance, shipping—you'll need to understand it all. The war has created opportunities for those positioned to seize them."

William's initial impulse was to resist—to assert independence against this predetermined path. But as Charles spoke of boardrooms and balance sheets, of influence and capital, William recognised the value of what was being offered: not just wealth, but power. Access to the machinery that moved the world.

"I'm not certain I'm suited to business," William said carefully, watching his father's expression tighten. "But I'm willing to learn."

Charles relaxed, misreading calculated acquiescence for filial obedience.

"Excellent. We'll start Monday."

Margaret laughed bitterly. "And so the next generation of Braithwaites is forged. Cold, calculating men who reshape the world to their liking."

William surveyed the dining room—the ancestral portraits, the heavy silver, the fine china—all symbols of a legacy built on ambition and ruthlessness dressed in respectability.

Home was not where love waited. It was where expectations were draped over your shoulders like chains, dressed up in fine manners and well-polished silver. And he, William Charles Braithwaite, would not wear their chains forever.

He smiled at his father, a perfect mask of compliance. Inside, something cold and patient unfurled.

Charles pushed back his chair with a satisfied smile. "I've some papers to review from London. Shall we continue this discussion tomorrow, William?"

"Of course, Father."

Charles departed with a stern glance at Margaret, who had already reached for the decanter. The door closed with a soft click behind him.

"Come, William," Margaret said, rising unsteadily. "Let's have a proper chat in the sitting room."

William followed his mother, selecting a leather-bound volume from the bookshelf before settling into a wingback chair in the far corner. He opened the book—Machiavelli's *The Prince*—though the words blurred before his eyes as he observed Margaret.

She perched herself near the fireplace, emptied her wine glass with practised efficiency, then reached for the crystal decanter of sherry. The radio played softly—a symphony broadcast, strings rising and falling like a restless sea. Margaret had been talking steadily for some time, drifting from the same old topics to topics—old neighbours, the war, rationing, the sacrifices they had made, the price everyone had paid. Her voice thickened by drink, laced with a brittle, shimmering tension.

William answered when necessary—nods and small monosyllables, careful not to provoke her.

"The Hartingtons lost their eldest at Dunkirk," she continued, swirling amber liquid in her glass. "And poor Evelyn Morton—her husband came back without his legs. Without his legs, William."

"Terrible," William murmured, turning a page he hadn't read.

But Margaret didn't want conversation. She wanted absolution.

"You've no idea what we suffered here," she said, her voice rising. "The bombs, the fear, the constant waiting for news. And what did we get for sending you away? For trying to keep you safe?"

She gestured wildly toward him, sherry sloshing over the rim of her glass.

"This... this coldness. This... look. As if we failed you somehow."

She struggled to her feet, the chair scraping loudly against the floor, and took a wobbling step toward him.

"We gave you everything," she hissed, growing angrier with each uncertain step. "Everything! And you come back looking at us like... like we're strangers to be studied."

Her foot caught the edge of the Persian rug. She staggered sideways, crashing into the low side table. Her cheek struck the corner, and the lamp rattled, toppled, and clattered to the floor.

Margaret let out a sharp cry—more frustration than pain—and sank onto the carpet in a tangle of skirts and indignation.

William rose instinctively, taking a half-step forward—hand half-lifted to help. But Margaret's head snapped up, her eyes wide and wild.

"Don't you touch me!" she shrieked, scrambling backward. "Don't you dare lay a hand on me!"

Footsteps pounded down the hall—Charles, summoned by the crash and the cry.

He burst into the room, took in the scene—the overturned lamp, the scattered books, Margaret's trembling form on the floor—and turned to William with thunder darkening his face and eyes.

"What the hell have you done?" he demanded.

William opened his mouth—no words came.

Margaret sobbed brokenly, pressing the back of her hand to her cheek in a trembling, theatrical gesture.

Not an outright accusation.

Not quite.

But enough.

Charles crossed the room in two strides. His hand found William's face with a short, brutal slap—the sound cracking through the room like the breaking of bone china.

William staggered a step backward, catching himself before he fell.

The blow wasn't vicious—not damaging—but it landed harder than fists: a judgment, a sentence, an unspoken declaration.

Margaret sobbed harder. Charles turned away from his son without another word, kneeling instead at his wife's side, gathering her in his arms.

William stood there for a moment longer, the taste of copper rising in his mouth.

He touched the corner of his lip absently, finding no blood, only the burning outline of Charles's hand.

The room seemed very small suddenly, very still, the edges of it closing in like a noose.

Without a word, he picked up his book from where it had fallen, straightened the toppled chair, and walked out—the click of the sitting room door behind him loud as a gunshot.

He mounted the stairs slowly, his body moving as if through water, heavy and numb.

He did not look back.

—◆◇◆—

William had just reached the landing when Charles's voice cracked through the house, low and commanding:

"Stay where you are."

The weight of it pinned William in place, his hand still resting on the polished bannister, his body half-turned toward the sanctuary of his room.

Footsteps pounded on the stairs. A door banged somewhere below. Margaret's sobs faded behind wood and stone. Only Charles remained now, and the judgment he carried with him.

Charles came into view — his face florid, jaw clenched so tightly that the cords of his neck stood out starkly against his collar.

He paused three steps below William, looking up at him with an expression that was not anger, but something worse: disappointment, solid as a blade.

"Your mother is not well," Charles said, voice low but cutting. "And I will not have her hurt under my roof. Not by anyone."

William stared at him, unblinking.

There was no point speaking. The verdict had already been delivered.

Charles climbed the last few stairs with slow deliberation, standing close enough that William could smell the faint trace of whisky on his breath — the constant, unspoken companion to the Braithwaite household.

Without warning, Charles's hand lashed out — not a slap this time, not a blow delivered in passion.

A shove, hard and deliberate, sending William stumbling back against the wall.

Not enough to injure.

Just enough to mark a line in the dust.

Just enough to say:

"You are smaller. You are guilty. You will submit."

William caught himself on the plaster, the sharp corner of the skirting board jabbing into his side.

He straightened slowly, his face a mask of calm.

Charles loomed a moment longer, breathing heavily, as if expecting protest, resistance, tears.

When none came, he turned sharply on his heel.

"Sort yourself out," he barked over his shoulder, the words tossed like garbage. "We'll speak again in the morning."

The sound of his footsteps receding down the stairs was hollow, final.

William remained where he was for a long moment, one hand resting lightly against the wall where the impact had jarred him.

No anger. No tears. No appeal.

Only the clear, cold knowledge settling into his bones:

There would be no sanctuary here.

No safety.

No justice.

Only the necessary performance of family—the brittle pantomime—until such time as he no longer needed them at all.

Without a sound, he pushed himself upright and walked the remaining steps to his room, closing the door behind him with the softest of clicks.

Not slamming it.

Not rebelling.

Simply... leaving them behind.

In every way that mattered.

◆◇◆

The door closed behind him with a soft click, shutting out the world beyond.

William stood in the centre of his old bedroom — the room that had been preserved like a shrine, a frozen memory of a boy who no longer existed.

The narrow bed, neatly made.

The shelves lined with books he no longer recognised.

The faded pennants on the wall — cricket clubs, seaside towns — relics of a life so distant it might have belonged to another boy entirely.

He crossed to the window and pulled the curtains back slightly, peering out into the night.

The garden below was empty, save for the faint yellow pools of light under the gas lamps. London slept, wounded and weary.

William let the curtain fall back into place.

Without undressing, he lowered himself onto the bed, the mattress sagging beneath his weight with a soft sigh, as if mourning his return.

The room smelled the same — dust, linen, the faint metallic tang of radiator pipes — but it held no comfort now. Only echoes.

On the nightstand beside the bed lay a small object—a smooth stone, worn nearly flat by time and water.

He picked it up, feeling its weight settle into his palm.

It was a river stone, taken from the stream that ran near the farm in Natal.

A piece of that brutal exile, a relic from the place where he had learned the first real lessons of life:

Pain. Endurance. Silence.

He closed his fingers around it tightly, feeling the coolness seep into his skin.

Grounding him.

Anchoring him.

Somewhere in the house below, a door slammed. Voices rose—Margaret's sharp and slurred, Charles's gruff and dismissive.

Another round of accusations, apologies, old ghosts reanimated for the thousandth time.

William did not move.

He felt nothing toward them now—no anger, no love, not even pity.

Only clarity.

The boy they had sent away had died somewhere far from here, beneath different stars, in the long years when no letters came, when promises turned to dust.

The boy they welcomed home tonight was a stranger.

Polite.

Obedient.

Carefully hollow.

A tool that could be wielded, for now, until the moment came when he no longer needed their shelter, their money, their names.

And when that day came, he would leave without a backwards glance.

He placed the stone back on the nightstand and lay down fully, staring up at the cracked plaster ceiling.

The old patterns were still there — shapes and maps traced over sleepless nights of childhood — but he no longer recognised them.

The silence deepened, stretching wide and cold.

He folded his hands behind his head, closed his eyes, and made no prayers.

None would have been heard anyway.

———————◀O▶———————

The bathroom was small and cold, lit only by the weak, yellow glow of a single wall sconce above the mirror.

Tiles cracked faintly beneath Margaret's knees as she knelt by the porcelain basin, her hands gripping the edges as if to anchor herself against a storm only she could feel.

The taste of wine and gin soured her mouth. The room tilted slightly when she closed her eyes, but the spinning had slowed now, leaving only the heavy, steady throb of a headache gathering behind her eyes.

She sat back on her heels, wiping at her face with trembling fingers, and stared at her reflection.

The woman who gazed back at her was not the one she remembered.

The carefully pinned hair had come loose in wisps around her temples.

The fine lines around her mouth, the faint puffiness beneath her eyes, the desperate, brittle sheen of tears barely held at bay—these were new, unwelcome visitors.

She looked tired. Older.

Lost.

A sob slipped from her throat before she could catch it—not loud, not dramatic, just a small, broken sound that seemed almost too soft for the tiled room to contain.

Margaret pressed both hands to her face, breathing raggedly against the coolness of her palms.

"What have I done?" she whispered into the hollow space.

Images tumbled through her mind — the dinner table, the forced laughter, the weight of Charles's expectations pressing down over them all — and then William's face.

So still.

So closed.

Not angry.

Not even hurt.

Worse—resigned.

And then her own voice, slurred and ugly, lashing out at him like a cornered animal.

The stumble, the fall.

The wild, shameful accusation — flung out not because she believed it, but because she had been too proud, too humiliated, too small to bear the weight of her own collapse.

And Charles, who hadn't hesitated.

Her boy—her only boy—struck down by the hand of the man he should have been able to trust most.

Because of her.

The memory of it rose in her chest like bile. She gagged, pressing harder against her face as if she could erase herself.

She could still feel the way William had looked at her when Charles's hand came down, not with anger.

Not even with hatred.

With nothing.

That emptiness terrified her more than any shouted accusation ever could have.

Margaret leaned against the cold ceramic of the sink, sobbing quietly, the sound absorbed by the tiles, the mirror, the unblinking gaze of her ruined reflection.

She had lost him.

Not tonight.

Not even five years ago, when she kissed him goodbye at the docks and watched the smoke and steam swallow him whole.

She had lost him in every moment she chose silence over apology, pride over truth, drink over courage.

And now, when she finally saw it clearly, it was already too late.

No apology would bridge the chasm she had torn open.

No confession would cleanse the stain.

She could still stand in his world, she supposed—still be "Mother," still be invited to ceremonies and celebrations in the hollow future Charles envisioned.

But she would never again be home to him.

Margaret pressed her forehead to the cold mirror, her breath fogging the glass.

"I'm sorry," she whispered, too soft for anyone but herself to hear. "I'm so, so sorry."

The mirror showed no mercy.

Chapter 11

Silhouettes and Shadows

William descended the broad staircase at Wraysbury the following morning, his footsteps precise and measured on the worn carpet. The night's sleep had been shallow, disturbed by half-formed dreams of salt water and distant voices. Now, the house was silent except for the mournful ticking of the grandfather clock in the entrance hall, marking time with relentless indifference.

In the breakfast room, his mother sat alone at the table, her hands wrapped around a teacup as if seeking warmth despite the mild summer morning. She looked up as he entered, her face composed now, the previous night's alcohol purged from her system if not her memory.

"William," she said, her voice carefully neutral. "There's eggs and toast if you'd like. Your father's already left for the office."

He nodded, helping himself to a modest portion before sitting across from her. The silence stretched between them, taut as piano wire.

"I was thinking," William said finally, his voice betraying nothing of the calculation behind his words, "about Gregory. I should write to him, let him know I've returned."

Margaret's teacup froze halfway to her lips. A flicker of something—pain? guilt?—crossed her face before she set it down with deliberate care.

"Oh, William." Her voice had softened, carrying a weight he hadn't expected. "I thought... I assumed you knew."

William paused, fork suspended above his plate. "Knew what?"

Margaret's fingers trembled slightly as she smoothed the tablecloth. "The City of Benares. Gregory's ship. It was torpedoed in the Atlantic. September 1940, just a few weeks after you left."

The information struck William like a physical blow. Gregory. His friend. The boy who'd stood beside him through everything, who'd given him the tin whistle as a parting gift.

"What happened to him?" William asked, his voice unnaturally calm.

"He was listed as missing, presumed..." She couldn't finish. "There were very few survivors. Only thirteen children made it out of ninety."

William set his fork down carefully. "When were you going to tell me?"

"I thought you knew. There were letters. We wrote to you in South Africa."

"I never received any letters." His voice was flat, controlled.

Margaret's eyes widened slightly. "None of them? We sent dozens."

William stood abruptly, turning to the window. Outside, a gardener was trimming the hedges, the rhythmic snipping a counterpoint to the sudden roaring in his ears.

"Gregory is dead," he stated, testing the words, searching for the expected pain, the grief that should accompany such knowledge.

But where there should have been anguish, he found only a curious emptiness. The boy who had cared for Gregory, who had treasured their friendship, seemed as distant to William now as the stars. That child had been left behind on the Liverpool docks, or perhaps buried somewhere in the red soil of Trewil Loop.

He should feel something. Rage at his parents for not ensuring he knew. Sorrow for his lost friend. Instead, he felt only a cold, analytical interest in his own lack of response.

"I'm sorry, William," his mother said, her voice breaking. "So terribly sorry."

William turned back to face her, studying her genuine distress with clinical detachment. He recognised an opportunity to appear normal, to maintain the facade of the son they expected.

"It was a long time ago," he said, injecting a careful note of resignation into his voice. "Five years. I'm not the same person I was."

Margaret looked up sharply, perhaps hearing the truth beneath his measured response.

"Still, he was your closest friend."

William nodded, performing the role required of him. "Yes. He was."

But as he resumed his seat and methodically finished his breakfast, William realised that Gregory's death—shocking as it should have been—was merely information to be processed, catalogued, and filed away. The noise of his homecoming, the challenges of navigating his new reality, had crowded out any genuine emotional response.

He was alone now. Truly alone. The realisation came not with fear but with a strange, cold clarity. No one would truly understand what had happened to him at Trewil Loop, how Jacques had reshaped him, hardened him against sentiment and weakness. Withheld his letters from home.

Perhaps it was better this way. No attachments meant no vulnerabilities. No expectations beyond those he chose to fulfil.

As his mother watched him with concern, William calculated his next moves with the precision Jacques had taught him. He would learn his father's business. He would accumulate knowledge, resources, connections. He would chart his own course, answerable to no one.

The boy who had once needed Gregory Talbot was gone. In his place stood someone new—someone who needed no one at all.

⸺◦⸺

The oak-panelled office of Braithwaite Enterprises stood on the third floor of a Portland stone building that had somehow survived the Blitz intact. While neighbouring structures showed the scars of German bombs—blackened facades, boarded windows, and in some cases, nothing but rubble-filled foundations—the Braithwaite headquarters remained pristine, as though war itself had respectfully kept its distance.

William sat in a leather wingback chair positioned near his father's mahogany desk, which dominated the room like a battleship. The desk was impeccably ordered: fountain pens arranged by size, papers stacked with military precision, a crystal decanter of amber liquid that caught the weak October sunlight. Behind the desk hung an oil portrait of William's grandfather, the company's founder, his stern gaze seemingly following every movement in the room.

The carpet beneath William's feet—a deep burgundy Persian—had been imported before trade routes closed during the war. The walls displayed hunting scenes and maps of far-flung territories where Braithwaite interests had taken root. A glass-fronted bookcase contained leather-bound financial records dating back decades, the company's history preserved like sacred texts.

Through the tall windows, William observed London's battered skyline. Cranes rose like mechanical giraffes above bombed-out districts. Workers in overalls cleared debris from streets still marked with white directional arrows from the blackout years. The city looked exhausted yet determined, like a boxer rising for the final round.

A discreet telephone sat on a side table, its black receiver gleaming. William had already observed three calls that morning—one from the Ministry of Supply, another from an American investor, and a third from someone Charles had addressed only as "the Minister." Each conversation had ended with his father's thin smile of satisfaction.

The wall clock—Swiss-made, with gold inlay—ticked towards eleven. Charles had been in the boardroom for nearly two hours now, leaving William to absorb the atmosphere of power that permeated every corner of the office.

On the desk lay yesterday's Financial Times, its headline announcing continued rationing despite victory celebrations. Paper rationing had reduced its size, but not its influence. Beside it sat a confidential memorandum regarding the conversion of wartime manufacturing to peacetime production—a challenge many companies were failing to navigate successfully.

Not Braithwaite Enterprises. The papers William had been permitted to review revealed a corporation that had not merely survived the war but thrived on it. While London burned during the Blitz, Braithwaite factories produced munitions at unprecedented rates. When shipping became perilous, Charles acquired warehouse space at premium locations, then leased it to desperate merchants at extortionate prices. When refugee labour became available, Braithwaite operations expanded overnight, paying minimal wages for maximum output.

Each crisis had been an opportunity. Each national sacrifice had yielded corporate gain. The company had doubled in size since 1939, its tentacles now reaching into shipping, manufacturing, property, and—most recently—the reconstruction contracts that would rebuild Britain's shattered cities.

The boardroom door opened, and men in expensive suits filed out, nodding deferentially to William as they passed. These were the lieutenants who had executed Charles's wartime strategy—men who understood that patriotism and profit were not mutually exclusive concepts.

Charles appeared last, shaking hands with a grey-haired man whose pinstriped suit couldn't disguise his military bearing. "The Minister will be pleased," the man said quietly. "Very pleased indeed."

Charles nodded, his smile revealing nothing. "England expects, Brigadier. Braithwaite delivers."

When they were alone, Charles turned to William, satisfaction radiating from him like heat from a furnace. "This," he said, gesturing to encompass not just the office but the empire it represented, "is what awaits you. Not the England they're rebuilding out there—something far greater."

William rose, his expression carefully neutral despite the surge of understanding that flowed through him. Here was power without pretence, ambition without apology. Here was a world where sentiment took a distant second place to strategy.

It felt like coming home.

⸺⬥⸺

The boardroom of Braithwaite Enterprises stretched beneath a coffered ceiling, its walls panelled in walnut that had darkened over decades of cigar smoke and whispered ambitions. Again, a portrait of the company's founder—William's grandfather—hung at one end, his severe expression surveying the table as though judging each man's worthiness to sit at it.

William, freshly seventeen as of the previous week, occupied a chair near the door—present but peripheral, exactly as Charles had instructed. "Observe, absorb, and above all, remain silent," his father had said that morning, straightening William's tie with hands that brooked no argument.

Around the gleaming mahogany table sat twelve men, each a carefully positioned piece on Charles Braithwaite's chessboard. Department heads, financial directors, and legal counsel arranged themselves according to an invisible hierarchy that William had quickly decoded during his weeks at headquarters. Nearest to Charles sat Hargreaves, the silver-haired Chief Financial Officer whose loyalty had been purchased decades ago with generous stock options. Opposite him, Richardson from Legal, whose expertise in navigating regulatory loopholes had proven invaluable during wartime contracts.

And then there were the uncles.

Duncan Braithwaite, fifty-one and corpulent, sat three seats from Charles, his jowls quivering slightly as he feigned interest in the quarterly reports. William had learned that Duncan controlled the shipping division—a position granted more from familial obligation than competence. His son Malcolm, twenty-six and Oxford-educated, was being groomed for greater responsibilities despite a drinking problem that the family politely ignored.

Edward Braithwaite, forty-four and rail-thin, occupied a seat near the far end, his bony fingers drumming silently on the tabletop. Edward managed the property portfolio with cold efficiency, though William had discovered through careful investigation that several prime acquisitions had mysteriously been diverted to holding companies that benefited Edward's son Peter rather than the main corporation.

"Gentlemen," Charles began, "our expansion into reconstruction contracts has exceeded projections by seventeen percent." He nodded toward Hargreaves, who distributed bound reports embossed with the Braithwaite crest. "The Minister has personally expressed his gratitude for our efficiency in clearing the East End sites."

William observed how his uncles exchanged glances—brief but loaded with meaning. Duncan's lips tightened while Edward's eyebrows rose fractionally. They were displeased, though anyone less observant might have missed it entirely.

"The American investment," Duncan ventured, his voice carrying a hint of challenge, "seems rather speculative given the current climate."

Charles smiled thinly. "The Americans understand that reconstruction presents opportunities that transcend borders. Their capital ensures we maintain controlling interest rather than diluting our position."

"Malcolm's analysis suggests alternative approaches," Duncan remarked, almost casually.

"How interesting," Charles replied with glacial politeness. "Perhaps Malcolm might benefit from collaboration with our financial team at some point."

The temperature in the room seemed to drop several degrees. William maintained a carefully neutral expression, though inwardly he recognised the manoeuvre for what it was—Charles deflecting Duncan's attempt to position Malcolm within the company hierarchy.

Edward cleared his throat. "Our assessment of the Liverpool properties indicates promising returns, particularly if we convert to residential rather than commercial."

William noted how Edward avoided looking at Charles directly—a tell that the Liverpool portfolio was likely another attempt to carve out territory beyond Charles's immediate oversight. The moves and countermoves continued throughout the meeting, a sophisticated game of corporate positioning with the Braithwaite legacy as the ultimate prize.

As the meeting concluded, William caught both uncles studying him when they thought he wasn't looking. Their expressions contained calculation, assessment, and something darker—the recognition of an obstacle to their ambitions. William held their gaze for precisely two seconds before returning his attention to his notes, his face revealing nothing of the strategies already forming in his mind.

Time, William knew, was his greatest ally. His uncles would expect him to act recklessly, to expose his ambitions prematurely. Instead, he would wait, observe, and prepare. After all, Jacques de Beer had taught him that patience was the deadliest weapon in any predator's arsenal.

⊸◇⊷

The meeting room emptied gradually, conversations trailing into silence as the last executives departed. Charles remained seated at the head of the table, his fountain pen tapping against the polished mahogany surface in a precise rhythm—three taps, then a pause, like the metronomic heartbeat of a predator at rest. He had not dismissed William, who understood the unspoken command to stay, having discerned over the last few weeks how to interpret his father's silences as clearly as his words. Richardson and Hargreaves also lingered, exchanging knowing glances that suggested foreknowledge of what was to come, their bodies angled slightly toward Charles in unconscious deference.

The late afternoon sunlight slanted through the half-drawn blinds, casting striped shadows across the table's gleaming surface and highlighting the silver in Charles's temples. A distant telephone rang somewhere in the building, then fell silent, emphasising the chamber's isolation from the world beyond its oak-panelled walls.

When the heavy oak door finally closed with a soft but definitive click, Charles leaned forward, folding his hands with the deliberate precision of a man accustomed to orchestrating lives. His dark blue eyes—calculating and cold—swept across the three faces before him.

"Gentlemen," he began, his voice pitched low despite the room's emptiness, each syllable weighted with authority, "we have matters of succession to discuss."

The word hung in the air—succession—with all its weight of inheritance, continuity, and power. It seemed to expand into the silence, filling the space between them with unspoken implications of dynasty and control. William felt three pairs of eyes assess him simultaneously, measuring his potential against some invisible standard that had been established long before his birth. Hargreaves's gaze was clinical, Richardson's speculative, and his father's—most unsettling of all—utterly inscrutable.

"William's education has suffered a significant interruption," Charles continued, directing his words primarily to Hargreaves, his fingers now perfectly still against the polished wood. "Five years in that godforsaken place has left considerable gaps. The war has taken much from everyone, but I will not allow it to claim my son's future. Cambridge will not lower its standards, even for a Braithwaite."

Hargreaves nodded, already producing a slim leather notebook from his breast pocket with practised efficiency. The silver-haired CFO's movements were precise, economical, the actions of a man who had anticipated this conversation for weeks, perhaps months.

"The entrance requirements remain rigorous, Charles. Latin, mathematics, and history at a minimum. The examinations will require comprehensive preparation—particularly the Latin compositions and mathematical proofs. Nothing less than excellence will suffice." He paused, tapping his fountain pen against the notebook. "The competition for places has intensified with returning servicemen seeking to resume interrupted studies."

"We have less than two years," Charles stated flatly, his tone brooking no argument or excuse. "My connections with the Admissions Committee will open doors, but William must cross the threshold on his own merit. The Braithwaite name must never appear diminished by charity or special dispensation. It would undermine everything we've built."

William maintained his composure, his ice-blue eyes betraying nothing of his inner thoughts, though inwardly he calculated the enormity of the task with cold precision. Five years of formal education compressed into twenty-four months, while simultaneously learning the business that would one day be his inheritance. The challenge stirred something in him—not anxiety, not fear, but a cold determination that settled in his chest like a stone. This was a test, the first of many, and he had no intention of failing.

"I'll arrange the necessary tutors immediately," Hargreaves said, making swift notations in his book. "The best in each discipline, regardless of cost. Former Cambridge dons with experience preparing candidates under extraordinary circumstances. Intense, private instruction six days weekly, with comprehensive assessments monthly to track progress. Might get it done." His last words carried the faintest hint of doubt—unusual for the typically assured financier.

Charles turned to Richardson, whose thin face remained impassive beneath steel-grey hair that seemed carved rather than grown. The Head Legal Counsel sat perfectly still, hands folded on the table, watching the proceedings with the detached interest of a chess master observing an opening gambit.

"Lionel, William requires more than academic knowledge. He must understand how power operates beyond textbooks—the unwritten rules that govern real influence." Charles's eyes narrowed slightly. "The machinery behind the machinery."

Richardson inclined his head slightly, the gesture containing both acknowledgement and complicity. "I understand perfectly, Charles." His voice was soft but carried effortlessly, the voice of a man accustomed to being heard in courtrooms and boardrooms alike.

"Teach him negotiation—not the theoretical nonsense they peddle at university, but the practical art of securing advantage. Show him how to read a man's weakness across a boardroom table." Charles's voice hardened, acquiring a cutting edge that sliced through the room's hushed atmosphere. "And introduce him to the right people. Quietly, discreetly. The sons of ministers, permanent secretaries, industrialists. The men who will occupy positions of influence when William takes his rightful place."

"A network of relationships built early bears fruit for decades," Richardson observed, studying William with new interest, as though seeing not the young man before him but the powerful figure he might become. "I'll begin with dinner at my club next Thursday. Lord Blackwood's son will be in attendance—he's apparently headed for the Foreign Office after Cambridge. The Cunningham boy might also prove useful—impressive family connections, and—as I said—I hear he's Cambridge-bound himself."

William absorbed this exchange without comment, his posture relaxed yet attentive, recognising it as the first move in a complex game of positioning that would span years, perhaps decades. His father was not merely preparing him for university; he was arranging the pieces for William's eventual assumption of power. The board was being set, alliances and connections mapped out with the same strategic foresight that had built Braithwaite Enterprises into an empire.

"And what of my uncles?" William asked, breaking his silence with a question that caused all three men to turn toward him sharply. The question hung in the air, unexpected and potentially dangerous—touching as it did on the unspoken power struggle within the Braithwaite family.

Charles's expression remained unchanged, though something flickered in his eyes—perhaps surprise, perhaps approval at his son's directness. He studied William for a long moment before responding, as if reassessing some internal calculation.

"Your uncles," he replied carefully, each word measured and precise, "will be managed. Duncan and Edward have their uses, but limited vision. Focus on your education and the connections Richardson establishes. The rest will unfold as it must." His tone suggested both finality and warning—this particular discussion would go no further today.

The implicit message was clear: the succession was already determined. William's path had been chosen. All that remained was for him to walk it with sufficient skill to justify his father's confidence—and to neutralise any obstacles, familial or otherwise, that might appear along the way.

— ◄O► —

The Athenaeum Club stood on Pall Mall like a Grecian temple transposed on London's heart, its stone façade gleaming pale against the evening sky. A massive Doric portico marked the entrance, beneath which men of consequence had passed for over a century. Inside, the air carried the complex bouquet of old leather, beeswax polish, and the ghost of countless cigars—scents that spoke of power and malice maintained across generations. The muted ticking of an ancient grandfather clock punctuated the silence, marking time as it had for the empire's elite since Victoria's reign.

William followed Richardson through the grand entrance hall, where Italian marble stretched beneath their feet and ornate plasterwork adorned the ceiling. Portraits of distinguished members gazed down from gilded frames, their eyes seeming to assess each newcomer's worthiness. The weight of history pressed down with almost physical force—judges, prime ministers, industrialists, and generals staring through the veil of time with expressions that suggested they found the present wanting.

"The club was founded in 1824," Richardson murmured as they climbed the sweeping staircase, his hand barely touching the polished mahogany bannister. "For men of science, literature, and art, though the definition has... expanded somewhat." His thin lips curved in the suggestion of a smile, revealing teeth yellowed by decades of expensive tobacco. "The waiting list spans decades, unless one has the right connections. Your father secured your future membership the week after your birth."

The dining room occupied the first floor, a space of cathedral-like proportions where conversation remained hushed despite the hundred or so men present. Crystal chandeliers cast a warm glow over tables draped in starched white linen, each setting arranged with military precision—silver gleaming, crystal winking in the subdued light. Waiters in black tailcoats moved with professional invisibility between tables, appearing precisely when needed and vanishing when not, their footfalls absorbed by the thick burgundy carpet.

"Lord Blackwood prefers the corner table," Richardson said, guiding William past members who nodded deferentially to the lawyer. Several pairs of eyes lingered on William, assessing Charles Braithwaite's heir with undisguised curiosity. "His son Lyle will join us shortly. Clever young man—headed for the Foreign Office after Cambridge. Pay attention to how he carries himself. In these circles, bearing communicates as much as words."

William absorbed the instruction silently, cataloguing it alongside the morning's intensive tutorial on differential equations and the afternoon's lesson in corporate tax law. Every interaction now carried dual purpose: immediate utility and future application. His father had made it clear—education extended far beyond Cambridge's lecture halls into these rarefied spaces where real power resided.

Lord Blackwood rose as they approached—a tall man with silver temples and the bearing of someone accustomed to authority. His dinner jacket fit with bespoke perfection across broad shoulders that had barely stooped with age. His handshake was firm, his assessment of William swift and penetrating, ice-blue eyes not unlike William's own making a thorough inventory.

"Charles Braithwaite's boy," he said, not quite a question. The words carried a weight of history William couldn't fully decipher. "I knew your grandfather. Formidable man. You have something of his jawline."

The conversation flowed into business and politics, the three men discussing the Labour government's nationalisation plans with the detached interest of naturalists observing an exotic specimen. William contributed sparingly but precisely, each comment earning a thoughtful nod from Richardson or Blackwood. The waiter appeared silently to pour wine, a vintage Bordeaux that Lord Blackwood approved with the barest inclination of his head.

Halfway through the first course—a delicate consommé served in Wedgwood china—William noticed a young man enter the dining room. Tall and fair-haired, he moved with a quiet confidence that drew attention without seeming to seek it. His dinner jacket was impeccably cut, neither ostentatious nor overly conservative. Several older members acknowledged him as he passed, and William observed how he returned each greeting with perfect calibration—respectful without being deferential, familiar without presumption.

"Ah, my son arrives," Lord Blackwood remarked, following William's gaze. "Late, as usual. Cambridge will do little to improve his punctuality, though much for his intellect."

Lyle Cunningham approached their table, apologised for his tardiness with an exact charm, and took his seat. His blue eyes met William's briefly—a moment of mutual assessment, neither warm nor cold but intensely curious. William recognised something in that gaze, a quality he couldn't immediately name but that resonated with his own nature—a particular kind of hunger, perhaps, carefully masked behind impeccable manners.

Throughout dinner, William and Lyle participated in separate conversations—William with Richardson, Lyle with his father—yet each remained aware of the other. William noted how Lyle spoke: precise, measured, revealing exactly what he intended and nothing more. When Lord Blackwood mentioned a diplomatic incident in Argentina, Lyle offered an analysis that suggested knowledge beyond what newspapers reported, his fingers toying absently with his signet ring as he outlined the geopolitical implications with unsettling accuracy.

Similarly, when Richardson prompted William to explain Braithwaite's position on the steel shortage, Lyle listened without appearing to, his attention seemingly fixed on his plate while his posture betrayed his interest. The slight tilt of his head, the momentary stillness of his knife and fork—subtle tells that William catalogued instinctively.

Neither young man addressed the other directly, yet by the meal's end, an unspoken recognition had formed between them—not friendship, not alliance, but acknowledgement of a kindred quality. They were alike in some essential way that distinguished them from the older men at the table, a shared understanding that power was not merely inherited but cultivated through patient strategy. The candlelight caught in Lyle's eyes as he glanced at William over the rim of his port glass, revealing a calculating intelligence that mirrored William's own.

As they departed, navigating between tables where men who controlled Britain's destiny lingered over brandy and cigars, Lyle nodded once to William, the gesture containing neither warmth nor challenge but something more valuable: respect. William returned it precisely, knowing they would meet again, and sensing that when they did, it would matter. In that brief exchange lay the foundation of something that would outlast the ancient club around them—a partnership forged not in friendship, but in mutual recognition of ambition's true face.

Chapter 12

The Sharpening Stone

William stepped from the train at Cambridge station, the October air sharp with promise and decay. A light mist clung to the platforms where students gathered in clusters, their voices creating a symphony of accents—the clipped consonants of public schools, the rolling cadence of northern counties, and the occasional American drawl from Rhodes scholars. Porter whistles punctuated the cacophony as smoke from the engine drifted across the scene like theatrical fog.

He claimed his trunk with ritual efficiency, ignoring the chaos around him. Unlike the other freshers who moved in packs, eyes wide with anticipation or anxiety, William stood apart—observing, calculating, cataloguing. This place would be his crucible for the next three years—maybe more, not a sanctuary of learning but a forge where he would hammer himself into something formidable.

The taxi wound through narrow streets that had witnessed eight centuries of ambition. William's gaze swept over medieval churches and Tudor shopfronts, past the Senate House where degrees had been conferred since before Columbus sailed, and along King's Parade where bicycles swarmed like mechanical insects. The ancient stones seemed to breathe history, exuding a quiet arrogance that matched his own.

"First time up, sir?" the driver asked, glancing in the rearview mirror.

"Yes," William replied, offering nothing more.

"Exciting times. First year that women are full members, you know. Five hundred years of tradition gone just like that." The driver snapped his fingers. "Mind you, they've been studying here since the war started—Girton and Newnham girls—but couldn't get proper degrees till now. Just certificates."

William absorbed this information silently, adding it to his mental inventory of Cambridge's power structures. The taxi turned onto Trinity Street, where students in undergraduate gowns billowed past like crows.

"Lots of ex-servicemen too," the driver continued into the silence. "Strange mix this year—boys fresh from school alongside chaps who've seen action in Burma. Makes for interesting tutorials, I'd imagine."

The taxi halted before massive wooden gates. Beyond them lay the First Court of St. John's College, a quadrangle of honey-coloured stone that had housed scholars since 1511. William paid the fare and hoisted his trunk onto the cobblestones, the weight familiar after years of farm labour at Trewil Loop.

He passed beneath the Tudor archway where generations of prime ministers, poets, and scientists had walked before him. The porter's lodge stood to his right, a bastion of college rules and traditions. Ahead, the court opened like a medieval vision—four ranges of buildings surrounding a perfect square of lawn that no undergraduate dared tread upon. Gargoyles leered from gutters, and mullioned windows reflected the weak autumn sun.

"Braithwaite? William Braithwaite?" A voice cut through his assessment.

A college servant approached, grey-haired and deferential. "I'll show you to your rooms, sir. Second court, staircase nine." William could sense his father's influence here.

They crossed the first quadrangle, footsteps echoing against stone that had witnessed plagues, wars, and revolutions with equal indifference. In the second court, even more magnificent than the first, sunlight illuminated the chapel's stained glass, casting jewelled patterns across the ancient flagstones.

"Quite the change from last year," the servant remarked as they climbed the worn oak staircase. "College was half-empty during the war. Then came the ex-servicemen on government grants—serious types, they are. Seen too much to waste time with undergraduate nonsense."

William's rooms occupied the second floor—a sitting room with leaded windows overlooking the court, a bedroom tucked behind, and a small study alcove. The ceilings were low, crossed with blackened beams that had witnessed four centuries of scholarly ambition.

"Coal allowance is limited, I'm afraid," the servant explained, gesturing to the fireplace. "Rationing still in effect. Your scout will bring hot water at seven. Dinner in the hall at six-thirty—formal dress required. Any questions, sir?"

William shook his head, and the man retreated, leaving him alone with the ghosts of previous occupants. He moved to the window, watching as new arrivals crossed the court below. Some travelled in groups, their laughter rising to his window; others moved alone, their faces set with determination. A cluster of women in undergraduate gowns passed beneath his window—pioneers in this ancient male domain, their presence a disruption to centuries of tradition.

From the river beyond the college grounds came the rhythmic splash of oars as a rowing crew practised on the Cam. Church bells tolled the hour, their bronze voices overlapping in mathematical precision. In the distance, he could see the spires of King's College Chapel rising like a stone prayer against the darkening sky.

William unpacked methodically, arranging his possessions with military precision. His books—economics, political science, mathematics—formed neat rows on the shelves. The walls remained bare, unlike the rooms he passed where photographs and posters already created shrines to home and identity.

He placed his father's gift—a silver letter opener engraved with the Braithwaite crest—on the desk, not with reverence but as one might position a weapon. Cambridge was not his destination but his instrument; these hallowed halls not a refuge but a training ground. While others sought knowledge for illumination, William sought it for armament.

As twilight deepened, the ancient stones of Cambridge settled into shadow. From his window, William watched lights appear in windows across the court, each one representing a rival, an ally, or merely an irrelevance in the great game into which he had come to participate, and to master. The mist from the river crept through the college grounds, curling around centuries-old stonework like spectral fingers.

Cambridge awaited him—not as an adventure, but as his battlefield.

Three weeks into Michaelmas term, Cambridge's ancient rhythms had begun to assert themselves. The tolling of chapel bells marked the hours, bicycles rattled over cobblestones, and the Cam flowed sluggishly beneath stone bridges as it had for centuries. William had settled into his academic routine with methodical precision, approaching each lecture and supervision as a tactical engagement.

Tonight, the Cambridge Union Society hosted its first major debate of the term. The Union's debating chamber—a Victorian Gothic temple to oratory—was packed to capacity, its tiered benches filled with students eager to witness verbal bloodsport. The motion before the house: "This House believes Britain's post-war reconstruction should prioritise social welfare over economic growth."

William slipped into a seat at the back, surveying the chamber as one might the terrain of war. The air hummed with anticipation, charged with the peculiar electricity that precedes intellectual combat. Around him, students in undergraduate gowns gesticulated over whispered arguments, their faces animated in the amber glow of the wall sconces.

The proposition speaker—a bearded economics student with NHS spectacles—was making his opening argument with evangelical fervour.

"Britain did not endure six years of total war merely to return to the inequities of the 1930s," he proclaimed, his Yorkshire accent cutting through the chamber's perfect acoustics. "The people demand—and deserve—the fruits of victory: housing, healthcare, education. Not as charity, but as a right."

Polite applause rippled through the chamber. William noted how the speaker's rhetoric leaned on emotion rather than evidence—effective for this audience, perhaps, but structurally weak.

The opposition's first speaker rose—a former RAF pilot still wearing his regimental tie. His counterargument centred on Britain's precarious financial position, the American loan, and the need for economic recovery before expanded social programmes.

"You cannot distribute wealth you haven't created," he concluded with military crispness.

The debate intensified as subsequent speakers traded increasingly barbed rejoinders. A Labour-supporting history student invoked the Beveridge Report with religious reverence. A Conservative economist from Trinity responded with dire warnings about national bankruptcy.

Then, from the opposition benches, a figure rose with unhurried confidence. William's attention sharpened instantly. Even before the young man spoke, the chamber quieted in anticipation.

Lyle Cunningham.

William had not seen him since their brief encounter at the Athenaeum Club over a year ago, but recognition was immediate. Lyle stood perfectly still at the dispatch box, his gown draped with classical elegance over a bespoke suit. His blond hair was immaculately styled, his posture aristocratic without effort.

"Mr President, honourable members," Lyle began, his voice carrying to the rafters without seeming to project. "I've listened with interest to the proposition's case for prioritising social welfare. Their argument contains much that is admirable and nothing that is practicable."

A ripple of laughter swept the chamber. Lyle waited for it to subside, utterly at ease in the spotlight.

"The proposition speaker asks us to choose between welfare and growth as if they were mutually exclusive. This is a false dichotomy born of economic illiteracy."

With surgical precision, Lyle dissected the proposition's arguments. He quoted Keynes and Hayek from memory, referenced obscure Treasury papers, and deployed statistics with devastating effect. Yet it wasn't merely his knowledge that commanded attention—it was the cool, almost predatory intelligence behind his delivery.

"Britain faces not a choice between compassion and prosperity, but a question of sequence," Lyle continued. "Build your economic engine before distributing its output. The alternative is well-intentioned bankruptcy."

When he turned to address the bearded proposer directly, his tone shifted to something more dangerous—polite contempt.

"The honourable member's plan would see us distributing increasingly thin slices of an ever-shrinking pie. I suggest he consult his economics textbooks—assuming he's opened them."

The chamber erupted in a mixture of applause and scandalised murmurs. The proposer's face flushed crimson.

From his position at the back, William studied Lyle's performance with clinical appreciation. This was not merely debate but domination—intellectual territory being claimed and held. Lyle's arguments were scaffolded with facts, but his true weapon was his absolute conviction in his own superiority.

As Lyle concluded to enthusiastic applause, his gaze swept the chamber and briefly locked with William's. A flicker of recognition passed between them—not the warmth of renewed acquaintance but the mutual assessment of equals recognising each other on the field.

The debate continued, but William's attention remained fixed on Lyle, who had returned to his seat with the satisfied air of a predator after a successful hunt. Their paths had crossed again, as William had suspected they might. Cambridge was, after all, where power was forged and alliances formed.

The question remained: were they to be rivals or allies in the years to come? Perhaps both. William understood instinctively that Lyle Cunningham was neither a man to underestimate nor to trust completely. Like himself, Lyle moved through the world with purpose, seeing others as either instruments or obstacles.

As the debate concluded with a narrow victory for the opposition, William slipped out before the crowd dispersed. He had seen what he came to see. In Lyle Cunningham, he had identified something rare: not a friend, perhaps, but a potential equal in a game that—for him—was only just beginning.

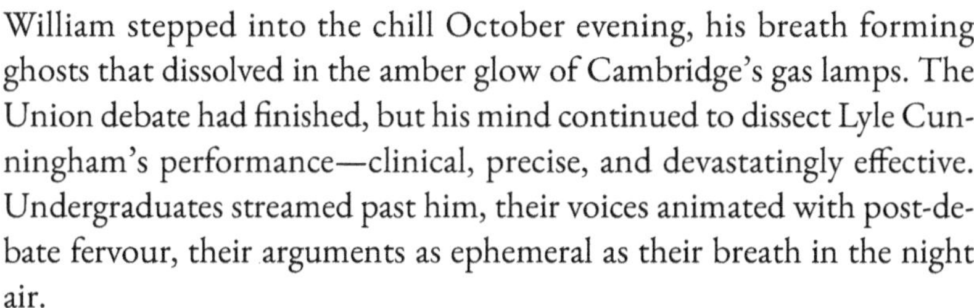

William stepped into the chill October evening, his breath forming ghosts that dissolved in the amber glow of Cambridge's gas lamps. The Union debate had finished, but his mind continued to dissect Lyle Cunningham's performance—clinical, precise, and devastatingly effective. Undergraduates streamed past him, their voices animated with post-debate fervour, their arguments as ephemeral as their breath in the night air.

He turned onto Trinity Lane, the ancient stone walls amplifying footsteps behind him. William didn't break stride or turn around. He had already catalogued the distinctive cadence—confident, unhurried, deliberate.

"Braithwaite." The voice carried the same commanding tone it had wielded in the debate chamber. "I thought that was you lurking in the shadows."

William pivoted, his face arranged in a mask of polite neutrality. Lyle Cunningham stood beneath a streetlamp, his blond hair catching the light like burnished brass, his college scarf casually elegant against his tailored overcoat.

"Cunningham. Impressive performance tonight."

"You didn't speak." It wasn't a question but an observation, perhaps even an accusation.

"I prefer to observe before engaging." William's tone was measured. "First rule of warfare."

Lyle's mouth curved into something between a smile and a smirk. "Is that what we're doing? Waging war?"

"Isn't everything?"

"How exhausting that must be." Lyle extracted a silver cigarette case from his coat pocket. He offered it to William, who declined with a slight shake of his head. "The African sun has hardened you, Braithwaite. Your father mentioned you'd been away."

William's expression didn't change, but he noted the casual reference to conversations with Charles Braithwaite. "South Africa. Not a place that rewards softness."

"Whereas Cambridge—" Lyle lit his cigarette with a matching silver lighter, the flame briefly illuminating his face, "—rewards those who know when to be hard and when to appear soft."

A group of undergraduates passed, their laughter echoing against the ancient stones. Neither man acknowledged them.

"Your argument tonight," William said, "about economic engines and output. Elegant, but it presupposes those controlling the engine have any interest in distributing its benefits."

"And you believe they don't?"

"I believe power, once accumulated, is rarely surrendered voluntarily."

Lyle exhaled a plume of smoke that caught the lamplight. "The cynicism of youth. How dreary."

"Not cynicism. Observation."

"Your father doesn't share your dim view. He sees Britain's recovery as an opportunity for everyone."

William allowed himself the faintest smile. "My father says many things in public."

Something shifted in Lyle's eyes—a flash of genuine interest replacing the practised charm. "Now that's intriguing. The son positioning himself to the right of Charles Braithwaite. I didn't think that space existed."

"I'm not positioning myself anywhere. I'm simply not burdened by the need to appear benevolent."

"Whereas I am?" Lyle's tone was light, but his gaze had sharpened.

"You're burdened by the need to be admired. Different affliction, same weakness."

Instead of taking offence, Lyle laughed—a genuine sound that momentarily transformed his calculated elegance into something almost boyish. "Christ, you're blunt. They really did send you to the colonies, didn't they?"

The exchange continued as they walked, their path taking them past Trinity College's Great Gate, its stone sentinels watching impassively as they had for centuries. Their conversation flowed with the rhythm of a fencing match—thrust, parry, riposte—neither man willing to yield ground, each testing the other's defences.

"Your father and mine have plans," Lyle said eventually, dropping his cigarette and crushing it beneath an expensive shoe. "For us, for Braithwaite Enterprises, for Britain's place in whatever world emerges from this rubble."

"And you intend to follow those plans?"

"I intend to improve upon them." Lyle's confidence wasn't boastful but matter-of-fact. "As I suspect you do."

They paused at a crossroads, Cambridge's spires silhouetted against the night sky behind them. In that moment, something unspoken passed between them—not friendship yet, exactly, but recognition. Two climbers eyeing the same peak, acknowledging that the ascent might be easier with ropes tied together, at least for part of the journey.

"The Copper Kettle, tomorrow at four," Lyle said. "They've somehow managed to secure actual coffee. We should continue this conversation."

William nodded once, neither eager nor reluctant. "Until tomorrow, then."

They parted without handshakes or further words, each turning toward their respective colleges. Behind them, the gas lamp flickered, casting their diverging shadows across the ancient cobblestones—separate for now, but destined to intersect again and again in the moments and years to come.

The Copper Kettle bustled with afternoon patrons—academics hunched over manuscripts, undergraduates debating philosophy, and a scattering of townspeople seeking refuge from the October chill. William arrived precisely at four, scanning the room with practised efficiency before spotting Lyle at a corner table, partially obscured by a potted fern.

"Punctual," Lyle observed as William slid into the chair opposite him. "A virtue I appreciate."

"Time is the one resource that can't be replaced or purchased," William replied.

A waitress approached, her manner brisk but pleasant. Lyle ordered coffee for both without consultation, adding, "And perhaps a plate of those shortbread biscuits." He waited until she departed before continuing. "I've secured us the most private table in a public establishment. One can be overheard anywhere in Cambridge, but here at least we'll see who's listening."

William noted the strategic positioning—backs to the wall, clear sightlines to both entrances. "You've thought this through."

"Always." Lyle's blue eyes carried a spark of amusement. "Just as you've already catalogued everyone in this room, assessed potential threats, and identified exits."

The coffee arrived, dark and aromatic in a way that had become rare during rationing. William took a measured sip, allowing the bitter warmth to spread across his palate before responding.

"Jacques—the Afrikaner who kept me—taught me to enter every room as if someone might wish me harm."

"Paranoid advice."

"Effective advice. His 11-year-old son was killed by a leopard."

They fell into silence as the shortbread arrived. Around them, conversations ebbed and flowed, fragments of academic discourse mingling with more mundane concerns. A clock ticked somewhere behind the counter, marking the passage of moments that would never return.

"I've been watching you," Lyle said finally. "In lectures, at hall, during debates. You speak rarely, but when you do, people listen. You don't seek approval, yet you accumulate followers. Interesting approach."

"I'm not interested in followers."

"Everyone needs allies."

"Allies, yes. Sycophants, no." William broke a piece of shortbread with precise movements. "And you? The golden boy of the debating circuit, darling of the professors, with your perfect manners and your family connections. What are you seeking?"

Lyle's smile tightened fractionally. "The same thing as you, I suspect."

"Which is?"

"More." The word hung between them, simple yet laden with meaning. "More than our fathers imagined. More than Cambridge can teach us. More than Britain currently offers."

The afternoon light slanted through the windows, catching dust motes in its golden beams. Outside, students passed in their gowns, laughing and arguing, oblivious to the quiet calculation taking place at the corner table.

"Our fathers," William said, lowering his voice, "built empires on the ruins of the last war. They think small—acquisitions, mergers, government contracts."

"While we think...?"

"Beyond borders. Beyond industries. Beyond the limitations they accept as immutable."

Something shifted in Lyle's expression—a recognition, perhaps even respect. "You don't just want your father's company. You want to transform it."

"The world is changing, Mr Cunningham. Britain is diminished. America ascendant. New powers emerging from the East. The old rules no longer apply."

"And the new rules?"

"Will be written by those bold enough to write them."

Lyle leaned back, studying William with new intensity. "Most of our peers are playing at politics, rehearsing for lives their fathers have already mapped out. But you're not playing."

"Neither are you."

Their eyes met across the table—blue against ice-blue—and in that moment, something unspoken passed between them. Not friendship, exactly, but recognition. Two predators acknowledging each other's territory, deciding that competition would be mutually destructive.

"Cambridge is merely a waypoint," Lyle said softly. "A credential to be acquired. The real education happens elsewhere."

"In boardrooms. In private clubs. In conversations that never appear in minutes or newspapers."

"Indeed." Lyle's finger traced the rim of his coffee cup. "My father has access to some of those rooms. Yours to others."

"And if we combined that access?"

The question hung quietly in the air, neither rhetorical nor entirely direct. Around them, the café continued its gentle hum of activity, oblivious to the pact being forged in their corner.

"There are many paths to the summit," Lyle said carefully. "Most climbers compete. Some fall. Others..."

"Form expeditions," William finished.

"Precisely." Lyle raised his cup in a subtle toast. "Not as friends, necessarily."

"Not as rivals, either."

"As... collaborators."

They didn't shake hands. They didn't need to. The understanding between them required no ceremony, no written agreement. It existed in the space between words, in calculated silences and measured glances.

As they finished their coffee and prepared to leave, the late afternoon sun cast their shadows across the table—separate yet aligned, distinct yet moving in concert. Neither man commented on it, but both observed. It was, perhaps, the perfect metaphor for what had just been established.

Not friendship. Not yet. But something potentially more valuable. An alliance.

------●------

The great hall of St. John's College gleamed beneath ancient wooden beams, transformed by candlelight into something approaching reverence. Long oak tables stretched across the flagstone floor, laden with silver and crystal that caught and multiplied the flames. Portraits of distinguished alumni gazed down from panelled walls, their painted eyes seeming to follow the movements of each black-gowned figure below.

William adjusted his academic gown over his dinner suit, noting how the heavy fabric settled across his shoulders like armour. Beside him, Lyle sat with perfect posture, the candlelight gilding his blond hair. Around them, the buzz of conversation rose and fell, punctuated by the occasional clink of cutlery against fine china.

The Master rose at High Table, the elevated platform where fellows and distinguished guests dined. A hush descended as he intoned the Latin grace: "Oculi omnium in te sperant Domine…" The words echoed beneath the vaulted ceiling, unchanged for centuries. William observed how some students mouthed along with practised precision while others shifted awkwardly, betraying their less privileged backgrounds.

"The eyes of all wait upon thee, O Lord," Lyle translated quietly as they sat. "A tradition since 1516."

William nodded, surveying the room. "Traditions endure while empires fall."

The soup arrived, carried by college servants moving with repetitious efficiency. At a nearby table, a third-year politics student held court, his voice carrying as he dissected the latest parliamentary debate. Two freshers leaned toward him, faces eager for approval.

"Thornfield," Lyle murmured, following William's gaze. "Father in the Foreign Office. Convinced he'll be Prime Minister by forty."

"And will he?"

"Not a chance. Too much ambition, too little subtlety."

William suppressed a smile. "You're cataloguing them all."

"As are you."

Across the hall, a group of women students sat together, their presence still novel enough to draw occasional glances. One caught William's eye briefly before returning to her conversation.

"Sarah Stevens," Lyle said, noticing the exchange. "Reading Law. Brilliant mind, they say."

"Your intelligence network is impressive."

"Merely observant." Lyle took a sip of wine. "Though I find myself caring less about these social taxonomies lately."

William raised an eyebrow. "A change of strategy?"

"Perhaps a change of perspective." Lyle's voice softened. "Do you ever tire of calculating every interaction?"

The question lingered between them, unexpectedly personal. William considered deflecting but found himself answering honestly.

"Sometimes. In Africa, everything was simpler. Brutal, but clear."

"How so?"

"You worked or you starved. You learned or you suffered." William broke a piece of bread. "Here, everything is veiled in politeness and tradition."

Lyle nodded slowly. "Cambridge is a game with unwritten rules. My father spent years teaching me how to play it."

"And yet you question the game."

"I question its purpose." Lyle gestured subtly toward their peers. "Look at them—jockeying for positions in debating societies, currying favour with tutors, forming alliances that will dissolve the moment they're inconvenient."

William watched a group of students laughing too loudly at a professor's joke. "Small ambitions."

"Exactly." For the first time, Lyle's smile reached his eyes. "It's rather refreshing to find someone who sees beyond the immediate prize."

The main course arrived—roast lamb with seasonal vegetables, served with a formality that bordered on ceremony. As they ate, their conversation drifted from politics to literature, discovering shared admiration for Conrad and Greene. When Lyle mentioned a passage from *The Heart of Darkness*, William finished the quote from memory.

"You surprise me, Braithwaite," Lyle said, genuine warmth in his voice. "I wouldn't have taken you for a literary man."

"Books were rare at Trewil Loop. When Marie—Jacques' wife—smuggled me a novel, I devoured it."

It was the first personal detail William had volunteered, offered without calculation or purpose. Something shifted between them, subtle but significant—the first foundation stone of what might, given time and trust, become friendship.

⟞⬧O⬧⟝

The formal dinner concluded with port and stilted conversation, but neither William nor Lyle had patience for the performative socialising that followed. They slipped away from the great hall, abandoning their gowns in their rooms before heading toward the Backs.

Moonlight silvered the path as they walked beside the Cam. The river moved with quiet purpose, dark and gleaming. Behind them, the colleges stood sentinel, their ancient stones softened by night. Here, away from the pressing weight of tradition and watchful eyes, Cambridge revealed a different face—one of shadows and possibility.

"My father would be appalled," Lyle said, breaking the silence. "Leaving networking opportunities to wander in the dark."

"Is that what we're avoiding? Opportunities?"

"Tedium, rather." Lyle's profile was sharp against the night sky. "Twenty minutes of Thornfield explaining how his summer internship at the Foreign Office positions him perfectly for a diplomatic career."

William's mouth twitched. "Fascinating."

"Excruciating." Lyle paused at the stone balustrade of a small bridge, looking down at the water. "The Cunninghams have been positioning themselves since the Restoration. My father had my life mapped before I could walk—Eton, Cambridge, the right clubs, the right connections."

"And you follow the map."

"I improve upon it." Lyle turned, moonlight catching in his eyes. "Old money has its advantages, but old thinking has limitations."

William remained silent, unwilling to offer reciprocal confidences. He'd revealed enough during dinner—one small truth about Trewil Loop. Even that felt like an error, a tactical miscalculation.

Lyle seemed to read his reticence. "You needn't worry. I'm not fishing for your secrets, Braithwaite."

"Everyone fishes for something."

"True enough." Lyle's laugh was unexpected, almost boyish. "But sometimes conversation is just conversation."

They continued walking, passing beneath the shadows of willow trees. A punt lay tethered at the bank, rocking gently with the river's movement. From somewhere distant came the sound of a piano, a nocturne drifting through an open window.

"My mother wanted me to study music," Lyle said, his voice lighter than William had heard before. "She found my aptitude for economics distressing. 'All that cold calculation,' she'd say."

"And is it? Cold calculation?"

"No more than chess or mathematics. There's elegance in it." Lyle glanced sideways at William. "You understand that better than most, I suspect."

William said nothing, but his silence was acknowledgment enough.

They reached a secluded bench beneath an ancient oak, its branches creating a cathedral of leaves above them. Lyle sat, stretching his long legs before him, suddenly looking more like a young man than the calculating strategist he presented to the world.

"I think we are alike, you and I," he said quietly. "Just... tuned differently."

William remained standing, wary of the intimacy implied in sharing the bench. "How so?"

"We both see the board rather than the pieces. We recognise the game extends beyond Cambridge, beyond our fathers' ambitions." Lyle looked up at him, his expression serious now. "But you play from necessity, while I play from choice."

The observation was uncomfortably perceptive. William felt the familiar coldness settle in his chest—the protective detachment that had served him since Trewil Loop.

"Does it matter why we play, if the outcome is the same?"

"Perhaps not." Lyle's gaze remained steady. "But knowing one's partner at the table has certain advantages."

The word drifted aimlessly between them—partner—neither a declaration of friendship nor a purely transactional proposal. Something rarer: an offer of alliance based on mutual recognition.

William considered it carefully, weighing risk against potential. Finally, he sat beside Lyle on the bench, the distance between them precisely calculated—close enough for confidence, far enough for dignity.

The night air carried the scent of river water and possibility.

The chapel steps were cold beneath them, the worn stone polished by centuries of genuflection and purpose. William and Lyle sat side by side as evening shadows lengthened across the quad. The last notes of evensong had faded half an hour earlier, leaving them in the peculiar silence that follows music—a silence that seems to hold echoes of what came before.

"What constitutes loyalty, do you think?" Lyle asked, his voice pitched low enough that it wouldn't carry. "Is it blind adherence to what's expected, or something more discerning?"

William considered this, watching a blackbird hop across the lawn. "Jacques—the farmer in Natal—believed loyalty was strength of purpose. Unwavering, regardless of circumstance."

"And you?"

"I think loyalty without judgment is just obedience." William's fingers traced an invisible pattern on the stone. "My mother was loyal to my father, even when it meant betraying herself."

He hadn't meant to say it, certainly not so plainly. The words seemed to materialise between them, unexpected and raw.

Lyle nodded, allowing the revelation to settle without pressing for more. "My family speaks of duty as though it's the highest virtue. The Cunningham name carries obligations spanning generations."

"The Foreign Office?"

"Among other expectations." Lyle's smile was thin. "A particular sort of marriage, a particular sort of life. All terribly respectable."

"And that's not what you want."

"I want to build something of my own making." Lyle looked up at the darkening sky. "Not merely occupy space in a structure designed by dead men."

The chapel bell tolled quarter past the hour, its resonance felt as much as heard.

"They sent me away to protect me," William said after a long silence. "But protection wasn't what I found."

It was as close as he'd come to speaking of what happened at Trewil Loop—the lessons learned through calculated cruelty, the slow death of the boy he'd been.

Lyle didn't look at him directly, offering the mercy of averted eyes. "We're all shaped by invisible hands, aren't we? Parents, circumstances, history itself."

"The question is whether we continue to let them shape us."

Their eyes met briefly, a moment of perfect understanding passing between them. Two men recognising in each other not just ambition or intellect, but the particular loneliness of those who see too clearly—and too early.

"No," Lyle said quietly. "That's not the question at all. The question is what we choose to shape instead."

⎯⎯⎯◇⎯⎯⎯

The university library at midnight had a particular quality—the scent of leather bindings and floor polish, the hushed rustling of pages, the occasional creak of ancient floorboards beneath the carpet. Yellow pools of lamplight illuminated islands of concentration amid the darkness.

William and Lyle had commandeered a corner table behind Medieval History, where the library's night porter rarely ventured. Papers and open books surrounded them like the aftermath of an academic explosion.

"Professor Harrington's face will be an extraordinary shade of puce," Lyle whispered, suppressing a smile as he reviewed William's latest paragraph. "You've dismantled his entire thesis on post-colonial economic theory."

"His argument has more holes than the Albert Hall," William replied, not looking up from his notes. "He spent forty minutes last Tuesday explaining why emerging nations can't possibly develop without British oversight. Pure imperial nostalgia masquerading as economics."

A student three tables away shot them a venomous glare. Lyle offered an apologetic nod before leaning closer.

"What I particularly enjoy," he murmured, "is that we're using his own cited sources against him. Harrington never imagined anyone would actually check his footnotes."

William's smile was cold and precise. "People rarely verify what they're told by authority figures."

"Your brutality needs my diplomatic touch, though." Lyle took the draft, crossing out several particularly savage lines. "We need to eviscerate his argument while appearing respectful of his position."

"Respectful?" William arched an eyebrow.

"Appearing respectful," Lyle corrected. "There's an art to academic assassination."

Somewhere in the stacks, a book tumbled from its shelf with a dull thud. Both men froze momentarily, then relaxed when no librarian materialised to investigate.

"We'll submit it as a joint paper?" William asked.

"Of course. Maximum impact, shared risk."

They worked in companionable silence for another hour, William supplying the razor-sharp observations that cut to the heart of Harrington's weaknesses, Lyle polishing them into arguments that couldn't be dismissed as mere student rebellion.

"Do you realise," Lyle said eventually, closing a reference volume with satisfaction, "this is the first time either of us has risked anything at Cambridge?"

William considered this. "A small rebellion."

"A rehearsal," Lyle replied, his eyes meeting William's with quiet understanding.

Neither needed to articulate what they were rehearsing for. The knowledge hung between them—a shared secret, the first of many to come.

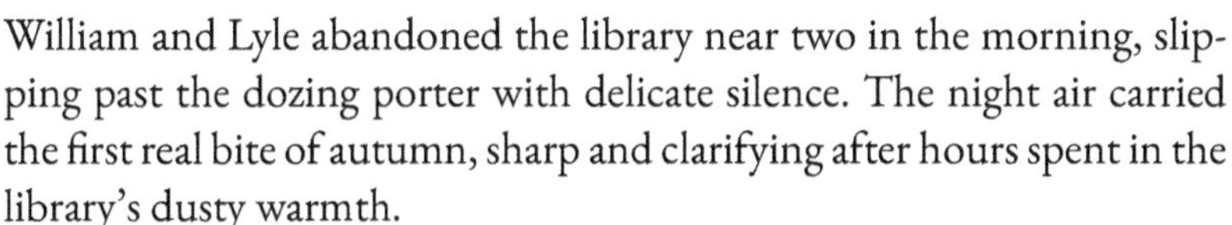

William and Lyle abandoned the library near two in the morning, slipping past the dozing porter with delicate silence. The night air carried the first real bite of autumn, sharp and clarifying after hours spent in the library's dusty warmth.

"Not finished yet," Lyle said, pulling William away from the path leading back to their college. "I've something better than sleep."

They moved like shadows across the darkened quadrangle, Lyle leading them toward a narrow doorway tucked behind an ancient buttress. A small key appeared in his hand.

"Borrowed from the chapel warden," Lyle explained with a thin smile that suggested the borrowing had been neither requested nor approved.

The spiral staircase within was treacherously narrow, worn smooth by centuries of feet. Their shoulders brushed the cold stone walls as they climbed, guided only by the weak beam of Lyle's pocket torch.

"Mind the last step," Lyle cautioned. "Nearly broke my neck the first time."

The door at the top opened onto the college roof. William stepped out, momentarily breathless—not from the climb, but from the panorama that stretched before him. Cambridge lay beneath them, a medieval dream rendered in stone and shadow. Moonlight silvered the edges of every spire and dome, while darkness pooled in the streets and courtyards below.

"Found this place in Michaelmas term last year," Lyle said, settling himself against a chimney stack. "Useful for thinking. No one ever comes up here."

From his coat, he produced a flat silver flask and two small cups that glinted in the moonlight.

"Macallan. Smuggled from town last week. The college statutes explicitly forbid spirits in residence."

"Another small rebellion," William observed, accepting the cup.

"One of many."

The whisky burned pleasantly, warming William from within as the October night chilled his skin. Below them, Cambridge slept—or pretended to. A few windows still glowed in distant colleges, marking other midnight scholars or quiet conspiracies.

"I've been thinking about what you said at the river," William said finally. "About shaping rather than being shaped."

Lyle nodded, his profile distinct against the night sky. "And?"

"I think we've been asking the wrong question. It's not what we choose to shape, but how far we're willing to go to shape it."

The whisky caught the moonlight as Lyle swirled it in his cup. "Most people imagine themselves capable of anything, until the moment arrives when they must actually do it."

"And you?"

"I suspect I'm capable of more than most." Lyle's voice was matter-of-fact, neither boastful nor apologetic. "You're the same."

William didn't deny it. The African night had taught him truths about himself that Cambridge's genteel corridors could never reveal.

"My father believes the future belongs to those who can rebuild what was lost," William said. "But he's wrong. The future belongs to those who build something entirely new from the ruins."

"The war changed everything," Lyle agreed. "The old men don't see it yet."

"They're still playing by pre-war rules."

"While we're writing new ones."

They fell silent, contemplating the sleeping city that had nurtured kings and poets, scientists and tyrants through the centuries. How many other pairs of young men had sat on these same rooftops, plotting futures that would remake the world below?

"To the new rules, then," Lyle said, raising his cup.

William considered, then shook his head. "To rules? No."

"What, then?"

"To victory."

Something flickered in Lyle's eyes—agreement, perhaps, or anticipation. "Victory," he echoed, touching his cup to William's.

They drank deeply, neither flinching at the spirit's burn. Below them, a clock tower struck three, the sound rippling across the sleeping colleges. In a few hours, the city would wake to lectures and tutorials, to the ordinary business of education. But up here, in the thin boundary between night and morning, William felt the first real stirring of purpose since leaving Africa.

Not friendship—that was too simple a word for what was forming between them.

Not loyalty—that implied a hierarchy neither would accept.

Something more complex, more dangerous.

An alliance forged not in affection but in the recognition of matched ambition. A partnership of calculation rather than sentiment.

Lyle refilled their cups without speaking. The whisky gleamed amber in the moonlight, like something ancient trapped and preserved.

Above the silent spires of Cambridge, two futures twisted together beneath a black October sky.

Chapter 13

Where the Silences Slept

The Eagle, dating back to 1667, a sanctuary of oak and brass, its low-beamed ceiling holding centuries of pipe smoke and whispered conspiracies. Sunlight streamed through diamond-paned windows, glittering dust particles that danced above crowded tables where students and dons alike hunched over coffee cups and dog-eared texts. The cold, taught, afternoon had brought half of Cambridge inside, a crush of tweed and wool seeking refuge from the unexpected chill.

William sat alone at a corner table, nursing a cooling cup of tea while annotating his political economy text. Again, he'd chosen this spot strategically—back to the wall, clear view of both entrances, positioned to observe without being obvious. Jacques'—and now Lyle's—lessons had not left him: *always know your exits.*

"Excuse me, is this seat taken? Everywhere else is full."

William looked up to find a beautiful, blond-haired, blue-eyed young woman standing before him, books clutched against her chest. Blonde hair caught in a shaft of sunlight that turned it almost incandescent. Her blue eyes met his with neither hesitation nor coyness.

"Please," he gestured to the empty chair.

She settled across from him with practiced grace, arranging her books with methodical precision: constitutional law, Woolf's *Three Guineas,* and a volume of Auden.

"Sarah Stevens," she offered, extending her delicate right hand.

William took it. "William Braithwaite."

"I know." A smile played at the corners of her mouth. "You sit with Lyle Cunningham at formal dinner. Second table from the high table, east side."

"You've been watching me."

"I've been observing everyone. It's what lawyers do; I'm told." She signalled to the harried waitress. "Though you two are rather hard to miss—the only ones who look like you're calculating everyone's value rather than simply enjoying your pudding."

William leaned back, reassessing. Not merely beautiful, but perceptive. Dangerous, potentially.

"And what value have you assigned us?"

"Oh, I haven't decided yet." The waitress appeared, and Sarah ordered coffee without breaking eye contact. "Your friend Cunningham's easier to read. Aristocratic ambition wrapped in intellectual veneer. You're more... opaque."

"Perhaps I'm simply boring."

"No one who has survived five years in Africa during the war is boring, Mr Braithwaite."

William's expression didn't change, but something cold slithered down his spine. "You've been making inquiries."

"Not actively. People talk. Especially about the boy who returned from exile and immediately aligned himself with the Cunningham heir." She opened her Auden, marking her place with a slender finger. "I find it curious that you chose him, of all people."

"Who says I chose him?"

"The way you watch the room together. Like generals surveying the terrain." Her coffee arrived, and she added a precise measure of sugar. "Though perhaps I'm being unfair. Perhaps you simply share a passion for poetry."

William closed his textbook. "Auden's a bit sentimental for my taste."

"What do you prefer?"

"Conrad. Greene."

"Heart of Darkness?" She raised an eyebrow. "How fitting."

"And you? Three Guineas suggests political leanings."

"I believe in questioning systems, not necessarily accepting them." She sipped her coffee, watching him over the rim. "Don't you find it odd that we've just emerged from a war against fascism, yet our own institutions remain so rigidly hierarchical?"

"You sound like a Marxist."

"And you sound like someone avoiding the question." Her smile softened the challenge. "But I'll allow it, since we've only just met."

Around them, the café buzzed with conversation and clattering cups. A group of engineering students argued loudly about bridge designs. Two philosophy wannabees debated existentialism by the fireplace. Yet William felt oddly isolated with this woman, as if they occupied a pocket of calm in the chaos.

"You mentioned Africa," he said carefully. "What else do people say about me?"

"That you're brilliant but cold. That professors find your essays unsettling in their precision." She tilted her head slightly. "That you speak Afrikaans when you're angry."

"I'm never angry."

"Everyone's angry about something, William."

His name in her mouth sounded different—not the formal address of professors or the calculated familiarity of Lyle, but something new. Something he couldn't quite categorise.

"Perhaps we should discuss something less contentious," he suggested. "Your interest in constitutional law, for instance."

"Now who's avoiding questions?" But she obliged, launching into an analysis of recent legal precedents that revealed both formidable intelligence and genuine passion.

William found himself responding in kind, their conversation flowing from law to literature to politics with effortless intensity. Her mind was quicksilver—challenging, probing, occasionally retreating only to advance from another angle. For the first time since returning to England, William felt fully engaged, even as part of him maintained clinical distance, assessing her as he would any potential ally or obstacle.

When the clock tower struck four, Sarah gathered her books with visible reluctance.

"Constitutional Law with Professor Milnerton," she explained. "Tedious but necessary."

"Perhaps we could continue this discussion tomorrow?" William surprised himself with the directness of his invitation. "Same time?"

Sarah paused, studying him with that penetrating gaze. "I'd like that. Though perhaps somewhere less crowded. The Fellows' Garden is lovely this time of year. Around 3pm?"

"Are students allowed there?"

Her smile turned mischievous. "Not technically. But rules are made to be... reinterpreted, wouldn't you say?"

As she turned to leave, William caught her wrist lightly. "One question. Why did you really sit here today?"

Sarah glanced at his hand, then met his eyes without embarrassment. "Because everyone else is afraid of you. And I find fear to be a terribly unreliable advisor." She gently extracted her wrist. "Until tomorrow, William."

He watched her weave through the crowded café, her blonde head disappearing into the sunlight beyond the door. Only then did William realise he'd been holding his breath.

⸺◈⸺

The Fellows' Garden presented a different world from the clamour of The Eagle—geometric hedges and ordered flower beds giving way to wilder, more secretive corners where ancient trees provided shelter from both sun and prying eyes. William arrived precisely at three, positioning himself on a stone bench with a clear view of both entrances. Now fast becoming an old habit.

Sarah appeared through the eastern gate ten minutes later, a vision in cornflower blue that complemented the autumn sky. She carried a small basket and moved with unhurried confidence past a startled gardener who clearly questioned her right to be there but lacked the courage to challenge her.

"You came," she said, as though there had been doubt.

"I said I would." William shifted slightly on the bench, making room without appearing eager.

"Most men say many things." She settled beside him, arranging her skirt with deliberate care. From her basket, she produced a small flask and two enamel cups. "Tea. Not as good as The Eagle's, but the company's more exclusive."

As she poured, William studied her profile—the determined set of her jaw, the intelligence in her eyes, the way sunlight caught in her hair. Something stirred in him, unfamiliar and therefore unsafe. He accepted the cup to occupy his hands.

"I watched the women's debate yesterday," he said, steering toward safer ground. "On the question of equal academic recognition."

"Did you?" Sarah's eyebrow arched delicately. "And what did the great William Braithwaite make of our feminine arguments?"

"I found Carmichael's historical analysis compelling. Richardson relied too heavily on emotional appeals."

"And where do you stand on the matter? Should women receive full academic honours, or merely be tolerated as decorative oddities?"

William considered his response carefully. "I find the entire controversy absurd."

"How very male of you to—"

"Not because women shouldn't have equal standing," he interrupted, "but because the question itself is meaningless. Either one has the intellectual capacity or one doesn't. Gender seems irrelevant to the equation."

Sarah studied him over her teacup. "You surprise me. I'd have thought you a traditionalist."

"I believe in meritocracy. The best mind should prevail, regardless of its housing."

"How refreshingly progressive." Her tone suggested she wasn't entirely convinced. "Though I wonder if you'd feel the same if women began outperforming men in your political economy seminars."

"I'd welcome the competition." William surprised himself with his sincerity. "Most of my classmates are intellectual lightweights playing at scholarship between cricket matches."

Sarah laughed, a sound both musical and unexpectedly genuine. "You're terribly arrogant, you know."

"I'm terribly accurate," he corrected, allowing himself the ghost of a smile.

They fell into conversation about the term curriculum, the relative merits of different colleges, and the pomposity of certain professors. William found himself speaking more freely than he had with anyone since returning to England—perhaps more freely than he ever had. Sarah listened with genuine interest, challenging his assertions without malice, building on his ideas rather than simply waiting for her turn to speak.

As afternoon light softened into evening gold, William experienced a strange sensation—as though something calcified within him was beginning to crack, allowing some warmth to seep through. It was uncomfortable. Alarming, even. Yet he made no move to leave.

"You're different today," Sarah observed, breaking a comfortable silence.

"Different how?"

"Less guarded. Yesterday you measured every word as if it might be used against you in court."

William considered denying it, then opted for honesty. "Perhaps I find you... unexpectedly trustworthy."

"High praise indeed from the man who appears to trust no one." She began packing away their tea things. "Not even your shadow-dwelling friend Cunningham."

"Lyle and I understand each other."

"Understanding isn't trust." Sarah's eyes met his, suddenly serious. "What happened to you in Africa, William? What made you build such formidable walls?"

The question should have triggered his defenses. Instead, William felt an unsettling urge to answer truthfully. He resisted it, but barely. "Another time, perhaps."

"Is that a calm promise?" There was no coquettishness in her question, only genuine interest.

"Yes," he said, surprising himself again. "I believe it is."

As they walked toward the gate, their hands brushed—accidentally at first, then with deliberate intent. William felt the contact like an electric current, foreign yet somehow essential. He didn't take her hand properly—that would be too overt, too vulnerable—but he didn't pull away either.

Something was shifting inside him, rearranging his carefully ordered interior landscape. The William who had returned from Trewil Loop would have recognised this as weakness and excised it immediately. But sitting with Sarah in the fading light, weakness seemed less threatening than isolation.

The gardener watched them leave with disapproving eyes, but William barely noticed. For once, his attention wasn't on potential threats or strategic advantages. It was entirely captured by the woman beside him, and the strange, fragile feeling taking root in his chest.

⸺◆⸺

Frost etched delicate patterns on the windowpanes of the tearoom where William and Sarah sat facing each other. Outside, Cambridge had transformed into a winter tableau—stone buildings dusted with snow, students hurrying across courtyards with scarves pulled tight, their breath visible in the December air. Inside, the warmth of the small establishment cocooned them from the approaching holidays and the inevitable separation they would bring.

William watched Sarah stir her tea, noting the precise, deliberate motion of her wrist. Three clockwise turns, never clinking the spoon against the porcelain. He'd memorised her habits over their weeks together, cataloguing them like valuable intelligence.

"You're staring again," Sarah said without looking up.

"I'm observing. There's a difference."

She smiled, a quick upward curve of her lips that had become increasingly familiar and attractive to him. "And what conclusions has the great observer drawn today?"

"That you're concerned about something." William leaned forward slightly. "Your left hand has adjusted your bracelet four times in the last ten minutes."

Sarah's eyes widened momentarily before she laughed. "Quite the detective. Though I'm not certain whether to be flattered by your attention or unnerved by your scrutiny."

"Both would be appropriate."

The admission floated between them, honest in a way William rarely allowed himself to be. Over the past months, their conversations had evolved from intellectual sparring to something deeper, more risky. Sarah had somehow slipped past defenses he'd spent years constructing, not by battering them down but by making him question their necessity—at least with her.

"I received my father's letter this morning," Sarah said, finally addressing what had been preoccupying her. "He's arranged several social engagements over the holidays. Apparently, the daughter of Justice Stevens should be paraded before eligible young barristers."

William's jaw tightened imperceptibly, and he felt a tightening of his gut. "And will you oblige him?"

"I'll attend. I'll converse. I'll even dance if absolutely necessary." Her eyes met his directly. "But I won't be entertaining any proposals, matrimonial or otherwise."

"Because you've set your sights on becoming the first woman appointed to the High Court bench?"

"That, yes, possibly." She paused, studying him. "And because I find myself rather preoccupied with a particular political economist with questionable social graces."

William felt something uncoil in his chest—not relief exactly, but its awkward, unsafe cousin. "Your father would disapprove."

"Undoubtedly. He believes the world is divided into those who uphold the law and those who manipulate it." Sarah leaned closer. "But he's wrong about the fundamental nature of things, isn't he?"

"How so?"

"The world isn't divided between the lawful and lawless. It's divided between predator and prey." Her voice lowered, intimate despite their public setting. "Most people stumble through life hoping not to be devoured. They trust in institutions, in rules, in the fundamental decency of others."

William nodded slowly. "And you don't."

"Neither do you." She reached across the table, her fingers brushing his. "That's why I'm drawn to, interested in you, William. You see the world as it is, not as we're told it should be."

For a moment, William allowed himself to be touched by her understanding and forthrightness. Jacques de Beer had taught him this truth through pain and deprivation, but Sarah had arrived at the same conclusion through keen observation and intellect. She wasn't damaged as he was, yet she understood.

"The law is merely a construct," she continued. "A useful one, certainly, and one I intend to master completely. But ultimately, it's a system created by predators to regulate the hunting grounds."

"And you intend to be a predator within that system."

"I already am." Her smile turned, conspiratorial. "Just as you are in yours."

William studied her face—the intelligence in her eyes, the determination in the set of her jaw. She was magnificent and beautiful, and for the first time since his return from Africa, he felt something beyond calculation stir within him. Sarah didn't soften his edges; she appreciated their sharpness while somehow making him feel human again.

"January will come quickly enough," he said, acknowledging their impending separation.

"Not quickly enough." Her hand covered his completely now, warm and certain. "But I'll be here when Lent Term begins."

"As will I."

The simple exchange carried the weight of promise between them. Neither spoke of missing the other or of writing letters—such sentimentality would have felt false. Instead, they acknowledged the gravitational pull between them, the certainty of their orbits realigning in the new year.

As they left the tearoom and stepped into the winter afternoon, William offered his arm. Sarah took it without hesitation, her grip firm through her gloves. They walked in comfortable silence across the frosted quad, two predators moving in perfect synchrony, each recognising in the other both an equal and something previously thought impossible—a sanctuary.

⸻◆⸻

They paused beneath the stone archway that led from college grounds to the street beyond. A light snow had begun to fall, dusting Sarah's hair with crystalline flakes that caught the fading afternoon light. For a moment, neither spoke, aware they stood at an intersection.

"My train leaves at half six," Sarah said, adjusting her scarf. "Father insists on punctuality, even during holidays."

William nodded, studying her face as though committing it to memory. "A trait I find admirable, if occasionally inconvenient."

Their bodies had drawn closer, an unconscious gravitational pull neither acknowledged. William's hand moved slightly toward hers, then stilled. The air between them seemed charged with something neither had anticipated when they first crossed paths months earlier.

Sarah tilted her face upward, her expression open in a way that made William's chest tighten uncomfortably. Her lips parted slightly, and for a suspended moment, the distance between them seemed both infinite and nonexistent.

They could cross it now—this final boundary. The thought occurred to them simultaneously.

Yet neither moved forward.

William's gaze flickered briefly to the ground, then back to her eyes. Something unspoken passed between them—an understanding that whatever was forming between them remained too precious, too fragile for hasty gestures. This connection, unlike any either had known before, deserved patience. Their mutual restraint wasn't born of hesitation but of respect for what they might become to one another.

"I'll see you in January," Sarah said finally, her voice steady despite the colour in her cheeks.

"Yes," William replied simply. He reached out, allowing himself to brush a snowflake from her sleeve—the briefest contact, yet somehow more intimate than any kiss could have been.

Sarah smiled, a genuine expression that transformed her face. "Happy Christmas, William."

"And to you."

She turned and walked away, her figure gradually disappearing into the swirling snow. William remained motionless, watching long after she had vanished from sight.

For the first time since Trewil Loop, he felt something akin to belonging—not to a place, but to a person. The sensation was unfamiliar, dangerous even, yet he couldn't bring himself to reject it. In Sarah, he'd found not just an intellectual equal, but someone who saw him clearly and remained unafraid.

He turned toward his rooms, the silence around him no longer empty but full of promise.

⋯⋯◇⋯⋯

William returned to his rooms with measured steps, the soft crunch of snow beneath his feet marking a rhythm that matched his thoughts. The college had emptied for the Christmas break, leaving the ancient stone corridors and courtyards in a stillness that suited his contemplative mood.

He lit the small coal fire in his grate and stood before it, watching the flames lick upward. Sarah's face remained in his mind, not as a fleeting impression but as something fixed and essential. He had not anticipated this. Women had always been abstractions to him—potential allies or obstacles, never individuals who might reach beyond his carefully constructed defences.

Yet Sarah had done precisely that.

William moved to his desk and pulled out a sheet of paper, not to write but to think more systematically. He began to map his future as he often did, a habit developed at Trewil Loop when planning provided the only certainty. His father's business would be his foundation, of course. Lyle would be his right hand—a partnership built not on sentiment but on mutual recognition of capability and shared vision. Together, they could extend beyond what either of their fathers had imagined possible.

But now, unexpectedly, a third point had emerged in his constellation. Sarah.

He considered her with the same clinical precision he applied to all elements of his life. Her intellect was formidable, her family connections useful though not exceptional. She possessed an unusual clarity of perception—she had seen through him immediately, recognised the calculations behind his every interaction. Most would have recoiled from such awareness. Sarah had stepped closer.

"Interesting," he murmured to the empty room.

William poured himself a measure of whisky and returned to the fire. The possibilities began to arrange themselves with satisfying elegance. With Lyle, he gained access to corridors of power his father had never fully penetrated. With Sarah, he would have not merely a wife but a shield—someone who could navigate the social terrain that had always felt foreign to him. Between them, he would stand protected, the core of a small but formidable alliance.

The arrangement was perfect in its symmetry.

Yet something else stirred beneath these practical considerations. William took a slow sip of whisky, allowing the unfamiliar sensation to surface, to saturate him. When Sarah spoke, when she challenged him or laughed at something he said, he experienced a warmth that had nothing to do with strategy or advantage. Her absence now created a peculiar emptiness he had never before acknowledged.

Was this love? The concept seemed alien, almost mythological—a weakness a drunken Jacques had warned against, a vulnerability his father would have exploited. William had long ago sealed himself against such attachments.

Perhaps it was simply recognition of a kindred spirit, someone who understood the world as he did. Perhaps it was merely the satisfaction of finding someone whose mind complemented his own. Or perhaps...

William set down his glass with uncharacteristic abruptness. The fire hissed and popped in the silence.

"I want her," he said aloud, testing the words. They felt right, true in a way few things had since his return from Africa.

He wanted her mind, her perspective, her strength. He wanted her beside him as he built something beyond his father's limited vision. He wanted her insights, her challenges, even her occasional opposition.

The decision crystallised with sudden clarity. He would marry Sarah Stevens.

Not immediately—that would be impulsive, and William was never impulsive. But he would begin the courtship properly when term resumed. He would approach it as he did all significant undertakings: with patience, strategy, and absolute commitment to the outcome.

William returned to his desk, pulled out his calendar, and turned to January 1949. He made a small notation on the first day of Lent Term, a private reminder of this moment of decision.

For the first time in years, perhaps since before the Llanstephan Castle, William felt something akin to anticipation. Not merely for what he would gain or accomplish, but for the presence of another person. Sarah had somehow become essential to the architecture of his future—not merely as an asset or an ally, but as something he had never permitted himself to imagine: a companion.

The snow continued to fall outside his window, transforming Cambridge into something pristine and unmarked. Tomorrow would bring new calculations, new strategies. But tonight, William allowed himself to consider possibilities that extended beyond power and control.

Tonight, he permitted himself to want—even need—someone.

Chapter 14

Shadow Choices

Lyle Cunningham leaned against the stone archway of Trinity Street, watching Sarah Stevens move through the January drizzle. She walked with purpose, her blonde hair tucked beneath a navy beret, her stride confident even as she navigated around puddles. A stack of books balanced against her side as she paused to greet another law student. When she laughed, Lyle felt something tighten in his chest.

He'd been watching her for months now. Not in a manner that would alarm anyone—Lyle was too sophisticated for such obvious surveillance. Rather, his gaze found her naturally in lecture halls and libraries, across quadrangles and in the Union chamber. She possessed a particular quality that drew attention without demanding it—intelligence worn lightly but unmistakably.

"Ridiculous," he muttered to himself, turning up his collar against the rain.

The infatuation had begun innocently enough. A chance encounter in the university library during Michaelmas term, where she'd reached for the same legal text he needed. Their fingers had brushed; she'd smiled and conceded the book with surprising grace. Later that week, he'd spotted her dismantling a senior professor's argument during a seminar with such precision that even the old man had looked impressed rather than offended.

By November, Lyle had found himself contemplating how he might orchestrate a proper introduction. He'd drafted and discarded several approaches, each seeming too calculated or transparent. The right moment would present itself, he'd decided. Cambridge was, after all, a small world. Their paths would naturally intersect again.

Then came that afternoon at The Eagle.

Lyle had entered the café intending to meet with a political society member, only to freeze at the threshold. There sat William at his usual corner table, deep in conversation with Sarah. Not the polite, performative dialogue of strangers, but something alive with genuine engagement. William—reserved, calculating William—was leaning forward slightly, his usual mask of indifference replaced by authentic interest.

And Sarah... Sarah was luminous.

Lyle had retreated without being seen, a strange hollowness forming beneath his ribs. He'd told himself it meant nothing. A chance encounter, perhaps. Yet in the days that followed, he'd observed their paths crossing with increasing frequency—in the library, walking across the commons, lingering after lectures. What began as coincidence had crystallised into pattern, and pattern into certainty.

William had beaten him to it. Without even trying.

Now, watching Sarah disappear around a corner toward the law faculty, Lyle permitted himself a moment of raw honesty. The feeling that had begun as intellectual appreciation had evolved into something more substantial. Something that, in anyone else, might be called yearning.

"Sentiment," he whispered, the word a judgment. "How terribly ordinary of you, Cunningham."

What troubled Lyle most wasn't the unrequited nature of his interest—he'd never been one to require reciprocation for validation. Rather, it was the uncomfortable recognition that Sarah had approached William, not the reverse. She had sought him out deliberately, which suggested something Lyle found difficult to accept: perhaps she saw in William what she did not see in him.

The rain intensified, forcing Lyle deeper into the shelter of the archway. He lit a cigarette, cupping the flame against the wind, and considered his options with characteristic detachment.

He could pursue Sarah despite her evident interest in William. Such a triangulation might prove temporarily satisfying to his ego, but ultimately destructive. William, for all his careful composure, would perceive it as betrayal. And William Braithwaite was not someone whose enmity one cultivated lightly.

Alternatively, Lyle could withdraw gracefully, preserving both his dignity and his alliance with William. This partnership—this friendship, if one dared call it that—held potential far beyond the ordinary connections that defined university life. Together, they might accomplish something significant. Something lasting.

The choice, when framed this way, was hardly a choice at all.

Lyle exhaled smoke into the damp air and straightened his shoulders. He would make this sacrifice for William, as he suspected he would make others in the years to come. Their association was worth more than a passing infatuation, no matter how compelling. He would bury these feelings for Sarah where they could harm no one—least of all himself.

A familiar figure emerged through the mist. William walked with his characteristic economy of movement, his expression unreadable to most observers. But Lyle had learned to read the subtle indicators—the slight lift at the corner of his mouth, the marginally quickened pace. William was looking forward to something. Or someone.

Lyle dropped his cigarette, crushing it beneath his heel.

"William," he called, stepping from the archway with a carefully composed smile. "I was just about to give up on you. Shall we proceed to the Union? I hear Thornfield is planning to challenge our position on the Marshall Plan, and I've several counterarguments that might interest you."

As William approached, Lyle felt the last ember of his interest in Sarah cool and darken. He had made his decision. Some sacrifices were necessary for greater ambitions. Some doors must remain closed so that others might open.

Besides, he thought as they fell into step together, what was sentiment compared to power?

⸻◆⸻

William matched Lyle's stride as they walked beneath the Gothic arches toward the Union. Rain beaded on their overcoats, the soft patter providing counterpoint to their footsteps on the ancient stones. For several minutes, they discussed Thornfield's likely arguments, though William seemed unusually distracted.

"Forgive me," William said finally, pausing beneath a covered walkway. "I'm not entirely present for this conversation."

Lyle noted the uncharacteristic hesitation in William's voice. "Something on your mind?"

William glanced around, ensuring their privacy. His face held an expression Lyle had never seen before—a curious mixture of calculation and something that might, in another man, resemble vulnerability.

"I've been meaning to tell you something." William straightened his shoulders slightly. "I've met someone."

"Met someone?" Lyle raised his eyebrows with focussed precision.

"A woman. Sarah Stevens. She's reading law." William's voice remained measured, but his eyes betrayed a spark of genuine animation. "We've been meeting regularly since late Michaelmas."

Lyle arranged his features into a mask of surprise, though the name stabbed through him with remarkable precision. "Sarah Stevens? I believe I've seen her at the library. Blonde, rather striking?"

"Yes, that's her." William's gaze grew distant. "She's... different, Lyle. Sharper than most. She sees things as they are."

"Someone somewhat like you, then," Lyle offered, his voice perfectly modulated despite the hollowness spreading beneath his ribs.

"Perhaps." A ghost of a smile touched William's lips. "Though with considerably better manners."

Lyle leaned against the stone pillar, affecting casual interest while carefully selecting his next words. "And this is serious, I take it?"

"I believe it could be." William's admission sank slowly between them, unadorned and significant. "She understands what we're trying to build."

The "we" didn't escape Lyle's notice. William was including him in this future, this vision. It was both consolation prize and confirmation of his value. He should feel honoured, Lyle supposed. And in some distant, analytical part of himself, he did.

"Well then," Lyle said, clapping William lightly on the shoulder, "I should meet this paragon who's managed to breach the formidable defences of William Braithwaite."

William studied him for a moment. "That's precisely what I was thinking. We're meeting at The Anchor tonight at eight. You should join us."

"I'd be delighted." The lie came easily, wrapped in the conviction that this was the correct move in their complex game of ambition and alliance.

They resumed walking, but William's pace slowed slightly. "You know, Lyle, I've never properly thanked you."

"For what, precisely?"

"For understanding what matters." William's gaze was direct now, penetrating. "Others would waste time with petty competitions, unnecessary rivalries. You've always seen the larger picture."

Lyle inclined his head slightly, accepting the compliment while wondering if William somehow knew—if this was acknowledgment of the sacrifice Lyle was making. But no, William couldn't possibly be aware of feelings Lyle had guarded so carefully.

"The larger picture is all that's ever interested me," Lyle replied smoothly. "Everything else is merely... distraction."

As they approached the Union building, William paused once more, his expression thoughtful. Something in Lyle's tone or posture had caught his attention—some microscopic fissure in the perfect façade. William's eyes narrowed slightly, his analytical mind working to identify the discrepancy.

Lyle met his gaze evenly, revealing nothing.

After a moment, William seemed to set aside whatever thoughts had formed. "Eight o'clock, then," he said. "Don't be late. Sarah values punctuality."

"Wouldn't dream of disappointing her," Lyle replied, pushing open the heavy oak door to the Union.

As they entered the crowded hall, William filed away his momentary unease for future consideration. There had been something in Lyle's response—something carefully controlled beneath the surface—that warranted observation. Not concern, precisely, but awareness. William would watch and wait. It was what he did best.

Lyle, meanwhile, calculated the precise amount of charm he would display that evening—enough to be pleasant but not excessive, enough to show appreciation for Sarah's qualities without revealing his own interest. He would endure the evening with grace, watching the woman he might have pursued engage with the man he had chosen as ally instead.

It was, he told himself, an honourable concession. A necessary sacrifice on the altar of greater ambition. And if there was pain in this choice, well—pain was merely information. Useful data to be processed and filed away, like everything else.

The debate hall buzzed with voices around them, oblivious to the complex currents flowing between the two men who had just entered—currents of ambition, loyalty, and unspoken sacrifice.

◆

The Anchor hummed with evening activity—students hunchbacked over pints discussing philosophy, professors unwinding after lectures, locals seeking refuge from Cambridge's persistent January chill. In a corner table near the window overlooking the Cam, William and Sarah sat in quiet conversation, a half-empty bottle of wine between them.

"Eight-oh-six," Sarah observed, glancing at her wristwatch as Lyle approached their table. Her tone was light but precise. "I believe punctuality was advertised as one of your virtues, Mr Cunningham."

Lyle removed his scarf with unhurried grace. "My sincerest apologies. The tutorial with Professor Milnerton ran unexpectedly long."

"Fashionably late," William interjected, gesturing to the empty chair. "Lyle understands timing better than most—when to arrive, when to speak, when to wait." The defense came naturally, surprising even William with its immediacy.

Sarah's eyes flickered between the two men, noting the ease with which William had spoken. "Then I shall defer to your judgment on the matter," she said, offering Lyle a smile that acknowledged something beyond her words.

Lyle settled into his chair with studied casualness. "William speaks too generously of my virtues while overlooking my numerous flaws."

"I doubt that very much," Sarah replied with a smile, pouring wine into Lyle's glass. "William strikes me as someone who catalogs flaws with remarkable precision."

The evening unfolded in layers of conversation—politics, literature, again the merits of different colleges. On the surface, three brilliant minds engaged in stimulating discourse. Beneath, currents moved in complex patterns only partially visible to each participant.

Sarah watched Lyle's hands as he spoke—elegant, controlled, never quite gesturing toward her directly. She remembered their first encounter in the library last term, when they'd both reached for the same volume of constitutional precedents. His fingers had brushed hers as he'd received the surrender of the book with perfect politeness. Even then, she'd noted how his gaze lingered a fraction too long, how his subsequent visits to the law library seemed timed to coincide with hers.

She'd observed him watching her across quadrangles and dining halls, always from a careful distance. The interest had been evident to her attentive eye—Sarah had grown up learning to read people's intentions like texts. What fascinated her now was watching that interest being deliberately, meticulously buried for William's benefit.

"Wouldn't you agree, Sarah?" William's question pulled her back to the present.

"I'm sorry, I was momentarily distracted," she admitted.

"By what?" William asked, his gaze sharpening with interest.

Sarah glanced between them. "By the remarkable nature of friendship," she said truthfully. "It's rare to see two people so perfectly aligned in their thinking."

Lyle raised his glass slightly. "To alignment, then."

As they continued talking, William found his attention divided. The conversation flowed easily enough, but something in Sarah's observation had triggered a new awareness. He began noticing subtle patterns—how Lyle's eyes never quite met Sarah's directly, how he directed his most insightful comments to William rather than to her, how he maintained a precise physical distance.

These were the behaviours of a man exercising discipline, not disinterest.

The realisation settled into William like a stone dropping through still water. Lyle—confident, calculating Lyle—harboured feelings for Sarah. Yet here he sat, deliberately sublimating those feelings out of loyalty to their alliance. William had encountered many forms of calculation in his life, but rarely had he witnessed sacrifice of this nature.

Unbidden, an image surfaced in William's mind—Gregory Talbot, imagined, standing on the deck of the City of Benares, tin whistle in hand, promising to play it across the ocean so William might hear. The memory carried an unexpected weight, a reminder of connection without calculation.

"William?" Sarah's voice cut through his thoughts.

He blinked, returning to the warmth of The Anchor. "Yes?"

"You disappeared for a moment there," she said, her expression curious.

William looked at Lyle, really looked at him—seeing not just the strategic ally he'd cultivated but something he hadn't expected to find again. "I was thinking about the nature of trust," he said quietly.

Lyle met his gaze with perfect composure, but William could now see the careful control beneath it. Something shifted between them in that moment—an acknowledgment never spoken aloud but understood nonetheless.

"Another round?" William suggested, his voice carrying a new warmth.

"Certainly," Lyle replied.

As William signalled to the barman, Sarah observed the subtle change that had passed between the two men. Whatever silent communication had occurred, she recognised its significance. The friendship forming before her was built on something substantial—not just shared ambition but mutual respect and, perhaps most surprisingly, genuine regard.

Sarah smiled to herself. In the complex equation of power and alliance she was considering, this variable would prove invaluable.

⸺◆⸺

The evening deepened around them as the pub grew quieter. A fire crackled in the hearth, casting warm light across their table now littered with empty glasses and the remnants of a shared plate of bread and cheese. Outside, Cambridge had fallen into darkness, the ancient stones of its buildings soaking in the secrets of countless alliances formed over the centuries.

"What I find most remarkable," Sarah said, leaning forward slightly, "is how so many people never look beyond the immediate advantage. They're so busy winning small battles, they lose sight of the war."

William nodded, his eyes reflecting the firelight. "My father built an empire that way—accumulating victories without vision. It's impressive but ultimately limited."

"And what is *your* vision, William?" Lyle asked, his voice carrying genuine curiosity beneath its polished surface.

William considered the question, turning his glass slowly. "To build something that outlasts not just me, but the century. Something that can't be dismantled by a single failure or betrayed by a moment's weakness."

Sarah studied him, her analytical mind dissecting his ambition. "You'll need protection," she said simply. "Not physical, perhaps, but legal. Structural."

"And tactical flexibility," Lyle added. "The ability to move in spaces where official channels fail."

The three exchanged glances, each recognising something essential in the others. Without formal declaration, roles were being established, territories staked not in competition but in complementary alignment.

"I've watched how the college deans handle complaints," Sarah continued. "They're masters at making problems disappear before they ever reach official channels. One word in the right ear, one document quietly amended."

"Legal firebreaks," William murmured appreciatively.

"Precisely," she nodded. "I could build those for us. Anticipate challenges before they materialise."

Lyle's eyes narrowed thoughtfully. "While I could ensure our operational *flexibility* remains uncompromised."

"And I provide direction," William concluded almost in a whisper, his voice carrying quiet certainty.

The landlord called last orders, breaking their momentary silence. Around them, other students gathered coats and scarves, their laughter and conversations creating a backdrop of normality that suddenly seemed distant from the world the three were constructing.

"I should think," Lyle said carefully, "that most partnerships fail because they're built on identical strengths rather than complementary ones."

Sarah nodded. "Or because they're founded on sentiment rather than clear-eyed assessment."

"Yet without some measure of trust, they're equally doomed," William observed. "Pure calculation only takes you so far."

They fell silent, each contemplating the delicate balance they were negotiating—between strategy and loyalty, between ambition and connection... between friends.

"I propose a principle," Sarah said finally, feeling the warm glow of the wine within her. "Whatever we build, we protect each other first. Not just our collective interests, but each individual within our circle."

"Even when it's inconvenient?" Lyle asked, his tone neutral but his eyes searching.

"Especially then," William answered for her. "Otherwise, what distinguishes us from the common opportunists populating every boardroom and government office?"

Lyle considered this, then nodded once, decisively. "Okay, Agreed."

The three finished their drinks as the pub prepared to close. Outside, the night air carried the bite of winter, their breath forming clouds in the darkness. They walked together along the cobbled street, their footsteps echoing against ancient walls.

"We should formalise this arrangement," William said as they approached the junction where their paths would diverge—Sarah to her college, William and Lyle to theirs.

"With contracts?" Sarah asked, a smile playing at her lips.

"With understanding," William clarified. "Clear boundaries, defined responsibilities."

"And absolute discretion," Lyle added.

Sarah nodded, pulling her coat tighter against the cold. "I'll draft something suitable. Nothing that could ever be found, of course."

"Of course," William agreed.

They paused at the intersection, standing in a triangle beneath a street lamp. No hands were shaken, no dramatic oaths sworn. Instead, three pairs of eyes met in silent acknowledgement of what had been forged—something beyond friendship yet more personal than mere alliance.

"Until tomorrow, then," Sarah said finally, looking down at her feet, almost a bow.

"Tomorrow," William confirmed.

As they separated into the darkness, each carried away a certainty that hadn't existed hours before. Whatever future awaited them—whatever triumphs or challenges—they would face it not as individuals but as something more formidable: a triumvirate of complementary strengths, bound by mutual ambition and, perhaps more surprisingly, by an authentic friendship.

The night closed around them, and Cambridge slept on, possibly unaware that something consequential had just been set in motion within its ancient walls.

Golden light spilled through the ancient elms, casting dappled shadows across the quad where fallen leaves spiralled lazily to the ground. The afternoon had that peculiar quality unique to early autumn—warmth without heat, brightness without glare—a perfect equilibrium between seasons that seemed to suspend time itself.

Beneath the spreading branches of a copper beech, three figures had claimed their territory with the casual confidence of those who belonged precisely where they were. William sat with his back against the trunk, a well-read, dog-eared copy of Machiavelli's *The Prince* open on his lap, though his eyes occasionally lifted to observe the passing students. Lyle reclined on the grass nearby, gesturing emphatically as he dissected the latest parliamentary white paper on industrial nationalisation. Sarah sat cross-legged between them, her law texts abandoned beside her as she listened to Lyle with a mixture of amusement and critical assessment.

"Attlee's premise collapses under the slightest scrutiny," Lyle insisted, his voice carrying the polished authority that had won him the presidency of the Union Society the previous term. "The steel industry cannot possibly function efficiently under state control."

"You're assuming efficiency is the primary objective," Sarah countered, tucking a strand of blonde hair behind her ear with an elegant gesture that hadn't existed in her repertoire a year ago. "Perhaps control itself is the point."

William's lips curved into the ghost of a smile. "Both of you are circling the actual issue," he said, his voice carrying that quiet certainty that made even professors pause mid-lecture. "It's about the appearance of progress while ensuring the old powers maintain their influence through new channels."

A group of freshers walked past, their eyes lingering on the trio with poorly disguised fascination. In the months since their alliance had formed, something had shifted in how the three carried themselves—a subtle magnetism that drew attention without seeking it. Their movements had become more economical, their silences more comfortable, their certainties more absolute.

"Do you remember," Sarah said after the freshers had passed, "how uncertain we must have all appeared during our first week? All those unwritten rules, all those invisible hierarchies."

Lyle laughed, a sound that contained genuine warmth when directed at his two companions. "Speak for yourself. I was merely... strategically cautious."

"You were petrified of Professor Harrington," William reminded him without looking up from his book. "You rehearsed your first tutorial question seven times in our room."

"A necessary preparation," Lyle defended himself with mock dignity. "And now he's writing me a recommendation for graduate study."

Sarah plucked a fallen leaf from the ground, examining its intricate veining. "It's strange to think how much has changed. Last autumn, I was desperately trying to prove, as a woman, that I belonged here at all."

"And now?" William asked, his ice-blue eyes meeting hers.

She smiled, the expression containing both warmth and steel. "Now I'm fairly certain most of *them* don't belong here with us at all."

The three exchanged glances of quiet understanding. In less than a year, they had moved from navigating Cambridge's labyrinthine social codes to subtly rewriting them. Doors that had been merely ajar now swung wide open; conversations that once excluded them now paused expectantly for their contributions.

"I've been thinking," William said, closing his book with deliberate care, "about what comes next."

"The master's programmes," Lyle nodded, sitting up straighter. "I've already spoken with Father about funding another two years."

"As have I," Sarah added. "Though mine required somewhat more persuasion. Father still believes a husband would be a more suitable accomplishment than a postgraduate degree."

William's expression hardened momentarily. "He'll understand the value of your education eventually."

"Or he won't," Sarah replied with a shrug that contained new confidence. "Either way, I'll be completing my studies."

A comfortable silence settled among them as they watched shadows lengthen across the quad. The university's ancient buildings glowed amber in the late afternoon light, their weathered stones bearing witness to centuries of ambitions similar to—yet fundamentally different from—their own.

"Perhaps we should think about our future arrangement," William said finally. "The undergraduate years have been fruitful, but the master's programmes will present new challenges."

Lyle considered this, his gaze thoughtful. "We'll be scattered across different faculties, with competing demands on our time."

"And we should be looking beyond mere continuation," Sarah added, her mind already tracing potential pathways. "These next two years will establish our foundation for what lies beyond Cambridge."

William's hand settled on the grass between them. Sarah's joined his a moment later, with Lyle's following.

"To what comes next," William toasted softly.

Their hands lingered together, shadows blending into one on the dappled grass. Cambridge carried on around them, its ancient routines unchanged, unaware of the quiet commitments forming beneath the copper beech—an understanding that would, eventually, extend far beyond these secluded college grounds.

Chapter 15

Shadows Dancing: Ashes and Vows

The trio's reputation had grown in their master's year. Where once they had been three ambitious students finding their way, they were now spoken of in guarded tones across Cambridge—not with fear exactly, but with a wary respect. Professors who had once dismissed them now sought their opinions, inviting them to small gatherings where the real decisions about department funding and research priorities were quietly made.

William observed this transformation with clinical satisfaction. Their influence had expanded through carefully cultivated relationships and strategic favours—a word here about a promising undergraduate, a suggestion there about a potential donor. Nothing so crass as outright manipulation, merely the subtle art of making others believe William's preferences were their own discoveries.

Yet for all his mastery of these social mechanics, William found himself paralysed by a surprisingly conventional dilemma.

The question of Sarah's hand in marriage had occupied his thoughts with increasing frequency. He had mapped the practical aspects with his usual precision—the timing, the strategic advantages, even the potential challenges from her family. What he hadn't anticipated was his own emotional response to the prospect.

"You've been distracted all evening," Lyle observed as they walked back from a dinner at their supervisor's home. Sarah had remained behind, engaged in conversation with the professor's wife about a legal matter.

William's gaze fixed on a distant point. "I've been considering the appropriate approach to Sarah's father."

"Ah," Lyle nodded, understanding immediately, a small smile breaking at the edge of his mouth. "The formal request."

"It presents certain... complexities."

Lyle studied his friend's profile. "The man is conventional but not unreasonable. Your family name and prospects will satisfy his practical concerns."

"It's not his response that concerns me," William admitted, the words feeling foreign in his mouth.

They paused beneath a streetlamp, its yellow light catching the frost forming on the cobblestones. Lyle waited, allowing the silence to draw out William's thoughts.

"I find myself..." William began, then stopped, searching for precision. "I find myself uncertain of the form such a request should take."

Something shifted in Lyle's expression—a momentary softening that vanished almost immediately. "William Braithwaite, master budding strategist of boardroom takeovers, undone by a simple question of matrimony?"

William did not smile. "There is nothing simple about it."

And there wasn't. William had dissected the most complex business arrangements before, he had anticipated and countered his opponents' moves several steps ahead, had built relationships based on calculated advantage. Yet the prospect of asking for Sarah's hand stirred something unfamiliar within him—a sensation both unsettling and strangely vital.

Later that night, alone in his rooms, William stood at the window overlooking the darkened quadrangle. The ancient stones of Cambridge had witnessed countless such deliberations over the centuries, young men contemplating futures with chosen partners. But William doubted many had approached the matter with his particular blend of calculation and unexpected vulnerability.

He had not anticipated how the thought of Sarah—not as an ally or an asset, but as a wife—would create this curious hollowness in his chest. It was not unpleasant, precisely, but it was unfamiliar. Disconcerting.

"This is merely a formality," he told himself, watching his breath fog the glass. "A necessary step."

Yet he knew it was more. Something had altered in the careful architecture of his plans. Sarah had ceased to be merely a component—or his friend—and had become... essential. Not just to his ambitions, but to himself.

William turned from the window, his reflection fragmenting in the glass. The realisation disoriented him. He had spent years constructing himself as a fortress—impenetrable, strategic, every emotion carefully managed. Now he found himself experiencing feelings he had no framework to process, no strategy to deploy against.

When had it happened? When had Sarah transformed from a calculated choice to a necessity? When had the thought of her absence become unthinkable?

William moved to his desk and methodically arranged his papers, seeking comfort in order. The sensation of being unmoored persisted. He had prepared for every contingency except this one—the possibility that in cultivating Sarah's affection, he had developed genuine feelings of his own. He was in love.

It was not weakness, he decided finally. It was evolution. Adaptation. The next logical development in his becoming. Yet logic failed to explain the tightness in his throat when he imagined kneeling before her, offering not just a ring but a genuine piece of himself—perhaps the first truly genuine offering he had made to anyone since childhood.

William Braithwaite, who had faced down hardened businessmen in his father's boardroom and navigated the cruelty of Trewil Loop without flinching, found himself afraid—not of rejection, but of the vulnerability inherent in truly wanting something he could not simply take.

⸻◆⸻

The spring sunlight dappled the water as William and Sarah strolled along the Cam, Cambridge's ancient buildings reflected in the rippling surface. Students punted lazily past them, their laughter carrying across the water. William walked with measured steps, his mind calculating various possibilities with each footfall.

"My father mentioned visiting next weekend," Sarah said, breaking their comfortable silence. "Mother insists on seeing me before term's end."

William nodded, seeing the opening he'd been waiting for. "Your parents visit often?"

"Not particularly. Father's practice keeps him occupied." She glanced sideways at him. "Though he's expressed curiosity about my... associations at university."

"Associations?" William raised an eyebrow, allowing a hint of amusement to show.

"His word, not mine." Sarah's lips curved upward. "He's rather traditional about certain matters."

They paused to watch a heron standing motionless at the water's edge, its reflection perfect in the still shallows. William considered his approach carefully.

"Traditional men often appreciate directness in important matters," he observed.

Sarah's eyes narrowed slightly. "And what important matters might warrant such directness?"

"Futures. Arrangements. Partnerships of significance."

She turned to face him fully now, her expression unreadable. "How clinical you make it sound."

William felt that unfamiliar tightness in his chest again. This wasn't proceeding as he'd anticipated. "Not clinical. Precise. Respectful."

"Is there something specific you're attempting to determine, William?" Her tone was light, but her eyes were watchful.

He measured his words carefully. "I've been considering the logical progression of our... arrangement."

"Our arrangement?" Sarah echoed, a smile playing at the corners of her mouth. "Is that what we have?"

William recognised the trap but couldn't quite navigate around it. "Our relationship, you and me," he amended.

"And what progression do you envision for this relationship?"

They resumed walking, crossing a small stone bridge. William felt unusually unsettled, his customary confidence failing him briefly. "I wonder if you've given thought to your plans after Cambridge."

"Naturally," she replied. "Though I suspect you're inquiring about something more specific than my legal career."

William stopped again, turning to face her directly. "Would you consider a more permanent arrangement between us?"

Sarah's eyes sparkled with something between amusement and affection. "Are you attempting to determine my receptiveness to a hypothetical proposal, William?"

Caught, trapped, ensnared, he didn't immediately respond.

"Because," she continued, "one might think you're attempting to secure a guaranteed outcome before risking the question itself."

"Efficiency," he offered weakly.

Sarah laughed then, the sound bright against the ancient stones. "My pragmatic William. Always needing certainty before committing to action."

She stepped closer, her voice softening. "What if I told you that certainty isn't always possible? That some leaps require faith?"

William felt exposed in a way he hadn't since childhood. "Faith has rarely served me well."

Sarah's expression gentled. She reached for his hand, an unusual public gesture for her. "Then perhaps it's time for new evidence."

She held his gaze steadily. "I have known since our third conversation that you were unlike anyone I'd ever met. By our seventh, I knew you were essential to whatever future I might build." Her voice remained measured, but emotion coloured her words. "I love you, William Braithwaite, not despite your calculations and strategies but alongside them."

William felt something shift within him—a door opening to a room he'd kept locked for years.

"And yes," she continued, "I would accept a proposal from you, should you ever find the courage to risk one without absolute certainty of the outcome."

William's grip tightened on her hand. "You've known all along."

"Of course." Her smile was both tender and triumphant. "Though watching you navigate this particular problem has been rather entertaining."

She glanced up at the sky, seemingly casual. "Perhaps you might accompany me next weekend when my parents visit. Father has expressed interest in meeting the man who's been occupying so much of my attention."

William caught the knowing look in her eyes. "That would be... convenient."

"Wouldn't it just?" Sarah replied, her smile widening. "A fortunate coincidence that provides exactly the opportunity you've been seeking."

William felt something unfamiliar bubble up inside him—not calculation or strategy, but simple joy. "You're rather formidable, Sarah Stevens."

"Yes," she agreed, linking her arm through his as they continued their walk. "That's precisely why we suit."

— ◆ —

The Orchard Tea Garden had been transformed for the evening, its daytime charm replaced by an atmosphere of quiet elegance. White linen cloths draped the tables, silver gleamed under soft lamplight, and discreet waiters moved with practised efficiency between the garden room and kitchen. For the Stevens family, the proprietors had arranged a private alcove—a small triumph of Sarah's careful planning.

Justice Damion Stevens commanded attention without effort. Tall and patrician, with the same ice-blue eyes he had passed onto his daughter, he carried himself with the unconscious authority of a man accustomed to pronouncing judgment. His wife Elizabeth sat beside him, her refined beauty softened by warmth that her husband's demeanour lacked. Sarah completed the tableau, poised and alert, occasionally catching William's eye with subtle reassurance.

"Cambridge agrees with you, Sarah," Elizabeth observed, taking a sip of wine. "There's a confidence about you that wasn't there at Christmas."

Justice Stevens nodded his agreement. "Your arguments have certainly sharpened. I found your paper on the limitations of parliamentary sovereignty quite compelling."

"High praise indeed," Sarah replied, "considering the source."

The first course arrived—poached quail eggs nestled on beds of asparagus, adorned with truffle shavings. William noted how Justice

Stevens inspected the plate with the same methodical attention he'd likely given to evidence in his courtroom.

"Mr Braithwaite," the Justice said, turning his penetrating gaze toward William, "Sarah tells me you spent the war years in South Africa. A remarkable experience for a child, I imagine."

William measured his response carefully. "It was transformative, sir. The landscape there possesses a brutal honesty that England lacks."

"How so?" The question came with judicial precision.

"The Drakensberg mountains don't pretend to be anything but what they are. The *veld* doesn't apologise for its harshness." William paused. "There's clarity in such environments."

The Justice nodded thoughtfully. "And the people?"

"Shaped by the land they inhabit. The Afrikaners I lived with value directness, sir. They've little patience for pretence."

"A quality you seem to have adopted," Justice Stevens observed, neither approving nor condemning.

The main course arrived—venison with a port reduction, accompanied by seasonal vegetables. The conversation shifted to politics, the changing landscape of post-war Britain, and the legal challenges of the emerging welfare state. William contributed judiciously, demonstrating knowledge without overreaching.

As the meal progressed, William noticed Justice Stevens studying him during moments when he thought himself unobserved. The scrutiny was neither hostile nor particularly warm—simply assessing, weighing, calculating.

When dessert plates had been cleared and coffee served, William caught Sarah's nearly imperceptible nod. She turned to her mother. "I believe Father mentioned wanting to see the garden's famous apple trees. Perhaps we could walk there while they're still visible in the twilight?"

Elizabeth Stevens, understanding the choreography at play, rose gracefully. "What a lovely idea."

As the women departed, silence settled between the two men. Justice Stevens added a precise measure of sugar to his coffee, stirred once, and set the spoon down with quiet deliberation.

"I suspect, Mr Braithwaite, that you've arranged this moment with some care."

William met his gaze directly. "I have, sir."

"Then perhaps we might dispense with preliminary conversation."

William nodded, appreciating the efficiency. "Justice Stevens, I wish to marry your daughter."

The older man's expression remained unchanged. "I'm aware of your father's position and the Braithwaite holdings. Your financial prospects aren't in question."

"I would hope that more than my financial prospects might be considered."

"Indeed." The Justice leaned back slightly. "Sarah is exceptional—intellectually formidable, morally grounded, and possessed of ambitions that extend beyond conventional expectations. She requires a partner who will neither diminish nor exploit those qualities."

"I agree entirely."

"Do you?" The question carried weight beyond its simplicity. "I've observed many men who claim to admire strong women, only to systematically undermine them once the relationship is secured."

William considered his response carefully. "Sir, I don't merely admire Sarah's strengths—I rely upon them. What I intend to build requires her particular intelligence and perspective. I would no more diminish her capabilities than I would sabotage my own."

Something shifted in the Justice's expression—not warmth, precisely, but recognition.

"That's perhaps the most honest answer you could have given," he said finally. "You speak of partnership rather than romance."

"I speak of reality, sir. Sarah and I understand each other with unusual clarity."

Justice Stevens studied him for a long moment. "There's something in you that wasn't formed in England, Mr Braithwaite. Something that carries both promise and peril." He set his cup down with precision. "Sarah sees it too, I suspect."

"She does."

"And still chooses you."

"Yes, sir."

The Justice nodded once, decisively. "Then you have my consent, though I suspect you would proceed regardless."

William allowed himself a slight smile. "I value tradition, sir. And beginnings matter."

"Indeed they do, Mr Braithwaite." Justice Stevens extended his hand across the table. "Indeed they do."

———◆○◆———

Elizabeth and Sarah returned to the table, their timing impeccable. Sarah's eyes met William's immediately, searching for confirmation. The almost imperceptible nod he offered was enough—she understood. Her shoulders relaxed slightly, the only visible sign of her relief.

"The apple trees are quite lovely," Elizabeth said, settling back into her chair. "Though they're past their best bloom now."

Justice Stevens poured his wife a fresh cup of coffee. "We were just concluding our discussion." His tone revealed nothing, but when he glanced at Sarah, there was a subtle shift in his expression. "I believe your young man has a proper understanding of the responsibilities he's undertaking."

Sarah's eyes widened slightly at the word "responsibilities"—her father's code for consent. She composed herself quickly, but not before William caught the flash of genuine emotion beneath her carefully maintained exterior.

"More coffee, William?" she asked, her voice steady despite the significance of the moment.

"Thank you, no," he replied, equally composed.

The conversation drifted to lighter topics—Cambridge traditions, the changing seasons, a recent exhibition at the Fitzwilliam Museum. Yet beneath this ordinary exchange, currents of understanding flowed between them all. Elizabeth spoke warmly of her own Cambridge days, while the Justice reminisced about legal cases from his early career. Throughout it all, William noticed the silent communication between husband and wife—a language of glances and subtle gestures built over decades of marriage.

Justice Stevens consulted his pocket watch. "I'm afraid we should consider making our way back to London. Early chambers tomorrow."

"Of course, Father," Sarah said. "The last train leaves at eight-forty."

As they stood, gathering coats and gloves, William felt an unexpected surge of something approaching happiness—not the calculated satisfaction of a successful negotiation, but something warmer and less familiar.

"Justice Stevens, Mrs Stevens," he said, the words emerging before he'd fully considered them, "I'd like to invite you both to the Braithwaite estate in Wraysbury. My parents would be honoured to meet you."

The Justice paused, his expression thoughtful. William recognised the careful consideration behind those ice-blue eyes—the same measured assessment Sarah employed when evaluating complex problems.

"When would you suggest?" he asked finally.

"Perhaps the weekend after next? I could arrange for a car to collect you."

Justice Stevens exchanged a glance with his wife—a silent conference conducted in the language of long marriage. Elizabeth nodded almost imperceptibly.

"We accept your invitation," the Justice said. "Though we'll make our own transportation arrangements."

"Excellent." William shook the older man's hand firmly. "I look forward to it."

Elizabeth kissed Sarah's cheek. "Do take care, darling. Your father and I will see you soon."

The Stevenses departed with dignified efficiency, leaving William and Sarah standing together in the soft evening light. They watched as the older couple disappeared around a corner, Justice Stevens' hand placed lightly at the small of his wife's back.

"Shall we walk back through the Fellows' Garden?" Sarah suggested.

They moved in comfortable silence until they reached the seclusion of the garden path. William's steps had an unusual lightness to them, his posture fractionally less rigid than normal.

"You're practically skipping," Sarah observed, her voice low with amusement.

"I assure you, I've never skipped in my life."

"Not physically, perhaps." She slipped her arm through his. "But I can feel it, William. You're... buoyant."

He didn't deny it. "Your father is an extraordinary man."

"Yes," she agreed. "And terrifying when he chooses to be."

"He didn't attempt to intimidate me."

"He wouldn't. That's not his style with those he respects." Sarah paused beneath a flowering cherry tree. "What did he say to you?"

"That you're exceptional. That I'd better not diminish you."

She smiled. "And what did you say?"

"That I rely on your strengths as much as my own."

Sarah's fingers tightened slightly on his arm. "Breathe, William," she whispered. "Your pulse is racing."

Only then did William realise how rapid his heartbeat had become. He inhaled deeply, feeling the cool evening air fill his lungs.

"I'm not accustomed to... this," he admitted.

"To what?"

"Getting what I want and actually wanting it." He turned to face her. "The two rarely align."

Sarah reached up and straightened his tie with precise fingers. "Well," she said softly, "you'd better become accustomed to it. Because I intend to say yes when you properly ask me."

William's usual mask of control slipped just enough to reveal genuine warmth in his eyes. "I should warn you—my parents are considerably less impressive than yours."

"I'm not marrying your parents," Sarah replied. "Now, shall we continue our walk? The porter locks the gate at nine."

They resumed their path through the garden, matching each other's stride perfectly, while Cambridge's ancient stones watched in silent witness to what they had set in motion.

⸻◆⸻

The late afternoon light streamed through the tall windows of the Braithwaite estate, casting long shadows across the drawing room's Persian carpet. Outside, the manicured gardens of Wraysbury stood in perfect order, a testament to the family's wealth and attention to detail. William observed the scene with clinical detachment, noting the precise arrangement of tea service, the careful positioning of chairs, the subtle signals of power and privilege.

Margaret Braithwaite sat with perfect posture, her hands folded neatly in her lap. William had noticed immediately—her eyes were clear, her movements steady. Not a drop of gin had passed her lips today. The realisation brought an unexpected sense of relief. Perhaps she understood the stakes of this meeting better than he'd given her credit for.

"Mrs Stevens, would you care for more tea?" Margaret asked, her voice carrying the warmth of a hostess who had entertained countless important guests.

"Thank you, yes," Elizabeth Stevens replied with equal polish. "You have a lovely home."

Sarah caught William's eye across the room, a silent communication passing between them. She looked entirely at ease, as though she'd been navigating such social waters her entire life—which, of course, she had.

The door opened, and Charles Braithwaite entered with purposeful strides. His bespoke suit bore not a single crease despite the long hours at his desk.

"Justice Stevens, Mrs Stevens," Charles said, extending his hand. "Please accept my sincere apologies for not greeting you upon arrival. Unavoidable business with our American partners."

Justice Stevens rose to his full height, impressive even among tall men. "No apology necessary, Mr Braithwaite. International commerce waits for no man, I understand."

The two men shook hands, each taking the measure of the other. William watched the subtle power play with interest—his father's firm grip, the Justice's equally unyielding response.

"I trust Margaret has been looking after you?" Charles took a seat beside his wife, his hand briefly touching her shoulder in a gesture that seemed almost affectionate.

"Splendidly," Elizabeth said. "She's been telling us about your collection of first editions. Quite remarkable."

The conversation moved through safe, neutral territory—books, gardens, the unseasonably pleasant weather. William noted the careful dance of politeness, the gradual warming as both families found common interests. Margaret spoke of her charity work with surprising animation, while Elizabeth described her involvement with the Royal Academy. Charles and the Justice discovered a shared interest in fly fishing.

"I understand congratulations may soon be in order," Charles said finally, addressing the unspoken purpose of their gathering. He glanced at William and Sarah, seated side by side on the Chippendale sofa. "Though I believe my son has yet to make a formal proposal."

"Father," William said, his tone carrying a rare note of warning.

Sarah placed her hand lightly on William's arm. "We've discussed the matter, Mr Braithwaite. The formal aspects will follow in due course."

"Young people today," Justice Stevens said with unexpected lightness. "They prefer to settle matters between themselves before involving parents."

"Indeed," Charles agreed. "Though some traditions are worth preserving."

The conversation shifted to practical matters—potential dates, venues, guest lists. William remained largely silent, observing how Sarah deftly steered the discussion, aligning their families' expectations with subtle skill.

"St. Margaret's would be appropriate," Elizabeth suggested. "Given both families' connections."

"The reception could be held here at Wraysbury," Margaret offered, surprising William with her enthusiasm. "The gardens are particularly beautiful in June."

"A summer wedding, then," Justice Stevens nodded approvingly. "Sensible timing, after Sarah completes her examinations."

Charles leaned forward slightly. "I believe this union represents more than just a marriage of two people. The Braithwaite and Stevens names together—there's significant potential there."

"I quite agree," the Justice said. "Our families share certain... values and aspirations."

William caught Sarah's eye again. She gave him the slightest nod, acknowledging what they both understood—their parents were already calculating the advantages of their connection, just as they themselves had done.

As evening descended, the staff lit lamps and drew curtains. Dinner passed with increasing conviviality, the initial stiffness melting away as both families recognised their alignment on matters of importance—position, influence, legacy.

After the meal, Charles rose from his chair. "Justice Stevens, perhaps you'd join me in my study? I've a rather excellent Macallan I've been saving for a worthy occasion."

"I'd be delighted," the Justice replied, following Charles from the room.

William watched them go, knowing that behind the closed doors of his father's study, the real negotiations would begin—not about a wedding, but about the future their families would forge together.

⬥

The grandfather clock in the hall struck midnight, its resonant chimes echoing through the sleeping house. Charles and Margaret had retired an hour earlier, followed shortly by the Stevens, who occupied the east wing guest rooms. The servants had extinguished most of the lights, leaving only the soft glow of a single lamp in the living room where William and Sarah remained.

William sat on the sofa with his arm around Sarah's shoulders, her head resting against him. The calculated performances of the evening had fallen away, leaving something neither had anticipated when they first began their alliance at Cambridge—genuine affection.

"They performed admirably," Sarah murmured, referring to their parents. "Your mother surprised me. I expected more resistance."

"She wants grandchildren," William replied simply. "And your father—I believe he sees more than he lets on."

Sarah nodded against his shoulder. "He always has. It's what makes him dangerous in court."

The crackling fire cast dancing shadows across the antique furniture. For once, William wasn't analysing the room for advantages or planning his next strategic move. Instead, he found himself tracing the contour of Sarah's hand with his fingertips.

"When did it change for you?" Sarah asked suddenly. "When did I become more than just a useful alliance?"

William considered the question with unusual honesty. "That day in the Fellows' Garden. You called me calculating, and instead of denying it, you said you found it comforting." He paused. "No one had ever seen me clearly before and stayed anyway."

Sarah turned to face him, her blue eyes reflecting the firelight. "You know what I value most about you, William? You never ask me to be less than I am. My intelligence isn't something to be hidden or apologised for with you."

"Why would I want you to be less?" William asked, genuinely puzzled. "It's your mind that I—" He stopped, the word catching in his throat.

"That you what?" Sarah pressed gently.

"That I love," he finished quietly, the word unfamiliar yet fitting.

Sarah reached up to touch his face. "We're quite the pair, aren't we? Everyone sees the calculation, the ambition. No one would believe we're sitting here like this."

"Let them underestimate us," William said, drawing her closer. "What's between us belongs to us alone."

In the quiet of the Wraysbury estate, they sat together, two formidable minds at rest in each other's company, their shadows merging on the wall behind them.

——◆◇◆——

Dawn arrived as a gentle whisper over Wraysbury, painting the landscape in watercolour hues of pearl and rose. Mist clung to the hollows of the estate grounds, curling around ancient oaks and softening the hard edges of the world. Through this ethereal veil, two figures moved with unhurried purpose across the dew-laden grass, their footprints momentarily dark against the silvered lawn before fading like memories.

William led Sarah along a barely visible path that wound away from the formal gardens, beyond the manicured hedgerows and into the wilder reaches of the estate. His steps were sure, following a route etched into his consciousness from childhood explorations. Sarah walked beside him, her cream coat catching the first true light of morning, her hand resting in the crook of his arm with casual intimacy.

The ruins appeared gradually through the mist—remnants of a medieval chapel that had stood sentinel on this rise for centuries before time reclaimed its stones. Broken arches reached skyward like supplicating fingers, while ivy embraced the weathered stonework in a centuries-long caress. William paused at the threshold, allowing Sarah to absorb the quiet majesty of this forgotten place.

Unbeknownst to the couple, their progress was observed from the east wing of the house. Through leaded glass windows clouded with morning condensation, a solitary figure stood motionless, tracking their journey with measured interest.

Within the ruins, William guided Sarah to a particular spot where an ancient stone altar remained largely intact, its surface worn smooth by countless seasons. Morning light spilled through a collapsed section of roof, illuminating specks of dust that danced in the air between them. He gestured to the surrounding walls, perhaps sharing some childhood tale or historical fact, his expression animated in a way rarely witnessed beyond their private moments.

Sarah listened attentively, her face tilted toward his, occasionally glancing at the architectural details he indicated. Her smile, visible even at this distance, held the quiet confidence of a woman certain of her place in the world—and in the heart of the man before her.

The observer remained perfectly still, breath creating small circles of fog on the windowpane, watching as William's posture shifted subtly. The young man's hand disappeared into his pocket, withdrawing something too small to discern from this vantage point. Then, with a grace that belied his usual calculated precision, William lowered himself to one knee before Sarah, taking her hand in his.

Time seemed suspended in the misty morning air. Birds continued their dawn chorus, oblivious to human rituals. A gentle breeze stirred the ivy on ancient walls. Sarah remained perfectly composed, her stillness speaking volumes. After a moment that contained worlds, she nodded once, decisively.

William rose to his feet and drew Sarah into an embrace that transcended their usual measured interactions. Her arms encircled his shoulders as his wrapped around her waist, lifting her slightly so that for a heartbeat, she was suspended above the earth. When they separated, their foreheads remained touching briefly, creating a perfect arch of connection.

From the bedroom window, Charles Braithwaite stepped back slightly, satisfaction warming his features. The scene below unfolded exactly as he had anticipated—perhaps even orchestrated. His son, once a distant and troubling enigma upon his return from Africa, now stood as the heir Charles had always envisioned. The Stevens girl would make a formidable addition to the Braithwaite dynasty, her legal mind and social connections complementing William's ruthless intelligence.

Charles nodded imperceptibly, a gesture of approval witnessed by no one. The morning light caught the silver at his temples as a smile—not of joy but of satisfied ambition—settled on his features. The path he had cleared for his son was being followed with precision. The Braithwaite legacy would continue, stronger than before, extending its influence through this strategic union.

In the ruins below, William and Sarah walked hand in hand through the ancient archway, returning toward the house. The mist began to lift around them, revealing the landscape in greater clarity. They moved in perfect synchronicity, two shadows merging into one as they traversed the sloping lawn, unaware of the approving gaze that followed their progress from above.

Chapter 16

Shadows Weave, Shape, and Set

Sunday arrived with the kind of gentle autumn sunshine that painted Wraysbury in golden hues. The engagement was barely twenty-four hours old, a private joy still being savoured, when William's black Bentley crunched across the gravel drive to collect Lyle from the station.

"I invited Cunningham for lunch," William had mentioned to his father the previous evening, almost as an afterthought. "He should meet everyone properly."

Now, as the Bentley returned, William and Sarah stood together on the portico, watching Lyle emerge from the vehicle. He wore a perfectly tailored charcoal suit that spoke of Savile Row without shouting it, a burgundy tie providing the only splash of colour. In his hand, a bottle of Château Margaux—Lord Blackwood's preferred vintage, William noted.

"Cunningham," William greeted him, extending his hand.

"Braithwaite." Lyle's grip was firm, his smile genuine. His eyes, however, flickered briefly to Sarah, registering something different about her—a subtle glow, perhaps, or the way she stood fractionally closer to William than propriety strictly required.

"Sarah," Lyle nodded, offering a slight bow that belonged to another century.

"We've news," Sarah began, but William touched her elbow lightly.

"Later," he murmured. "Let's get through the introductions first."

Inside, the drawing room hummed with pre-luncheon conversation. Justice Stevens stood near the fireplace, discussing something with Charles while their wives sat together on the Chesterfield.

"Father, Mother," William said, commanding the room's attention without raising his voice. "May I present Lyle Cunningham. Lyle, my parents, Charles and Margaret Braithwaite."

Charles stepped forward immediately, his handshake vigourous. "Cunningham. Your father is Cecil, Lord Blackwood, yes? We've crossed paths at the Carlton."

"Indeed, sir. He speaks highly of your shipping ventures."

"And Justice Stevens, Mrs Stevens," William continued. "Sarah's parents."

Something passed across Justice Stevens' face—recognition, perhaps wariness. "Cunningham," he said, his voice measured. "I believe I've had the pleasure of your father's company before the Lords. The Fisheries Bill, was it not?"

"The very same," Lyle acknowledged with a slight incline of his head. "He mentioned your formidable opposition to the coastal access clauses."

"Formidable but ultimately unsuccessful," the Justice replied, a hint of irony touching his lips.

Margaret Braithwaite observed the exchange with a glass already in hand, her eyes slightly unfocused. "Do sit down, Mr Cunningham. Simmons will announce lunch shortly."

At the dining table, conversation flowed easily between disparate tributaries. Charles and Lyle discovered mutual interests in post-war German reconstruction, while Justice Stevens occasionally interjected with legal perspectives. Margaret, seated beside Elizabeth Stevens, had begun sharing thoughts about flower arrangements and guest lists—details that seemed oddly premature to those not yet privy to certain news.

When the main course arrived, William cleared his throat. The table fell silent.

"Sarah and I have an announcement," he said, his voice steady. "Early this morning, I asked Sarah to become my wife, and she has done me the honour of accepting."

A chorus of congratulations rose from those who hadn't yet been informed. Lyle's face remained perfectly composed as he raised his glass.

"To William and Sarah," he offered. "May your union bring you everything you desire and deserve."

Only Justice Stevens noticed the slight emphasis on the final word, the infinitesimal tightening around Lyle's eyes. The Justice had spent decades reading witnesses, discerning truth from fabrication, and what he saw now was masterful concealment—pain submerged beneath perfect social performance.

"We're thinking June next year," Sarah added, "after we've completed our studies."

"The rose garden will be perfect then," Margaret said to Elizabeth, her words slightly slurred. "William used to hide there as a boy."

Charles observed the dynamics unfolding with clinical detachment. He noted how Lyle's attention remained fixed on William even when addressing others, the subtle deference in his posture. Here was loyalty of a kind rarely seen—a young man who had clearly sacrificed personal desire for friendship's sake. Such devotion could be useful.

"Cunningham," Charles said during a lull, "William tells me you've quite the head for strategy. Perhaps you might join us tomorrow at the London office? I'd value your perspective on our West African ventures."

Elizabeth Stevens, quiet throughout most of the meal, missed nothing. Her gaze travelled from Margaret's trembling hand as she reached for her wine glass, to Charles's calculating assessment of Lyle, to her husband's perceptive observation of the young trio. She saw the bonds forming and breaking, the alliances shifting like tectonic plates beneath the polite veneer of a Sunday lunch.

Most clearly, she saw her daughter—brilliant, ambitious Sarah—who had secured not just a wealthy husband but a power base from which to launch her own ambitions. Elizabeth caught Sarah's eye across the table and offered a small, knowing smile. Sarah returned it with equal understanding.

The meal continued, plates cleared and replaced with dessert, while beneath the surface of cordial conversation, the future began to take its shape.

The morning light slanted through the tall windows of Braithwaite Enterprises, casting long shadows across the polished marble floor of the reception area. William, Sarah, and Lyle stood in a loose triangle as they waited for Charles to collect them from the lobby. The building hummed with post-war purpose—telephones ringing, typewriters clacking, leather-soled shoes clicking against stone as messengers darted between departments.

"Impressive," Sarah murmured, her gaze taking in the gleaming brass fixtures and the imposing company crest mounted behind the reception desk. "One might almost forget there's still rationing outside these walls."

William's expression remained neutral, though his eyes registered her observation. "Father believes in projecting permanence, especially when the world outside is in flux. Worth considering that rationing will eventually come to an end, and we have to be ready for that."

Charles emerged from the lift. "Ah, excellent. You're all here." He gestured expansively. "Welcome to the nerve centre of Braithwaite Enterprises. Shall we begin?"

The tour proceeded methodically through departments—accounting, legal, shipping, and commodities trading. At each stop, Charles introduced the trio to department heads who invariably addressed only William and Lyle, with cursory nods to Sarah.

On the executive floor, they encountered Duncan Braithwaite emerging from his office, his corpulent frame filling the doorway.

"Nephew," he said, his smile not quite reaching his eyes. "And this must be the fiancée we've heard about. Congratulations are in order, I suppose."

"Uncle Duncan," William replied evenly. "May I present Sarah Stevens and Lyle Cunningham."

Duncan's gaze flicked dismissively over Sarah before settling on Lyle. "Cunningham? Lord Blackwood's boy?"

"The same, sir," Lyle answered with perfect courtesy.

"Interesting friends you're making, William," Duncan commented, his tone suggesting the opposite. "Your father always did have an eye for useful connections."

Edward Braithwaite appeared silently beside his brother, as if materialising from the woodwork. His thin frame and watchful eyes provided a stark contrast to Duncan's bluster.

"William," Edward nodded, his bony fingers adjusting his tie. "I understand congratulations are in order. Miss Stevens, a pleasure." His eyes lingered on Sarah with an unsettling calculation before shifting to Lyle. "And Mr Cunningham. How is your father finding the Lords these days?"

"Tedious but necessary, I believe is his usual assessment," Lyle replied smoothly.

Edward's thin lips curved upward. "Indeed. Well, we mustn't keep you from Charles's grand tour."

As they continued down the corridor, Sarah leaned closer to William. "Your uncles seem...invested in your activities."

"Like vultures circling a carcass they hope is dying, keep an eye on them", William replied quietly.

They arrived at the boardroom where Hargreaves and Richardson were waiting. Richardson looked up, recognition flickering in his eyes as they met Lyle's. The two men exchanged subtle nods—acknowledgment of their previous meeting at the Athenaeum and the circles they both navigated.

"Miss Stevens," Hargreaves began, "perhaps you'd be more comfortable in the anteroom while we discuss business matters? Miss Pemberton can arrange tea."

An executive secretary stepped forward, hand extended toward Sarah. "This way, Miss Stevens. The ladies' sitting room is quite lovely."

William's hand settled lightly on Sarah's lower back. "That won't be necessary." His voice was quiet but carried an unmistakable edge. "Sarah will remain with us. Her legal insights will prove valuable, particularly regarding our expansion plans."

"But surely—" the secretary began.

"Miss Stevens will be joining the discussion as my guest and future wife," William continued, his tone ice-clear and brooking no argument. "She graduated top of her class at Cambridge Law and has already consulted on matters that would make your head spin, Miss Pemberton. She stays."

Charles observed the exchange with interest, a flicker of approval crossing his features. "William is quite right. Miss Stevens, please take a seat. Hargreaves, have another chair brought in for Mr Cunningham."

Richardson's eyebrows rose fractionally before his face resumed its professional mask. "A progressive approach, William. Most refreshing."

Sarah took her seat with composed dignity, but William caught the brief pressure of her hand against his—silent acknowledgment of his intervention.

As the meeting commenced, Lyle watched the dynamics unfold with growing certainty. William had not merely defended Sarah; he had demonstrated the precise calibre of leadership Lyle had gambled on—decisive, uncompromising, and forward-thinking. The alliance he had chosen, even at personal cost, was proving sound.

"Now, Mr Cunningham," Charles said, spreading a map of West Africa across the table, "William tells me you've some thoughts on our operations in the Gold Coast and Nigeria."

Lyle leaned forward, fully committed now. "Indeed, Mr Braithwaite. With independence movements gaining momentum, I believe there's an opportunity to position Braithwaite Enterprises not as a colonial remnant but as a development partner."

Charles's eyes narrowed with interest. "Go on."

As Lyle outlined his vision, he felt the weight of his decision—to throw his lot in completely with the Braithwaites. The sacrifice of his feelings for Sarah seemed a small price to pay in exchange for the empire they would build.

◆◇◆

The clock tower struck three, its chimes echoing through the hushed atmosphere of the Squire Law Library's reading room. The sound lingered in the air, mingling with the subtle symphony of academic labour—the whisper of turning pages, the occasional scratch of pen against paper, the soft creak of ancient wooden chairs. Nearly empty now, the library had witnessed a gradual exodus as most students retreated to their colleges under Trinity Term's mounting pressure.

Sarah closed the final volume of case law with a decisive thud, sending a small cloud of dust specks spreading out in the slanting lamp light. The distinctive scent of aged paper, leather bindings, and furniture polish hung in the still air, overlaid with the faintest trace of chalk dust that seemed permanently embedded in Cambridge's academic spaces.

"Finished?" William asked without looking up from his economic projections, his voice barely above a whisper in deference to the library's sacred silence.

"For now. Though I'll need to revisit Blackstone's commentary on sovereignty before my meeting with Professor Harwood tomorrow." Sarah massaged her temples, where a dull ache had been building for hours. "He's determined to find fault with my position that international corporate entities are becoming de facto sovereigns in post-colonial territories."

"Because it's true," Lyle murmured from behind his stack of financial journals, his words almost lost in the distant sound of footsteps echoing across the marble floor. "*And* because he sits on three corporate boards that benefit from precisely that arrangement."

The library's afternoon light filtered through leaded windows, casting medieval patterns across the polished oak table and their modern ambitions. Dust particles floated lazily in the golden beams, occasionally disturbed by a passing scholar or the gentle draft from an ancient window frame. The radiators ticked and sighed, struggling against the perpetual Cambridge dampness that seemed to seep through the stone walls.

For weeks, they had claimed this corner table, surrounded by towers of references and dog-eared notes. Their master's theses had become their singular focus—the final academic hurdle before their real work began. The evidence of their scholarly dedication was everywhere—empty tea cups with tannin stains marking the hours, discarded pencil shavings, crumpled drafts of abandoned paragraphs, and the faint smell of coffee gone cold.

William's thesis on economic leverage in post-colonial markets had drawn quiet concern from his supervisor, who questioned whether such "realpolitik" belonged in academic discourse. Sarah's examination of corporate sovereignty challenged fundamental assumptions about nation-state primacy. Lyle's analysis of banking structures as tools for political influence had already earned him a discreet job offer from the Treasury.

"We should break for dinner," William said, checking his watch. The soft metallic click of its clasp seemed unnaturally loud in the library's quiet. "My brain's beginning to circle the same paragraph."

The heavy weight of fatigue pressed down on all of them, evident in their slumped shoulders and the dark circles beneath their eyes. The library clock ticked relentlessly, marking the passage of precious hours as deadline pressure built like a physical presence around them.

Sarah gathered her notes with meticulous precision, the rustling papers sounding like autumn leaves in the hushed space. "I can't. Professor Harwood wants my revised chapter by morning, and I've three more cases to integrate."

"I'll bring something back for you," William replied. The casual domesticity of the offer stalled between them—not a question but a certainty.

Lyle observed this exchange with the detached neutrality he had perfected over the past year. "I should finish these projections as well. Perhaps you could bring something for both of us?"

William nodded, closing his leather portfolio with a soft snap that punctuated the silence. As he left, his footsteps faded into the distance, leaving Sarah and Lyle to continue working in comfortable silence, their intellectual partnership transcending the unspoken complications between them. The library settled back into its academic rhythm—the turning of pages, the scratch of pens, and the persistent ticking of the clock marking time against the looming deadlines that defined their scholarly existence.

⸺◇⸺

At Wraysbury, Margaret Braithwaite studied fabric swatches with unusual sobriety while Elizabeth Stevens reviewed the guest list.

"The blue is lovely with the silver," Elizabeth commented. "Though perhaps too cool for a June wedding?"

Margaret's fingers trembled slightly as she reached for her teacup instead of the gin decanter. "Charles always said blue was the Braithwaite colour. Royal blue, specifically."

"And what do you prefer, Margaret?"

The question caught her off-guard. Few people asked Margaret's preferences anymore. "I rather like the cream with gold accents. Warmer, somehow."

Elizabeth made a note. "Cream and gold it is, then. We'll save the blue for accents—napkins perhaps, or the ribbon on the favours."

Margaret blinked, surprised at having her opinion not just heard but adopted. "You don't think Charles will mind?"

"I think," Elizabeth said carefully, "that this is primarily Sarah and William's day, and secondarily a celebration for the mothers who raised them. The fathers will have their moment when contracts are signed and businesses merged."

A small, genuine smile crossed Margaret's face. "You're quite right, of course." She hesitated, then added, "I haven't always been... present... for William. The war was difficult."

Elizabeth touched Margaret's hand lightly. "We all survived as best we could, Margaret."

"Some better than others," Margaret replied, glancing at the untouched decanter.

"Twenty-eight days now, isn't it?"

Margaret nodded, surprised that Elizabeth had noticed. "Charles doesn't believe I'll manage through the wedding."

"Then we shall prove him wrong," Elizabeth said simply, turning back to the guest list. "Now, about the Cunninghams—they'll need to be seated at the primary table, I think. William was quite insistent about Lyle's importance."

"Charles says the boy has promise. Excellent connections."

Elizabeth's pen paused. "Yes, though I wonder if that's all. The three of them seem... unusually aligned."

Margaret considered this. "William has always been... strategic in his friendships."

"As has Sarah," Elizabeth acknowledged. "Though I believe there's something more substantive here. Something being built."

Outside the window, gardeners prepared the grounds for the June celebration, pruning roses and clearing pathways with methodical precision. The estate would be immaculate by wedding day—every detail arranged, every surface polished, every appearance maintained.

Margaret followed Elizabeth's gaze. "Do you ever worry about them? About what they might become?"

Elizabeth set down her pen. "Constantly. Sarah has always been brilliant but never... warm. And your William—"

"Has his father's ambition without his father's restraint," Margaret finished quietly.

The two women sat in momentary silence, the weight of maternal concern hanging between them.

"Well," Elizabeth finally said, returning to the list, "at least they'll have each other. And young Cunningham seems a steadying influence."

Margaret nodded, though uncertainty lingered in her eyes. "Yes, they'll have each other. God help whoever stands against them."

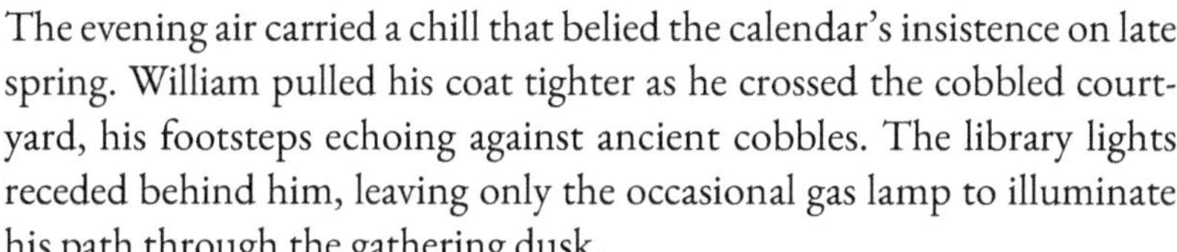

The evening air carried a chill that belied the calendar's insistence on late spring. William pulled his coat tighter as he crossed the cobbled courtyard, his footsteps echoing against ancient cobbles. The library lights receded behind him, leaving only the occasional gas lamp to illuminate his path through the gathering dusk.

Trinity's clock tower struck the half-hour, the sound hanging momentarily before dissolving into the ambient murmur of distant conversations and closing doors. William calculated the quickest route to Fitzbillies, where he could secure something substantial enough to fuel Sarah and Lyle's continued academic exertions.

As he rounded the corner past the Senate House, a figure detached itself from the shadows of a doorway. The man stood with casual deliberation, positioned precisely where William couldn't avoid him without obvious evasion.

"Evening," the man said, his voice carrying a faint accent William couldn't immediately place. "Lovely night for a walk."

William slowed, maintaining a calculated distance. The stranger was lean, dark-haired, with intelligent hazel-green eyes that seemed to assess rather than merely observe. He wore a simple but well-tailored jacket, the collar turned slightly against the evening chill.

"It is," William replied neutrally, noting the man's satchel—academic, but worn beyond what a typical student might carry.

"Braithwaite, isn't it? William Braithwaite."

William's posture shifted imperceptibly. "You have me at a disadvantage."

"Schenker. Avner Schenker." He offered no hand to shake. "Modern History and Political Science."

"I don't believe we've met."

"We haven't." Schenker's smile was brief, calculated. "Though I've observed your work with interest. Your thesis on economic leverage in transitional markets is... provocative."

William remained still, his mind cataloguing possibilities. The man's knowledge of his unpublished work suggested either academic connections or something less transparent.

"Academic interest only?" William asked.

"There are those who find your perspective valuable beyond academic circles." Schenker glanced toward the chapel, then back to William. "The world is realigning itself. New powers emerging, old structures weakening. Men with vision are needed."

"Men with vision are always in demand," William replied. "The question is: whose vision are they serving?"

Schenker's expression remained unchanged, but something flickered in his eyes—a reassessment. "You stand at an interesting threshold, Mr Braithwaite. There are opportunities for someone with your... particular insights."

"I find thresholds overrated," William said. "They're merely artificial boundaries. I prefer to determine my own points of transition."

A half-smile touched Schenker's lips. "Indeed. Though even self-determined men occasionally benefit from doors being opened."

"And what door might you be offering to open?"

"One that leads to rooms where real decisions are made. Beyond boardrooms and parliamentary chambers."

William studied him, recognising the careful language of recruitment. "You seem to be standing at your own threshold, Mr Schenker. Tasked with bringing in new talent, perhaps? I wonder if you fully understand what you're attempting to acquire."

Something shifted in Schenker's demeanour—a fractional narrowing of the eyes, a slight tensing around the mouth. He hadn't expected William to reverse their positions so smoothly.

"I understand enough," Schenker replied.

"I doubt that." William's tone remained conversational, but carried an edge. "You wouldn't be approaching me in shadows if you truly understood."

Schenker paused, reassessing. "Perhaps we could continue this conversation in a more suitable setting."

"Perhaps," William acknowledged. "Though I find timing crucial in such matters. And this isn't the right time."

"And when might that be?"

"When I decide it is." William glanced at his watch. "Now, if you'll excuse me, I have colleagues waiting."

Schenker nodded, accepting the dismissal with grace that suggested experience with strategic retreats. "Until our paths cross again, Mr Braithwaite."

"I expect they will," William replied.

As William continued toward Fitzbillies, he felt Schenker's gaze following him. The encounter lingered in his mind—not a threat, precisely, but a variable to be considered. Someone was watching them, assessing their potential. Whether as assets or obstacles remained to be seen.

By the time William returned to the library with a brown paper bag containing sandwiches and a thermos of coffee, he had already filed Avner Schenker away—not as an immediate concern, but as a thread to be traced back to its source when the time was right.

Sarah looked up as he entered, her eyes immediately detecting something different in his bearing.

"Everything all right?" she asked.

"Perfectly," William replied, setting the food on the table. "Just a small reminder that we're being noticed."

Lyle raised an eyebrow questioningly.

"It seems," William said, pouring coffee into three cups, "that we aren't the only ones with plans for the future."

Chapter 17

Shadows before the Wind

June unfurled over Cambridge like a half-hearted promise, the English summer sky neither committing to brightness nor surrendering entirely to grey. On the lawns outside the Senate House, black-gowned graduates clustered in shifting constellations of laughter and whispered farewells. Parents clutched programmes like precious artefacts, cameras capturing moments already fading into memory.

Sarah, William, and Lyle stood apart from the main crush, a deliberate few paces removed from the celebration's epicentre. Sarah's posture betrayed quiet satisfaction, her first-class honours a validation rather than a surprise. Lyle tugged at his collar, the formality of the day sitting on him like an ill-fitted costume.

"All that pomp for a handshake and a rolled piece of paper," Lyle observed, scanning the ceremony's remnants with mild disappointment. "I was rather hoping for something more... transformative. A secret handshake at the very least, perhaps a whispered password to the halls of power."

Sarah smiled. "Disappointed the Master didn't anoint you with sacred oil?"

"It would have justified the ridiculous hat."

William remained silent, his gaze fixed not on the people but on the Senate House itself—the weathered stone, the weight of centuries, the architecture of power. His expression wasn't cold, merely detached, as though mentally he had already stepped beyond this threshold.

A movement in the crowd caught his attention. Avner Schenker moved with quiet purpose among the graduates, pausing to speak with a chemistry student who had published a notable paper on molecular structures. William watched the brief exchange, noting how the student's initial confusion gave way to attentive interest.

"Our friend is recruiting," William said quietly.

Lyle followed his gaze. "The one who approached you last term?"

"Schenker. Yes." William turned to Lyle. "You should make his acquaintance."

"Should I?" Lyle's eyebrow arched with interest.

"Find out what he's planning. Who he represents." William's tone was measured. "He's collecting minds for someone's purpose. I'd rather know whose."

Sarah's fingers tightened almost imperceptibly on her degree scroll. "He's been watching all three of us. I've noticed him in the library. Always with different students, never the same conversation twice."

Professor Harwood passed by, offering them a wave more collegial than the deference he'd shown during their examinations. "Congratulations, all of you. The faculty's loss is the world's gain, I suspect."

They nodded their acknowledgements, the brief exchange underscoring what they already knew—Cambridge had been merely a staging ground, valuable for its weight in others' estimations rather than any transformation it had wrought within them.

"Shall we?" Sarah suggested, gesturing toward the gate.

They began walking slowly across the lawn, allowing the moment its proper weight. Around them, the rituals of departure played out with predictable emotion—tearful embraces, promises to write, photographs preserving smiles that would soon fade into nostalgia.

The trio exchanged no such sentiments. There were no goodbyes to make. Their alliance transcended this place, had always been oriented toward what lay beyond these ancient walls.

As they reached the path that led to the gate, Lyle paused and looked back once at the Senate House, its pale stone gleaming against the darkening sky.

"Do you think we'll miss it?" he asked, a rare note of sentimentality in his voice.

William looked over his shoulder, his gaze sweeping across the lawns where they had plotted and planned over the years.

"We'll miss who we were," he said. "But not for long."

Sarah slipped her arm through his, her touch both possessive and steadying. The diamond on her finger caught what little light remained in the day.

And as they stepped through the gate and down onto the uneven street beyond, it was as if something unspoken had been folded up and placed gently in memory. Not discarded, merely archived—a foundation upon which they would build what came next.

Behind them, Cambridge continued its centuries-old ritual of releasing minds into the world. Before them stretched London, boardrooms, power, influence, the world—the empire they had mapped out in library corners and midnight conversations.

The clouds shifted overhead, neither breaking nor gathering. A perfect English compromise of a sky, non-committal and patient.

Unlike the three figures moving steadily away from it, already rehearsing in their minds the roles they would soon assume.

⚬

The weeks that followed were awash with activity—fabric swatches exchanged with urgent whispers, folded letters delivered by hand, engraved invitations dispatched to carefully selected addresses, and whispered phone calls that stretched into the early hours, each word weighed for its implications. A wedding, yes—but more than that. An event. A moment. A declaration of intent.

Sarah had initially resisted the scale of it. She had always imagined something more modest, something warm and understated. But as the machinery of preparation whirred into motion, so too did the realisation that this would not be an ordinary union. Not in meaning. Not in scope. Not in consequence.

"Who you marry," William had said one night, his voice low and certain, "is one thing. Who attends the wedding—that's legacy."

And he was right.

They secured not a cathedral, but a private chapel on the Kentish estate of a family friend—ancient stone, ivy-wrapped arches, and a bell tower that hadn't rung in decades. Workers swarmed the grounds daily. It would be restored for the occasion. Not ostentation, but symbolism. Renewal. Power reclaimed.

Sarah handled the ceremony with her mother. The vows. The readings. The music. Everything intimate.

William and Lyle handled the guest list with Justice Stevens and Charles.

It began innocently enough. Family, of course. Close friends. Faculty. But then came the subtle, precise additions: a retired Chancellor of the Exchequer who had taken a quiet interest in William's graduate work. A South African mining magnate who had once written to Lyle about a speculative investment fund. An Italian banker with rumoured Vatican ties. The daughter of an East African diplomat, with whom Sarah had shared a term. Her father, it was noted, was interested in financing infrastructure projects in post-colonial states.

Each name added not just to the count, but to the weight of the event. Phones rang constantly. Couriers arrived with sealed envelopes. It became clear—even to those on the periphery—that this wedding was not simply a social affair. It was a gathering of minds. Of influence. Of future power, not yet fully visible, but already undeniable.

Lyle managed the RSVPs with almost clinical focus, keeping a ledger with marginal notes that looked more like a chessboard than a party plan. His desk perpetually covered with telegrams, responses, and requests for clarification.

Braithwaite Enterprises—various company officers attending.

De Beers proxy—attending.

Representative from the House of Lords—tentative (dependent on health).

French attaché—confirmed. Curiosity noted.

He worked alone most nights, lit by lamplight, the windows of his study steamed over from the damp. Occasionally, he would pause over a name and stare into the distance, his pen unmoving.

This was not about favour or fashion. This was placement. Alignment.

When Sarah asked him once whether it made him uncomfortable to treat a wedding like a negotiation, he had smiled gently.

"It's not a negotiation, necessarily," he said. "It's a signal."

She had nodded. She understood.

Even her dress was a statement—Parisian silk, yes, but not designer-branded. Commissioned quietly from a couturier known for dressing women of state. Fittings occurred at odd hours, with fabric samples arriving under cover of darkness. Elegant, stark, and entirely hers.

William, for his part, became quieter in the weeks before the ceremony. Not withdrawn, but watchful. He moved through the fittings and formalities with the calm of someone who knew he was walking toward a different kind of life.

"Are you nervous?" Sarah had asked one evening, as they walked along the river, coats drawn close.

"No," he had said. "I'm aware. That's different."

She took his hand, and they walked in silence for a while.

The house they would live in had already been chosen—a townhouse in London's Holland Park, discreetly elegant, with enough room for dinner guests and war rooms. Decorators and security specialists came and went. William had asked Lyle to take one of the upper floors for himself. "At least until you decide to run the IMF," he'd joked flippantly.

But it wasn't really a joke.

The day before the wedding, as the final deliveries arrived and the chapel grounds were cleared of ivy and stone dust, Lyle stood in the gallery overlooking the nave. The stained-glass windows caught the light of the descending sun. Rows of chairs, still empty, waited in perfect symmetry.

He watched the workers, the decorators, the florists. Watched as each piece fell into place.

Behind him, Sarah appeared, soft-footed and tired.

"Is it what you imagined?" she asked.

Lyle didn't answer immediately.

"No," he said finally. "It's more."

She stepped beside him.

"I thought you'd say it was too much."

"It is. But it's right."

They stood a moment longer, watching the space that tomorrow would be filled with so many faces—some known, some unknowable.

Sarah turned to him. "Thank you, Lyle. For everything."

He looked at her, eyes thoughtful. "Don't thank me yet."

Then, with a faint smile, he added, "Wait until the speeches."

———◦———

The restored chapel doors were still closed, but the air inside was already charged—like a breath held before an oath is spoken. The windows, tall and arched, caught the soft light of the dying afternoon and threw it across the flagstone floor in golden blades. Candles flickered in sconces and candelabras, their light steady and unwavering. The scent of beeswax and roses lingered beneath the incense.

It was a room built for sacred things.

Lyle stood at the front in a sharply cut suit of navy wool, collar crisp, eyes calm. He wore no flower on his lapel, no pin of lineage—nothing that declared anything except readiness. To his left stood the officiant, a retired bishop with a voice like old parchment and eyes that missed nothing.

The guests had taken their seats in silence, as if entering not just a ceremony, but a contract. There were no murmured conversations, no tittering cousins. Only the quiet sound of breath and the occasional creak of wood under careful shifting.

In the third row, a retired Chancellor adjusted his cufflinks. Behind him, an attaché from the French Ministry took discreet mental notes. Across the aisle, a South African mining magnate whispered something to the daughter of a diplomat. They all knew this was no ordinary wedding.

It was a preview, an alignment.

And then the music began.

Not loud, not triumphant. Strings, low and steady. A single cello line, mournful and noble, followed by the warm lift of a piano. It was not a bridal march. It was a prelude to something consequential.

Sarah entered. Her arm affectionately draped over her father's forearm.

She wore a gown of ivory silk—no lace, no train. Just clean lines and elegance made tangible. Her hair was gathered at the nape of her neck, pinned with a single pearl comb. She held no bouquet.

She did not look down. She looked ahead—at William, already waiting for her at the front, his posture still, his expression composed but lit from within.

He wore a tailored three-piece suit in charcoal grey. No tails, no frills. A single cufflink of polished hematite, and his grandfather's watch. There was a timelessness about him—something ancient and yet untested. He did not smile when he saw her.

But something in his eyes broke open.

She stopped before him, and for a long moment, they simply stood there—neither reaching for the other, nor looking away. The room faded. The guests blurred. Only the silence between them held.

Damion Stevens turned towards his eldest daughter, his eyes light pink from what welled deep down within him. He held her hands in his for a brief moment, then, quietly acknowledging William, released her for the last time.

Then the officiant spoke.

His words were not the usual liturgy. They had written the vows themselves—pared down, lean, fierce in their simplicity.

Sarah's voice, when she spoke, was low and clear.

"I vow to speak truth, even when silence tempts me.

To build, when it would be easier to inherit.

To choose you, not because I need to, but because I always will."

William took a breath. His voice was steady.

"I vow to protect you without possessing you.

To listen when power would tempt me to speak.

To walk beside you—not in front, not behind."

No one moved. Not a cough, not a whisper. Even the candles seemed to lean in.

The officiant did not ask if anyone objected.

He simply nodded, and said, "Then let it be done."

And they kissed—briefly, reverently, delicately. Not as a finale. As a beginning.

The chapel bell rang once. Outside, the trees swayed slightly. And the guests, still quiet, rose to their feet in slow succession—not to applaud, but to bear witness.

William took Sarah's hand. They turned, side by side.

And for the first time in the entire day, he smiled.

———◆———

The reception unfurled like a tapestry woven of silk and steel. Beneath the glass canopy erected over the estate's south lawn, chandeliers cast warm light across tables draped in cream damask. Champagne flowed from crystal fountains, and waiters glided between clusters of guests bearing silver trays of canapés too artful to be merely food.

Sarah had changed from her wedding gown into something equally striking—a sleeveless sheath of midnight blue silk that caught the light with each movement. A single strand of pearls graced her neck, and sapphire drops hung from her ears, gifts from William's mother that morning. Her hair remained elegantly pinned, but now with a silver comb inlaid with lapis lazuli. She moved through the crowd with a measured grace, her smile calibrated perfectly between warmth and dignity.

William remained in his charcoal suit, the only concession to festivity a glass of champagne in his hand that he rarely sipped from. His eyes constantly found Sarah across the room, not with the dazed look of a besotted groom, but with the focused attention of a partner tracking their counterpart's movements in a choreographed dance.

"Extraordinary match," murmured Lord Harrington to the French attaché as they watched the couple. "The Stevens girl brings the legal mind the Braithwaites have always lacked. And connections to the judiciary that can't be bought."

The attaché nodded. "My government is particularly interested in their West African ventures. Perhaps we might discuss..."

Three tables away, Charles Braithwaite shook hands with the South African mining magnate. "The marriage is just the beginning. We're repositioning our interests in the Transvaal next quarter. William has some rather innovative ideas about resource extraction."

"I'd be keen to hear them," the magnate replied, slipping a business card into Charles's breast pocket. "Perhaps next week at my club?"

Margaret Braithwaite, sober and composed in pale gold silk, engaged a cabinet minister's wife in conversation about charitable foundations while her eyes tracked William's progress through the room. Justice Stevens leaned against a marble pillar, watching his daughter navigate a conversation with two banking executives, pride and concern warring in his expression.

Sarah touched the elbow of an American investor. "William and I were just discussing your position on the Singapore development. Perhaps you might join us for dinner next month?"

The investor nodded eagerly. "I'd be delighted. Your husband's analysis of the shipping regulations was remarkably prescient."

William, meanwhile, stood with a group of older men near the champagne fountain. "The opportunity isn't in manufacturing," he was saying. "It's in controlling the distribution networks. The Empire may be contracting, but the pathways remain."

Lyle moved between these constellations of power and influence, observing, connecting, occasionally whispering something in William's ear or catching Sarah's eye across the room. He was everywhere and nowhere, essential yet invisible.

Then came the soft, persistent chime of silver against crystal. Conversations paused. Heads turned.

Lyle stood on the small dais near the head table, glass raised. His navy suit caught the light, making him appear almost sculpted from shadow.

"Ladies and gentlemen, if I might have your attention."

The room settled. Waiters paused their circuits. William and Sarah moved to the centre of the gathering, standing close but not touching.

"They say politics makes strange bedfellows," Lyle began, his voice carrying effortlessly. "And finance makes even stranger ones. I've spent enough time in both worlds to confirm this is absolutely true."

Stifled laughter rippled through the room—light, genuine.

"But tonight, I am not an academic. I am not an economist, nor am I a cynic... or even a dangerous man to sit next to at dinner."

A beat.

"I am simply the man who stood closest to the groom for the last six years—literally, and often emotionally—trying to decipher whether he was a genius, a machine, or just quietly planning to overthrow half the global supply chain."

More laughter. William smiled, eyes down.

"Now, he's gone and done something truly astonishing. He's married someone who makes even him seem normal."

The laughter, now fuller, touched with affection.

"Sarah, you are brilliance wrapped in elegance. And mercy on the rest of us if you two ever decide to form a sovereign state."

He raised his glass.

"To fire and intellect. To love that plans, and plans that love to win. To William and Sarah—who deserve each other in the best and most dangerous ways."

Applause rang out, echoing beneath the glass canopy. William's hand found Sarah's, their fingers interlacing with newfound confidence. Their eyes met, and for a moment, something genuine passed between them—a current of understanding that ran deeper than strategy, sharper than ambition.

In that moment, they were not just allies, not just friends and partners, but something rarer and more formidable: two people who saw each other completely and chose each other anyway.

The guests raised their glasses, unaware they were witnessing not just a union, but a coronation of a kind.

◆○◆

The last ember of the celebration faded with a whisper. The candles, guttering low in their crystal holders, offered more scent than light. The marquee stood hollow now—no longer a stage, just a structure, the echo of laughter clinging faintly to its seams.

On the terrace beyond, William stood with one hand in his pocket, the other curled loosely around a glass of whisky. The air was colder than expected, the kind that made your breath visible but didn't quite reach the bone.

He welcomed it.

The lawn before him stretched into the darkness, framed by hedges and low stone walls. Somewhere, a fountain trickled faintly. Beyond that: fields, trees, the hush of the estate. Above: the clean, endless dark.

Behind him, footsteps—light and familiar.

Lyle.

He didn't speak. Just came to stand beside him, mirroring his posture, gaze turned to the horizon. He held no glass. He didn't need one.

After a long pause, Lyle said, "You handled yourself well tonight."

William's mouth twitched. "Thank you."

"That guest list—those conversations—you understand what they mean, don't you?"

"I do."

"They weren't watching a groom tonight. They were watching a variable. Trying to calculate how dangerous you might become."

William took a slow sip.

"I'm sure they're right to wonder."

Another silence passed, companionable.

Sarah's voice joined them a moment later, soft from behind. "So this is where the real reception is happening."

They turned to her. She stepped onto the terrace wrapped in a pale shawl, her heels now discarded. Her hair had begun to fall from its pins. She looked more herself now than she had all day.

William reached for her hand, and she moved to stand between them. The three of them stood in a line, shoulder to shoulder, facing the fields.

Lyle glanced between them. "We'll be talked about. Studied. There will be memos written about this night, I'm sure."

"I know," Sarah said. "That's why I wore silk and not sequins."

William chuckled.

She looked up at him. "Are you ready?"

He didn't answer right away.

Instead, he looked out—at the darkened land, the future coiled beneath it like a waiting flame. Then he looked at Lyle. At Sarah.

The people who knew him best. The people who would shape everything.

The people he trusted.

And then he said it.

"Now," he said, "we start to build."

He turned to Lyle, a faint glint in his eye.

"And let's not wait to be asked," he added. "Let's be the question."

No one replied.

They didn't need to.

The stars blinked overhead in the stillness.

And the world, far beyond the fields, waited.

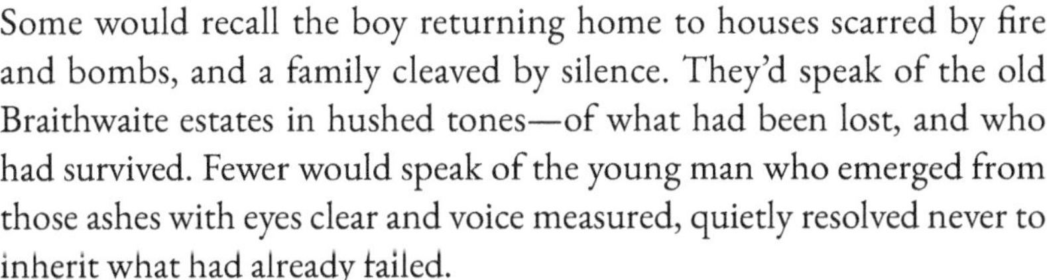

Some would recall the boy returning home to houses scarred by fire and bombs, and a family cleaved by silence. They'd speak of the old Braithwaite estates in hushed tones—of what had been lost, and who had survived. Fewer would speak of the young man who emerged from those ashes with eyes clear and voice measured, quietly resolved never to inherit what had already failed.

Others would remember the pact. Not formal. Not written. Just two friends—William Braithwaite and Lyle Cunningham—seated across from one another in a borrowed seminar room, sharing coffee gone cold and a vision still forming. Not of power, but of structure. Of a world reassembled, piece by deliberate piece, beneath their hands.

And always, there was Sarah.

Not the ornament at a statesman's side, not the footnote in another man's legacy. She was the gravity that held their orbit, the fulcrum between ambition and restraint. Brilliant, discerning, and utterly unwilling to stand in shadow. When she and William married, it was not the merging of romance, but of minds, of codes—of futures.

Together, the three became something the world didn't yet have a name for. Not a dynasty. Not a cartel. Not even a partnership.

A presence.

They moved carefully, at first. Quietly. No headlines. No proclamations. Just dinners attended, meetings observed, names noted. Systems studied, not to be destroyed, but to be inherited differently.

And the world—so often slow to notice—began to adjust, and something new began to emerge.

There were some who said it started at Cambridge. Others who traced it back further to the African *veld*. But those closest to the matter would later agree: the foundations were laid in silence. In the gentle closing of doors. In glances across marble floors. In candlelight, and pact, and promise.

What would follow, in time, would not be a war in the traditional sense. But something subtler. More patient. A reshaping.

And as a part of their story closed, and the winds of another world began to stir elsewhere—far away, under different skies—those three figures stood, for now, together.

Still.

Decided.

And quietly... inevitable.

⸺◆O◆⸺

"Light gives the shadow its form; warmth gives the wind its breath. And yet, it is the shadows in the wind that reshape this world—hiding light, stealing warmth, leaving silence in their wake."—Author

Shadows in the Wind

Others in this Series

The five books, of this four-book saga are:

Corpus Quadripartitum (all four books in one)
Book 1: Tenebris Ordior
Book 2: Aurora Inter Tenebras
Book 3: Malitia Adolescit
Book 4: Quisque moriatur ut vitam perseveret